THE FOUR KINGDOMS

THE FOUR KINGDOMS

Book One

A.R. RISCH

To order additional copies of this book, contact:
Xlibris Corporation
1-888-795-4274
www.Xlibris.com
Orders@Xlibris.com
104921

CONTENTS

The Four Kingdoms 8

Prologue 13

Rosegarden 23

Dragon's End 32

West Watch 47

Icestorm Castle 54

Rosegarden 67

Dragon's End 80

Autumn Way 90

Snow Cap Mountains 101

Elf Forest.. 112

Southern Sea 122

West Watch 134

Snow Cap Mountains 151

Crystal Keep 159

Fire Harbor 167

West Watch 178

Icestorm 186

Rosegarden 195

Epilogue 203

Character Overview.. 211

A Note on Chronology...

The Four Kingdoms is told through the eyes of characters that are sometimes hundreds of miles away from one another. Some chapters cover a day, some only a couple hours, others might cover a month. The narrative cannot be strictly sequential; sometimes important events are happening at the same time at opposite sides of the country.

A.R. Risch

This Book is for my grandma Vivian,
my mom Kathy and my husband Mark.

THE FOUR KINGDOMS

The North

*Icestorm Castle

Capitol of the North—
House Mathis

+ **Frostfall**—House Beckman

+ **Snowflake Landing**—House Degoyler

+ **The Horseshoe**—House Gribbens

+ **North Star**—House Landrum

+ **Thor**—House Schmitt

+ **The Pines**—House Perrenot

+ **Giant's Keep**—House Goldberg

+ **Rivercross**—House Wiker

The East

* Rosegarden

Capitol of the East—
House Carrender

+ **Dolphinkeep**—House Turk

+ **Acorn Hill**—House Merriman

+ **Crystal Keep**—House Hearon

+ **Golden Rock**—House Chitwood

+ **Lionsgate**—House Stoddart

+ **Spring's End**—House Mullen

The South

*Dragon's End Castle

Capitol of the South—
House Cvetkovich

- **Bloodstone**—House Smeltzer

- **The Vipers**—House Malliett

- **Serpent Tongue**—House Filoso

- **Gator Swamp**—House Brunson

- **Fire Harbor**—House Hugart

- **Summerkeep**—House Hamstra

- **Sun's End**—House Chittick

- **Foxrun**—House Beckom

- **The Red Islands**—House Kouns

The West

*West Watch Castle

Capitol of the West—
House McCue

- **Forest End**—House McCorkle

- **Eagle Nest**—House McCowan

- **Autumn Way**—House McClure

- **Leaflanding**—House McMahon

- **The Sword**—House McNeely

Key for the Four Kingdoms:

* = Castles

✦ = Cities

— = Road

X = Village

(=) = Crossing or Bridge

Trees = Forest

Triangles = Mountains

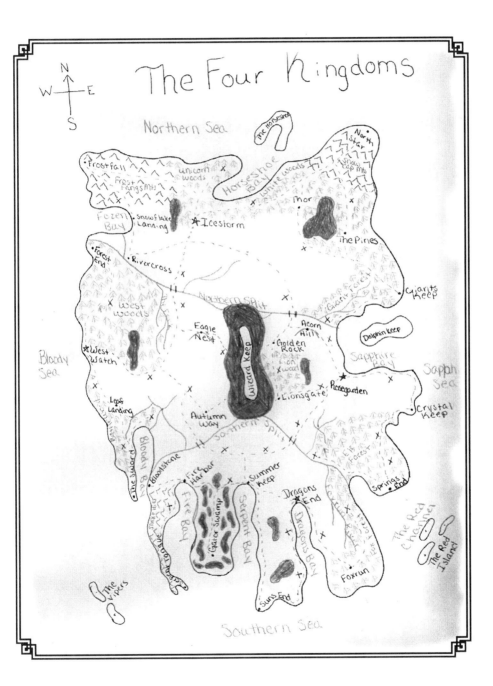

PROLOGUE

King Finn was getting dressed in his chamber for the hunt. Three days had passed since they received word of bear attacks in the village between Icestorm and North Star. Thirty villagers have been killed so far. His ward Connor Wiker was helping him when the knock came at the door. "Enter" said the King. A tall dark haired man with dark eyes dressed in armor came through the door. It was the King's brother Ser Brian Mathis.

"You summoned me, Your Grace" said Ser Brian.

"Yes, I want you and Fergus to stay behind to guard the Queen" the King replied.

"Your Grace, surely the Queen will be safe at the castle, you will need guards in the woods. The bears are one thing, but there's more than bears in those woods." Ser Brian was shocked by the suggestion. He had been looking forward to getting out of the castle to ride his stallion through the snow and kill things.

"I am sure she will be safe, but I need you and Fergus to make sure of it! This is not a suggestion!" The King had been surprised when his wife had told him last night after their love making that she was with child, *she might have the next King in her belly*, he thought and he wasn't going to take any chances. Ser Brian's face was starting to redden and the King could see the anger in his brother's eyes. "Brian, who can I trust more than my own brother to keep her safe?" the King knew he wanted to go but his Queen was more important.

"As you command, Your Grace" Ser Brian turned on his heels and walked swiftly out the door.

After Connor fastened his cloak around his shoulders, he made his way to the yard. As he walked out the door into the cool air, it had started to snow and the sky looked darker to the North. The hounds were gathered at the gate with fifty men on horses. Connor brought the King's stallion, a big silver beast with a white mane that was braided with ribbons as blue as the lake. The blanket under the saddle was the same blue with the Unicorn of his house embroidered on all four corners. Connor bent down and cupped his hands for the King's foot. The King swung himself in the saddle, and Connor handed him his spear. The King spurred his horse and rode toward his men, Connor following close behind.

"We stay together, it looks like a storm's coming from the North and we don't want to get caught in it and get split up" the King announced. The Master of Arms, Ser Miles rode up on the King's right as the group headed through the gate. As they rode under the wall that surrounded Icestorm, the King looked up. He had lived in this castle his whole life, yet looking up at the great wall still took his breath away. The wall around Icestorm was white marble and reached over one hundred feet high. If it snowed heavy, you didn't even know it was there until you ran into it. On the outside of the wall there were carved unicorn's running and fighting. The big steel gate closed loudly behind them and they were off towards the woods.

As they entered the woods, the snow started falling heavy, *how am I to find a bear in a snow storm*, the King thought. The hounds were leading the way, noses on the grounds and tails straight up. "The hounds have a trail," Ser Miles said to the King, "they will find the bears' cave and we can smoke them out."

"If it keeps snowing like this, they will lose the trail," the King said, annoyed at how the snow was sticking to his beard and eyelashes. He was use to snow, but he knew how hard it was to try and hunt in it. Deep into the woods the hounds kept going. They were still many miles from the village. The King had doubts the hounds even had the right trail. He didn't see a bear traveling that far just to eat.

The deeper they went the heavier the snow fell. It was still morning, but it looked like evening in the forest. The men even lit torches so they could see one another. "Should we set the tents before it gets worse?" Ser Miles asked the King.

"We haven't gone far enough, what will my people think of my protection if I only hunt for two hours?" the King replied. He knew that Ser Miles was right, but he wasn't going to waste the day in a tent when his people were being torn apart by bears. So they moved on. The snow had brought their pace down to a crawl, but the hounds didn't seem bothered by it and appeared to still have the trail.

By midday they stopped to warm up and eat. Connor went to gather some wood and brush for a fire while the King spoke with Ser Miles. "Do we know how many bears we are hunting?" the King asked.

"No, all the villagers that were killed were found afterwards with no beast in sight. All the killing was at night most were in bed" Ser Miles answered.

"The villagers that died, what were they doing out at night?" the King was annoyed at that. If you live in the woods and you are stupid enough to go out at night, what do you expect to find?

"No one knows, may haps they heard a noise and went out to check on it" Ser Miles always had an answer for everything. If you asked him why the sky was blue he would come up with some explanation.

"So we are hunting for bears, and it might not even be bears that did this! If no one saw the beast that killed all those people, how do they know it was bears? And why am I just now finding this out?" asked the King, you could hear his anger in his voice.

"I was told you were informed of everything Your Grace" Ser Miles was getting nervous and started shifting back and forth.

"The only thing I was told was there are some bears that have killed thirty villagers. Not that the beast that killed them might not even be a bear, or that no one saw any of them get killed!" the King's voice got louder with every word. By that time Connor was back and had made a fire, not a large fire, but large enough to get warm. The King left Ser Miles and went over to the fire to warm his hands. About the time he was getting the feeling back in his fingers, Connor brought a skin of wine, some white bread with nuts, and salted beef.

The horses were saddled, the hounds gathered, and the fire was smothered. The King was the last to mount his horse. The King rode to the front by the hounds and led the hunt. Ser Miles was to his right, Connor to his left, and the other fifty men close behind. The snow was falling so heavy now that he could not see the trees next to him or in front of him. The King had to put all his trust in his stallion and hoped there wasn't a tree root or rock in their path. Half the men had torches and he could make out a light glow from maybe ten of them. It had gotten colder, a damp heavy cold almost suffocating.

"How are we to find the beast if we can't see in front of us?" the King asked Ser Miles.

"The beast is likely still miles away, hopefully the snow will let up by then. The hounds will find the beast, all we have to do is kill it."

"And how are we to kill it if we can't see it?" the King was looking forward to this answer, *might be I finally have a question he doesn't have an answer for,* he thought.

After a long silence, the answer came, to the King's disappointment, "We can see the hounds below us, that's close enough to kill." The King said nothing, he didn't want to risk another stupid response to make him lose his temper.

The King and his men were passing a skin of strong wine between them so at least they would be warm on the inside. The wine burned with every drink. The wine had also lifted the King's spirit a little, his head was getting light and the snow wasn't bothering him as much. The woods were black. It had been one hour since the midday meal and it seemed the middle of night. The snow still fell, hiding everything more than five feet away. The hounds still had their nose to the ground and tail straight up. They were heading northeast and would reach the village by night. The woods were dead silent. The King hadn't seen a living animal all day. *They took shelter from the storm,* he thought, *may haps we should do the same.*

The King was not one to give up. He wanted to find this beast and kill it so he could get home to his wife. "How long till we reach the village?" the King asked.

"By night, at the least, at this pace we will be lucky to be there that soon" answered Ser Miles. The snow was packed in Ser Miles beard, and when he answered some of it fell away and the King tried to keep a straight face.

"You are starting to look more beast than man Miles, may haps you're the one killing the villagers" the King said with a smile, "I should just kill you so I can go home."

Ser Miles did not seem amused with that, but at least he had no answer. The snow was letting up some and didn't seem as thick as it had an hour past.

"Should we quicken pace, Your Grace?" Connor asked "The snow is not falling as hard, we might make it to the village after all." The King gave a nod and spurred his horse to a trot, the fastest he dared to go with the snow that deep.

As the group came to a clearing the King announced "We will rest here a while," and dismounted his stallion. The King handed the reins to Connor and walked around the clearing to get his legs to stop tingling from the ride. The rest of the men were dismounted and gathering wood for fire. Ser Miles walked up to the King with a wine skin in hand.

When he offered it to the King he asked "Should I have the men set the tents?"

"I will think on it and let you know after we eat," the King said and walked away with the wine. The King liked Ser Miles but was in no mood to talk to him. The King walked on through the woods. He wished it wasn't snowing so he could see the tops of the trees and maybe a cloud or even better, the sun. He would be much happier if he could see the sun. He turned and made it back toward the clearing.

A large fire was burning in the middle of the clearing and the men gathered round it to feel the warmth. The King walked toward his men and when he got ten feet away he could smell meat cooking.

"I caught a rabbit!" Connor came running up and announced. Connor was glowing with pride, his red cheeks were balled up from the big smile on his face. The King smiled and gave a nod, *one rabbit won't feed fifty men,* he thought, but he would not ruin Connor's joy. Every man got a bite of rabbit. It was more teasing than anything. They all knew if they were home they could be eating a whole rabbit. The men also saw how proud Connor was about his kill, so every man thanked Connor for the meat and smiled at him.

The King went to Ser Miles after they ate and told him to have the men start setting up the tents. Ser Miles was grateful for that, "If the gods are good, it will not be snowing on the morrow" Ser Miles said, and the King hoped it true. While the men were setting the tents the King sat by the fire and finished off another skin of wine.

"Your tent is ready, Your Grace" Connor said, but when the King stood he stumbled toward Connor. The boy's eyes got large and his mouth fell open as he held up his hands to try and stop from being squashed by the King.

"It's alright, I'm not going to fall on you. I didn't realize how much wine I had drank until I stood," the King told the boy.

"Let me help you to your tent, Your Grace" Connor pleaded.

"No Connor, I am fine thank you" the King answered and stumbled toward his tent.

The King woke to sun coming through the blue fabric of the tent, giving the whole tent a blue glow. King Finn tossed the furs off of him and stood to stretch out the cramps from the night. The thumping in his head was a reminder of the wine he had drank the night before. He found Connor at the end of the furs and shook him awake. Connor looked at the King with red eyes and sat up. Connor's brown hair had looked like he rolled around the whole tent, sticking straight up and to the side.

"Help me get dressed," the King said to the boy.

"Yes, Your Grace." and with that Connor shot right up and hurried around the tent to find the King's clothes.

After the King had dressed he stepped outside the tent. He felt the cool morning breeze and sun on his face, *this is hunting weather* he thought and walked to the nearest tree to piss. While still lacing up his breeches he turned around and was nearly blinded by the sun reflecting off the silver on his tent. His tent was a massive thing. Blue as a winter lake with two white Unicorns on the top and trimmed in silver. On the top was a silver spike. He walked toward the smell of roasting meat and found a boar over the fire.

"Did you kill this one too?" he asked Connor.

The boy blushed and replied "No, Your Grace, some of the men went out before dawn and came back with it, Your Grace."

The King broke his fast on wild boar, cheese, white bread with nuts and wine. Rested and full the King was quite pleased, even the thumping in his head had left.

"I would like to continue on to the village as soon as possible. Have the men start breaking down the tents and getting the horses ready," he told Ser Miles

"Aye, Your Grace."

Even Ser Miles is less annoying, he thought with a smile. They were off within the hour, the hounds with noses to the ground and tails straight. The King was leading the hunting team again and this time he could see the whole forest. Pines so tall they seemed to kiss the clouds. Squirrels were running through the branches of the tall pines and crows flying in the sky above. The sun's light made yellow lines through the branches of the trees and touched the snow covered ground below. It was much warmer than the day before and not a snowflake in sight. The men seemed better spirited also talking to one another as they followed their King.

The King and his men reached the village midday, when the sun was right above them. The village was small with no walls to surround it. One stone road ran through the middle of the village. On either side of the road were simple one room hutches made of wood.

"Ser Miles, have the men stay behind, outside the village. You and Connor come with me," the King said.

"Men guard the outside of the village!"

The King entered the village, Ser Miles on his right and Connor on his left. They rode down the stone road toward the temple at the end of the village. Passing villagers in simple garb and scared looks on their faces. He could see the fear in their eyes as they rode by. They passed the inn which was the biggest structure in the village. The inn looked more like a barn than an inn with only two stories. When they got close to the temple, they could see the bodies.

King Finn swung down from his stallion and walked to the first body on the ground. It was a man, half his face had been ripped off, his organs were hanging out his belly and one arm was ripped off at the shoulder. The second body was a woman with her neck ripped open, all her blood stained hair was sticking to her face, and half of her right leg was gone. The third was a child and the King could not tell the sex from the looks of it. Based on the size the King guessed the child to be around six. The child was ripped in half right under the ribs. The King was so distracted by the bodies that he didn't even see the Priest that was standing in front of him.

"This is the Brown family, Your Grace," the Priest announced. The Priest was an old man with no hair on the top of his head and brown splotches on his scalp. His beard was gray with some white and went down past his belly. His skin hung loose on his face and his hands looked all bone.

"A whole family? Is this the first multiple killing?"

"No, Your Grace, every killing has been at the least two and up to five. This is not the worst some of the bodies were so mutilated that we couldn't identify them at first. Your Grace" the Priest answered.

"Take me to where they were found," ordered the King.

The Priest led the King, Ser Miles and Connor behind one of the hutches toward the front of the village. Behind the hutch the snow had been dyed red. Some of the blood melted the snow to the ground below and pooled in the dirt.

"Your Grace, paw prints," Ser Miles announced, and King Finn went to where he was standing. "That's no bear tracks, Your Grace. Big enough as a bear, but the tracks are wrong," Ser Miles said his face had turned almost gray.

"Looks like wolf tracks, but no wolf is big enough to leave tracks that size," the King observed. "No one heard or saw the beast?"

"The whole town heard, but no one dared to check on it or we would have more bodies. No one saw though, all their windows were shut. Your Grace," the Priest answered.

This is worst than I thought the King thought. "Ser Miles, looks like the tracks lead toward the mountains. Have the men get ready and get the hounds I want to track this thing while the trail is fresh."

"Aye, Your Grace," Ser Miles replied and ran off.

The hunting party headed off into the woods toward the mountains. The hounds followed the bloody paw prints about ten feet, and then the snow must have washed all the blood off the beast and left perfect white prints in the snow. The prints were the size of a man's head. The King could not imagine a wolf that size *has to be as big as a horse* he thought.

The hounds were howling and barking, "Ser Miles, find a way to shut the stupid hounds up! The beast will hear us coming!" the King said, annoyed.

Ser Miles shouted some command in a different tongue and the hounds silenced. The party was heading northeast toward North Star. The pines were getting thicker and the road thinning, they had to ride two across which made a long line of the hunting party. Two hours after they left the village, they came upon the mountains.

The mountains were light gray with white tops to them, most had no trees. The King knew the road through the mountains was hard, at times you had to get off your horse and lead it. The King had traveled to North Star often and was familiar with the road, but dreaded traveling it every time. The hounds veered off the road after the first mountain. They had to slow down the horses over the rough land. The King could see the fear in Connor, he had turned white. He was shivering and sweating at the same time.

"Connor, I want you to go to the back of the hunting party. You do not need to be in the front," the King said to the boy.

"But I am your ward, Your Grace, I go where you go," Connor replied almost a whisper.

"I have Ser Miles with me and I would like you in the back. I need the skilled hunters in the front with me," the King said. Connor looked disappointed but relieved. He nodded and turned toward the back of the line.

Once they reached the third mountain, the hounds found a cave at the base of it and stopped. The King dismounted, "Tie up the horses and have Connor stay with them," the King told Ser Miles. Once all the party was dismounted and their horses tied, they lit the torches and headed into the cave. The King had to duck to enter the cave, but once inside it opened to a wide chamber that was at the least ten feet high. The chamber had four passages. "We are going to have to split up. Ser Miles choose two of your best," the King said. Ser Miles chose and the rest were split up by four. The King took the second passage to the right.

The tunnel was wide enough for three men to walk side by side. The King held out his torch which lit enough to see twenty feet in front of him. The stones echoed their foot steps down the passage and pebbles were falling from above them, raining on their heads. They came across a boulder in the path that came up to his waist and the men had to climb over it. As the men followed the King down the tunnel, the dark hung around them and the air became thick. The King had his torch in his left hand and his spear in his right. The steel tip of the spear pointed in front of him reflecting the light. They came across another chamber with two passages. They must have already walked a mile into the mountain. The King stopped and stuck his torch in both passages and could not see the end. The King knew they would have to split up again and was not happy about it.

The King took seven men down the passage to the left, and the other six took the passage to the right. The air was so thick it was hard to breathe. The smoke that the torches put off did not help. The passage weaved like a snake; in and out, right and left, up and down.

"Aaaahhhhhhaw!" A blood curdling scream came echoing down the passage from behind them. All the men quickly turned around, spears up and ready. Not a minute later, more screams came so loud the King's ears rang and a shower of pebbles fell on them.

"Head back!" the King yelled and pushed his way to the front, going back the way they had came.

The King hurried the pace almost to a run, hoping some of his men were still alive, but doubting it by the screams. He heard something, "Stop," he said as one of his men ran into the back of him and the King dropped his torch. When the torch hit the ground the fire went out. The King turned around and grabbed the torch of the man that had run into him, *if I live through this I will beat the shit out of you*, he thought. When he turned back around with the torch, glowing eyes blocked the path in front of him. He could not make out what kind of animal it was, it stayed in the shadow, and all he could see were the eyes.

From behind he heard "Rrrrrrrrrrrrrrrrrr" a low rumble of a growl. The man behind him whispered "they are behind us too." The men made a circle, their spears pointed out, all of them shoulder to shoulder. They were out numbered by the beast. The most they could hope for was to kill one and scare the rest of them off. Then out of nowhere, a gust of wind came down both ends of the passage. They were in complete darkness. *What demons from the hells are these*, the King thought? There was nowhere for the wind to come from. What had caused the gust? The men's breathing turned hard and shallow as they waited for the first beast to attack. They had started swinging their spears in hopes of striking one. Then the man whose shoulder was pressed to the right shoulder of the King went down. He could hear his head hit the ground and the man's hand brushed the King's calf as he was dragged away. The King moved in and found that his seven was now only four, one man to his back, one man to his right and two to his left. *What the bloody hell.*

The King was thrusting his spear down and to the side. The only good it did was hit the men's spears beside him. Then each man on both sides of him let out a scream. The one on his right grabbed his leg and he was being pulled away. The King tried to grab the man's arm, but he was gone. The next thing he knew, a sharp pain went into his right leg and he could feel the blood trickling down the back of his leg. The King struggled to pull his leg free, trying to ignore the pain not wanting to scream. With a wet ripping sound his leg was free. The King put his hand down to his leg. His calf was ripped clean off. The King felt the warm blood gushing from his leg and his head started to spin. He fell, the loss of blood was too much.

Something grabbed his foot, the sharp teeth digging through the bone. This time he did scream. He had dropped his spear. He was punching the beast in the head. Claws came up and ripped at his left eye. Then his head was in the strong jaws . . . .

ROSEGARDEN

Maggie was running through the garden that the castle got its name from. Roses of pink, red, peach, yellow and white were mixed in together. The royal children of the castle have always played in the maze of roses. Maggie was trying to hide from her siblings and she could hear them yelling and laughing behind her. She was looking behind her when she turned the corner. She ran right into hard golden armor. The impact knocked her right on her ass. She looked up to see who she had run into and saw her cousin Ser Jaron standing over her with a frown and his eyebrows pushed together. Ser Jaron was the son of her father's brother, Lord Jared, and had the same features as the rest of her family. Golden hair in curls, deep blue eyes and skin the color of cream.

"Princess Margery, you should watch where you are running," Ser Jaron said to her.

"Beg pardons, cousin," she replied and got up of the ground.

"Your Queen mother craves words with you and your siblings. She is in the Throne Room waiting." Ser Jaron informed her.

"I will head there right away," Maggie said and ran off toward the castle.

The courtyard outside the castle was full of servants hurrying about with their duties. Her father, the King of the East, was having his annual tourney in two days and the last preparations were keeping everyone busy. She weaved her way through the servants across the yard. The massive golden castle stood in front of her. The castle was built with yellow stone that had a golden sparkle to it when the sun hit it. It was one big structure with eight towers sticking out from all around. The middle tower was the biggest, by far, reaching so high from the top you could see all the way across Sapphire Bay.

That tower was named the King's Tower and was Maggie's fathers; the Throne Room was at the base of it. Next to the King's Tower was the Queen's

Tower; where her mother's chamber were, along with a smaller dining hall, a library, a kitchen and the Queen's servant quarters. Behind the King's Tower was a much shorter tower called Rose Tower where the royal children's chambers were. To the left of Rose Tower was Sapphire Tower that was Maggie's uncle's tower, Prince Alexander. To the right of Rose Tower was Gold Tower that belonged to her uncle Prince Teagan and his family. The tower between the Queen's Tower and Gold Tower was Lord Jared's tower who was uncle to her father, that tower was called Thorn Tower. The other two Towers were Diamond Tower and Amethyst Tower, those were full of servants and knights and part of them was for highborn guest.

Maggie ran up the steps to the entrance, two big oak doors were pushed open. The doors into the castle were big enough for a giant to walk through without ducking his head. Around the doors were golden roses and the handles were golden vines. Once in the castle, the floor was a reddish marble, great pillars of the same marble reached from the floor to the ceiling. There were big red and gold tapestries hung from the ceiling and blew with the breeze that was coming through the open doors. When Maggie entered the Throne Room, her Queen mother was sitting on her smaller throne to the right of the King's throne. Both thrones were gold with a vine of golden roses growing around and through them. The King's throne had golden thorns on the rose vine, and the Queen's throne had golden leafs. Both thrones had red velvet cushions filled with feathers.

"Maggie look at you," the Queen said as Maggie entered the room. "Your hair is a mess, your gown is dirty and your face is all red. You are a woman now and you are required to act like one. You will not be playing children's games anymore; you will act like a proper lady should."

Maggie was four and ten and had already had her first blood. Since then she had heard this speech daily. She didn't feel like a woman, she felt the same. Being a "proper lady" seemed boring; she would rather play with her brothers and sisters.

"Yes, Your Grace," Maggie replied and bowed her head. "Ser Jason said you craved words with me," Maggie knew there was more to be said.

"Your father's tourney is in two days and you are the eldest of his children. You will be dinning with the adults this year on the left of your father and you are required to mind your manners." The Queen stated. "The tourney starts on the full moon and ends at the next full moon, so our guests will be here awhile. This year will not be like last year, your presence is required at all events and dinners your father attends. This is the first tourney that you will be a woman at and you are to act like one."

Maggie thought all that would make a rather boring month but replied "I will do all that is required of me, mother."

"Very good, go to your chambers and get washed and changed," the Queen insisted.

So Maggie bowed and left the Throne Room and headed toward her chambers. She walked the hall that lead to Rose Tower. Servants were hurrying about with their hands full, some with clothes others with food.

Maggie grabbed one of the servants by the arm "Can you find my chamber maids and have them meet me in my chamber."

"Yes, Princess right away," the servant replied and ran off.

Maggie was in her chamber when her chamber maids Tansy and Violet came in. "Tansy fetch water for my bath. Violet help me get out of this gown," Maggie said to her maids.

Her water was ready and steaming by the time Violet had helped her get undressed. Maggie slide into the hot water, the heat from the water made her fair skin turn pink. Her maids washed out her hair and scrubbed the dirt and sweat from her skin. After her bath her maids dried her and helped Maggie step in to a pink gown. The gown was a soft shiny silk with pink pearls around the neck, sleeves and the bottom. The sleeves were tight from the shoulder to the elbow, and then stretched down to her waist. The neck was a V neck and if she had full breasts they would show beautifully, but Maggie's breasts were just starting to fill out so Maggie thought the gown look stupid on her. Violet laced the gown up tight so Maggie's curves would show.

Once dressed Maggie sat down on an oak stool in her chamber, Violet was pining Maggie's golden curls on top of her head. Ladies in the East always wore their hair up, only children wore their hair down. Once all of Maggie's hair was up, a thin golden crown was placed in front of her hair. The crown had three small golden roses with rubies in the middle. Maggie stood in front of the looking glass and did not recognize the woman starring back at her. A beauty with golden curls surrounding her heart shaped face, with big sky blue eyes and plump pink lips. The silk gown showed all her curves and shaped her breasts. Her mother was right, she was a woman now.

Maggie entered the small dining hall. During the tourney they would feast in the Great Hall, but until then they would have their meals in the small one. Her King father was at the head of the table with her Queen mother to his right. The rest of her siblings had not made it yet and her father was talking to his brother Prince Alexander down the table.

When she approached her father he stood to welcome her into an embrace, with his mouth by her ear he whispered "you look very beautiful Maggie."

"Thank you father," she answered blushing and took her seat to his left.

Shortly after her younger brother and heir to the throne, Jon, entered the dining hall. Jon was two and ten, and six inches shorter than Maggie. His golden curls touched his red cloak on his shoulders, he had the same color breeches as the cloak and a vest made of golden fabric. Jon greeted their father and mother and sat next to the Queen. Kate the youngest of the royal children followed close behind Jon. She was wearing a pink dress with red roses embroidered onto it, and her hair was tied away from her face with a pink ribbon. Kate's golden curls flowed down her back to her hips. She greeted father and kissed him on both cheeks then greeted her mother the same and took a seat next to Maggie. Jason came awhile later with his golden hair a mess and his face red from running. He was ten and the wildest of all the children. Jason wore simple brown breeches and a red vest with a rose broach over his heart.

"Forgive me for being late father, I lost track of time." The King gave a nod and Jason took his place by Jon.

At the foot of the table was their father's uncle Lord Jared, his wife Lady Jaquelyn to his right. To Lord Jared's left were his son Ser Jaron and his wife Jazmyn and their children Burton and Byron. Next to Lady Jaquelyn sat Lady Hallie who was wife to Prince Teagan. Next to her were her children Hanah and Harding, then Prince Teagan who was the King's youngest brother. Prince Alexander the King's brother sat next to Kate.

The serving wenches walked around the table pouring wine to the adults and goat's milk sweetened with honey for the children. They filled Maggie's chalice with sweet strawberry wine. The first course was mutton soup with carrots, celery and onions, that came with a dark rye bread. Maggie sampled to soup, but enjoyed the wine more. Her father was talking to her uncles about the tourney and going over the games. A singer was in the corner playing his harp to a jolly tune and Maggie was listening to his song more than listening to her father talk.

Once the bowls were taken away the servers brought a plate of mixed fruit and different cheeses. She nibbled on a pear and some of the yellow cheese when her uncle Teagan asked "Maggie are you looking forward to the tourney?"

Not really Maggie thought but answered with a smile "I can hardly wait."

Then her uncle turned his attention back to her father. Maggie ate all the fruit and all the yellow cheeses; she didn't care for the other cheese. She was eating the last bite of fruit when the servants brought a roasted swan on a big golden platter. They carved the swan as the servers were clearing the plates from the fruit and cheese. The swan was very tender and moist. With the swan the servers piled squash on everyone's plate. The last course was tarts filled with raspberries and dusted with sugar.

Once all the plates were cleared and all glasses emptied, her family bid good night and left the hall until her parents and siblings were the only ones left at the table.

"Jon, Jason and Kate head up to your chambers and change for bed. Maggie I would like to speak to you," the King told his family. The children hurried off and the King, Queen and Maggie were the only ones at the table.

"Maggie, you have turned into a very beautiful woman," her father said to her.

"Thank you, father."

"This will be the first year that you are available," her father said.

Maggie didn't like this she could feel her stomach start to twist "available for what?"

"Available for marriage," her father said, "there will be many high born men that will want your hand. The tourney is the perfect opportunity for them."

Maggie could not believe what she was hearing, she knew once you became a woman you got married to a man your family approved of, but she did not expect it to be this soon.

"I want you to give these men a chance, Maggie. Dance if they want to dance. Talk to them if they talk to you first. And mind your manners. You need to act like a lady," her father continued.

Maggie knew there was no arguing with him, he was the King and use to getting his way. "Yes father, I would very much like to find a husband," she said. It was not what she was feeling but she had found out saying what you felt didn't always work out. The conversation would go a lot quicker if she told her father what he wanted to hear.

"May I return to my chamber father? I am very tired and would like to be well rested for the tourney," Maggie asked her father.

"You may, good night Maggie."

"Good night father," she said and kissed him on both cheeks. "Good night mother," she said to her mother and kissed her as well, and left the hall.

Maggie did not feel like going back to her chamber so she headed toward the courtyard. Two guards stood in front of the massive oak doors with spears crossed in an X.

"Let me through ser, I want to visit the temple before bed," Maggie said to one of the guards.

"I am sorry Princess, but no one is to pass without the King's order."

"I do not remember my father declaring that Princesses are to take orders from knights!" Maggie was getting tired of people telling her what to do and she was not going to let some knight tell her what to do! "You will let me through or I will go to my father and get that Ser taken off your name!" Maggie said, hoping the knight would believe her threats.

"I am sorry Princess but until I get the order from your father you will not go through this door," the Knight answered, he was not going to budge.

Maggie turned and walked away. Maggie was so frustrated she was almost in tears, she walked swiftly to the Rose Tower. When she came to the stairs of the tower they were lit with a torch after every fifth stair. Maggie was out of breath by the time she reached her chamber on the eighth floor. When she entered her chamber she found her maids Violet and Tansy getting her room ready.

"Get me out of this gown."

"Right away miss," Violet answered and started unlacing the back of the gown.

When the gown fell away from Maggie it looked like a pink puddle on the floor. Maggie sat on the stool and let Tansy take her hair down and brush through the tangles.

"Leave me," Maggie said, her maids bowed and left the room. Maggie got in to bed, pulled the blankets to her chin and cried herself to sleep.

The cool morning air woke Maggie with a shiver. She opened her eyes, but did not want to get out of bed. *May haps I could sleep through the tourney* she thought, knowing that it was not going to happen. Maggie got out of bed and went to her window. The sun was just coming over the horizon and the sky was pink, orange and red then turned into different shades of blue as it reached across the land. She could see the bay below, and to both sides were magnificent gardens speckled with different colors of flowers. Maggie was sitting on her window seat when her maids came in.

"Violet I would like the lavender gown today, with the amethyst spider web for my hair," she told her maid.

Violet hurried to get everything. Maggie's maids dressed her in a lavender silk gown, with white lace and amethyst beads sewn around the neck and sleeves. Around her waist was a silver chain that almost touched the floor. Her hair was piled into the silver and amethyst spider web, with strands of curls kept out around her face. Once Maggie was dressed she headed toward the small dining hall to break her fast, and face her family.

The morning meal was always served one hour after sunrise and she knew it would be close to time. Maggie was the last to enter the small hall. Her family was already at there seats with the only open chair to her father's left.

"Forgive me father and mother for running late," Maggie said when she approached her parents.

"Nonsense, the others just got here," her father replied with a smile, "have a seat and we can start."

Maggie took her seat and the course began. The servants had squeezed juice from oranges and were filling everyone's chalice. Servers brought boiled eggs, a white bread with wild berries and fruit. Maggie was cracking her egg when her Queen mother asked "Maggie I was hoping you could accompany me today as I check on the preparations."

"I would love to mother," she replied, she didn't have anything better to do. She ate her egg, fruit and some of the bread and waited for everyone else to finish their meal.

Everyone had left the small hall except Queen Helen, Maggie, Lady Hallie, Lady Jaquelyn and Lady Jazmyn.

"We have six highborn families that will be staying with us in Diamond Tower. The lowborn knights and the houses arms with have tents set up in the court yard. All highborn knights in the tourney will be dinning with us in the Great Hall. We need to figure out the seating arrangement so as not to offend anyone," the Queen started, "Dolphin Keep has Lord Balder Turk, his wife Lady Caelie and their two children. Acorn Hill has Lord Huginn Merriman, Lady Charla and three children. Crystal Keep has my Lord father, my Lady mother and my oldest brother. Golden Rock has Lord Geirrod Chitwood, Lady Vanessa, their oldest son and his wife. Lionsgate has Lord Herman Stoddart, Lady Kacey and their three children. Spring's End has Lord Midir Mullen his wife Lady Rachelle and their son Rolland."

"That is two and twenty high lords, we can fit them all at one table," said Lady Hallie.

"Do we know how many knights will be in the tourney?" Lady Jazmyn asked the queen. Lady Hallie and Lady Jazmyn were the Queen's younger sisters, and married to the King's brother and cousin. All three women looked a lot alike as they all had large deep blue eyes, heart shaped faces and pail skin. The Queens hair was golden curls like Maggie's, but her sisters had a darker gold hair that looked more like honey and no curls.

"We have at the least ten lowborn knights from villages, plus each highborn house has one champion, plus all of our King's Guard," the Queen answered "so two and twenty at the least."

"We always have knights that travel from the other kingdoms too," said Lady Jaquelyn "so I would say at the least fifty knights total."

"The five hundred gold pieces the King is giving to the winner is sure to attract many," said the Queen, "I say we have the Royal table, then one for the high lords and three for the knights. We can always add tables if more sign up for the tourney."

"I agree," said Lady Hallie.

"Me too," Lady Jaquelyn agreed.

"Yes, that should be enough. What about the meals," asked Lady Jazmyn.

"I have ordered the cooks to take care of that. I have enough to do than to worry about courses," the Queen answered.

"Maggie, I have also been thinking of possible husbands for you," the Queen said with a smile. Maggie hadn't been paying much attention to the rest of the talk, but that brought her attention right away.

"Who have you thought of mother?" Maggie was curious who she would be given to, she knew all the high born families and never found any of the boys her age interesting.

"There is Charles Merriman of Acorn Hill; he is the heir and six and ten years old. His younger brother is four and ten, but I will not marry you to someone who has no claim. Kayden Stoddart of Lionsgate is five and ten and the heir to his father's city. Rolland Mullen is twenty and the heir to Spring's End. Caelan Turk is five and twenty and the heir to Dolphin Keep." The Queen went down her list.

"Which do you favor mother? Which city would be a better match? Any of the Lords would be happy to join the royal family I am sure" Maggie tried to say with out being rude, but she was so annoyed and her mother heard the defiance in her voice.

"Your father and I thought you would like to have some input, but we don't have to give you a choice if you do not appreciate what we are doing for you," the Queen said firmly.

"Beg pardons, mother I am just nervous about being betrothed is all." Maggie said with a blush.

"Maggie, every woman has been in your spot. You are lucky you have such a high list, everyone I have named is heir to a city," the Queen said gently.

"Yes mother, but in your situation you went from being a Lady to a Queen. I am going from being a Princess of Rosegarden to a Lady of a city. Being the eldest it is a step below my current position," Maggie said to her mother.

The Queen's expression changed from anger to pity. "Maggie, I will speak with your father about this. In all the history of the Four Kingdoms no one has ever joined kingdoms. There is no doubt you would make a great Queen, and you are already a great Princess." the Queen told Maggie.

"King Abhay of the South has two sons; his brother Prince Amar has two sons also. King Cynon of the West has three sons, and his brother Prince Cadogan has one. May haps His Grace will welcome the alliance, no doubt it would make our kingdom stronger," said Lady Jaquelyn to the Queen.

"Yes, it would help our kingdom to join houses with another. I will speak to my husband before our evening meal," the Queen was deep in thought it was plan on her face. Maggie wasn't sure that was what she meant to do, she wanted to stay in her castle, but she would rather stay a Princess or become a Queen than be a Lady.

DRAGON'S END

Xolan, the Red Wizard of the South, was standing beside King Abhay, the King of the South, in the throne room during court. The King was sitting on a massive stone throne that had a dragon perched on the top. The dragon was standing on hind legs with wings spread out toward the walls. Its head looked upon the court and it had large red rubies for eyes. The spear shaped tail curled around the throne to the floor. The King wore a red jerkin with his chest bare beneath it. His black breeches covered the tops of his serpent skin boots. His crown was red gold and in the shape of many flames as his raven black hair fell from beneath it with a braid on both sides that met in the back of his head. Xolan was in a red robe, with no sleeves, that drifted down to the floor in waves of silk. He had his great staff with a huge crystal on top of it in his left hand, and his ring on his right pointer finger. His ring was magnificent, in the shape of a snake curled around a red tiger's eye. Xolan's peppered beard met the middle of his stomach and his peppered hair was tied in the back. His hard black eyes were starring at the prisoner that had been brought before the King.

Ser Dakarai Ramey and Ser Kojo Jioner stood beside the prisoner and Ser Thabo Andre and Ser Ime Merrion behind. The prisoner was a huge man at least six and five feet tall, with big muscled legs and arms. His chest was wide and there were so many muscles on his shoulders they swallowed his neck. His olive skin was scarred and his black hair a tangled mess. He wore just a dirty brown tunic and his hands were bond in front of him. The people called him the Black Bull. The Black Bull had been riding around Fire Harbor raping women and killing their husbands, then stealing any valuables they had. The King had sent half his guard to hunt down the Bull and bring him to justice. It had not been easy. The Bull had killed two of the King's men while trying to escape.

"You are charged with rape, murder, theft, and murdering the King's own guard which is treason. What do you have to say?" Asked the King, in a stern voice.

"They got what was comin to 'em," the Bull answered in a raspy voice.

"The penalty for rape is your manhood, the penalty for theft is your hand, and for murder the penalty is sacrifice! You have brought death and despair to my country and you will pay dearly for it!" The King said in a loud voice, his face was turning red and Xolan thought he was about to get up and kill the man himself.

"I will let you choose your fate, Ser Sefu the die," the King held out his hand. Ser Sefu Hanlin brought out a cubed die with six sides to it, on each side was a different animal, and one side was blank. What ever side the die landed on, you would face that beast and have a chance of life. If you got the blank side you lost your head. The King stood and walked toward the prisoner. Ser Dakarai and Ser Kojo grabbed the prisoner's arms. The King put the die in one of the Bull's massive hands and stepped back.

The Bull stared at the King with hatred, his dark eyes trying to cut through the King.

"You roll or I roll, would you not rather decide your own fate than me do it for you," the King said meeting the Bull's eyes.

The Bull dropped the die to the floor. It rolled across the floor and hit the steps that lead up to the throne, wobbled and stopped a picture of a dragon pointing up toward the sky.

"You will face the dragon. If you live you are free, but first you must pay for your other crimes. Ser Dakarai make sure his manhood is removed along with his right hand. In two days you meet the dragon." With that the prisoner was dragged from the hall.

"Xolan walk with me," the King said as he headed toward the door behind the throne. Xolan followed close behind the King and waited for the King to start talking. They walked out the door, to the stairs. Xolan followed the King up the stairs to the third floor were the King turned to the right and took the fourth door on the left. They entered a room with a single table and three chairs, it was the King's "decision room" they called it. The King would sit for hours in this room and when he came out he would always have an order.

"Sit with me my friend," the King said and sat himself down in an oak chair. Xolan took a seat across from the King. "You have been with me many years and with my father before I was born. Tell me what brings such evil into the world?" The trial had been hard on the King. He never showed it until he was alone, *a King must be strong,* he would say.

"There have always been evil men, since the beginning of men. You can not have light without dark or white without black. You have many good men in your kingdom, Your Grace," Xolan said.

"Every evil man I kill, another takes his place. It is common knowledge I do not take crimes lightly, the punishment alone should be enough to scare them," the King answered.

"They do not think of the punishment until they are caught, Your Grace," Xolan stated.

The King took off his crown and placed it on the table. There was a dent in his forehead where the crown had sat. "Then we will change that. Have the villages notified that the Bull will meet the dragon in two days. Tell them that I command their presence! They will see what happens when you test my justice," the King ordered.

"Your Grace, I think they would find it more amusing than frightening."

"You do not think they fear the dragon," the King asked puzzled.

"They do, but they will be amused at the sacrifice part. They will see it as an adventure to come to the kingdom and see the dragon. They will be excited and gay. They care not for the Bull and most villages don't even know who he is. I say have the commons from Dragon's End, word will spread."

"May haps you are right old friend, I was getting carried away. What is your suggestion on crime?" The King asked.

"Have all the High Lords double their guard, with more knights about people will be more cautious."

"You are right. Have it written up for my signature and seal so we can send it out. Also let the commons know of the sacrifice. Thank you for your council. Now if you would excuse me I have to get ready for the midday meal with my family. I will see you at council after noon," the King said.

"Yes Your Grace," Xolan bowed and left the room.

Xolan took the stairs down to the bottom floor and walked the hall to the Flame Tower where his chambers were along with Sage Zuri and most of the other council members. Xolan made his way toward Sage Zuri's chambers, when he reached it he knocked on the door and waited for answer. Sage Zuri opened the door. He was shorter than Xolan and younger a man of five and forty. Zuri had short cropped black wavy hair and kept no beard. Above his eyes were huge bushy eyebrows. His face was narrow and his nose long and pointed.

"Xolan, to what do I have the pleasure?" Zuri asked with a friendly smile.

"His Grace would like it written that the High Lords must double their guard. Also His Grace would like the commons of the capitol to know that the Black Bull will meet the dragon in two days and all is welcome to come."

"I will have it ready for His Grace for council. Would you care for some wine Xolan?"

"Wine would be most welcome, it is an extremely hot day," Xolan answered and walked into Zuri's chamber.

Zuri wore a robe much like Xolan, but his was orange silk with a yellow sash tied about his waist. Zuri poured two chalices and handed one to Xolan.

"My thanks," Xolan said as he took the wine and took a sip. It was a dark summer wine and very sweet.

"How is His Grace today? Did the trial go well?" Zuri asked.

"Trials always weigh heavy on His Grace. He loathes so much despair being brought upon his people. The Bull had no regret in his eyes. He said all those people got what was coming to them. The Bull did not even object to the ruling or beg for his life. There is only evil in that man," Xolan answered.

"I am sure he will be begging for mercy soon," Zuri said with a smile. "What was the punishments, if I may ask?" Zuri was a curious man but very wise.

"His manhood and right hand is to be removed, and then he rolled the die on the dragon," answered Xolan.

"He will have a hard time facing a dragon with one had," Zuri had a wicked grin.

"He would have a hard time facing a dragon with both hands," Xolan laughed and Zuri joined in.

"Are we to hear anything interesting at council today?" Zuri was full of questions.

"I have not heard any new news. The docks are full of trading ships, we lost two guards to the Bull, other than that I am not sure what will come of today," Xolan answered. He had been too busy with the King this morning he hadn't talked to anyone else.

"Well, I better get started on those documents for council," Zuri said then emptied his chalice.

"I will see you then," Xolan said and left the room.

Xolan was weary and wanted to rest before council, so he headed to his own chambers. His servants Kwasi and Kwame were inside setting his meal on the table.

"My Lord, the servants from the kitchen just brought your meal up," Kwasi told him, Xolan nodded and sat at the table. It was a simple meal of fish cooked with spicy peppers, corn bread, and some hot cheese. After his meal Xolan sat by his window and read the histories of the Four Kingdoms until it was time for council.

When Xolan entered the council room most of the Lords were already seated. Lord Rajesh Smeltzer, the Master of Coin, was seated to the left of Xolan's chair. Lord Rajender Maillett, the Master of Arms, was at the end of the table. Lord Anand Filiso, the Commander of the Guard, was seated across from Lord Rajesh. Then Lord Kalyan Brunson, the Commander of Goods. To his left was Lord Raj Hugart, the Commander of the Docks. Then Lord Aravind Hamstra, the Master of Word. Lord Jitinder Chittick, the Chief Captain, was sitting next to Lord Punit Beckom, the King's Justice. Lord Yash Kouns, also the King's Justice, sat at the other end of the table. Sage Zuri sat across from Lord Punit. The King and his brother Prince Amar the King's Hand, walked in after Xolan took his seat. The King sat to Xolan's right and Prince Amar sat to the King's right.

"If you haven't heard, the Black Bull will meet the dragon in two days. I have also ordered his manhood and right hand be removed for rape and theft," the King announced to his council.

"Then we should start calling him the Black Cow, since he will no longer be a man," Lord Punit said with a smile. Lord Punit was a tall skinny man, with a long face, long arms and long legs. He had dark black hair to his shoulder and a short trimmed beard. His eyes were set close together in between his beak shaped nose.

"I am sure he would like that, he might not scare so many people being a Cow," Lord Yash said. He was always a cheerful man for being part of the King's Justice. Xolan thought he just liked killing and if so he was in the right position. Lord Yash was the opposite of Lord Punit, he was short, no taller than five feet and chubby. His round dark face had two chins, and was surrounded by his dark curly hair. He was clean shaven, had tiny eyes and a round nose.

"What other news or issues have arrived?" The King asked. It was obvious he no longer wanted to think about the Bull.

"There are problems in the Bloody Bay. The Sword and Bloodstone is at each other's throat about the trading ships coming in. Supposedly the ships dock at The Sword first and trade, then move on the Bloodstone. So Bloodstone is saying they are taking all the goods from them," announced Lord Raj.

"Write up a letter to Lord Smeltzer and tell him that we are not going to start a war over trading ships," said the King. "That should stop them for a while. The South has more ports than the West so they get what goods they can. Suggest Lord Smeltzer to go to Fire Harbor for the goods he cannot get from the ships."

"I will have it written out and ready for your seal before days end, Your Grace," said Lord Aravand.

"The King in the North has yet to be found and is presumed dead. His wife Queen Ana is with child and bout to burst from what I hear. If she does not have a son, I fear there might be a rebellion in the North," said Lord Aravind. Being Master of Word, he knew every rumor, truth and talk of all four kingdoms. It was said that he could find anything or anyone. He was a plump bald man of many years. His beard had gone all gray and made his skin look darker than it was. He had large, gray bushy eye brows and big, round brown eyes. He never wore armor but simple robes or tunics. Today Lord Aravind was in a bright green tunic that came to his knees with a golden belt about his waist and a golden chain at his neck. All his fingers had a ring on them and he had a golden armband on both wrists.

"I care not for matters in the North, we are far enough away they will not trouble us," the King said.

"Your Grace, we lost two guards to the Bull and I need to replace them," stated Lord Anand.

"Promote two from the Capitol Guard to the King's Guard," said the King "You can hold try outs and pick whom ever you like."

"My thanks, Your Grace," Lord Anand replied.

"A trading ship has come in from the islands with silk, lace and jewels and I thought your Queen might enjoy having a look, Your Grace," said Lord Raj.

"I will speak to her tonight and let you know on the morrow her decision. Anything else?"

"Your Grace, I have the documents to all the High Lords to double their guards and it is ready for your signature and seal," announced Zuri.

"Yes, is there anything else I need to sign and seal today?" the King asked.

"Yes, Your Grace, the East has asked that you allow passage from the Split for their tourney. I have them here to send to the guards at the crossing," replied Zuri.

"Very well, it could not hurt for some of my people to come back with a little gold from Rosegarden. We are much better with a lance in the South, though I am sure the East would disagree," the King said, "But we cannot afford to lose any of our knights here at the capitol with the sacrifice only two days away. Lord Anand, you must let your men know they are not to attend this tourney in the East, I need them here."

"Yes, Your Grace, you will have all the swords you command," replied Lord Anand.

The King signed and sealed all documents then said, "If that is all, I have other matters to attend." With that the King stood and left.

Xolan left the council room and headed towards his chamber. He was halfway there when his servant Kwame came running up to him.

"My Lord you have a message, I have been trying to find you," Kwame said and handed the rolled paper to Xolan.

Xolan unrolled the paper and it said, *Lord Hugart is riding from Fire Harbor to see that justice is done to the Black Bull. He requests His Grace King Abhay of Dragon's End and King of the South to provide the hospitality of his house. Lord Hugart is traveling with his Lady wife and their five children and one hundred guards. His guards have tents if there is not room enough for them. Lord Hugart will be arriving on the morrow. He thanks His Grace ahead of time for the hospitality.*

Xolan rolled up the paper, "have the servants get the guest chambers ready. Lord Hugart will be arriving on the morrow."

"Yes, My Lord," Kwame said and ran off.

Xolan found Ser Dakarai and Ser Kojo standing outside the King's chamber.

"Is his Grace inside?" Xolan asked Ser Dakarai.

"Yes, My Lord," the knight replied. Ser Dakarai wore red gold armor with a white tunic underneath. He had the yellow cloak of House Cvetkovich fastened to his shoulders. His long sword at his hip, the hilt came up to his chest and the tip was three inches from the floor. Ser Dakarai always kept his hand on his swords hilt. Xolan knocked on the door and waited for a reply.

"Enter," he heard from inside. Xolan entered the King's chamber and found the King and Queen Kala sitting at the balcony drinking wine.

"Your Grace," Xolan bowed and kissed Queen Kala's hand. The Queen was a rare beauty. Tall and slender with straight raven black hair that flowed down past her waist. She had a long face with big black eyes, a small nose and a beautiful mouth. Her breasts were plump and the top of them were sticking out the top of her dress. The golden chain around her neck held a great ruby and made her copper skin glow.

"Xolan have you missed me?" The King asked with a smile.

"Your Grace, I have just received word that Lord Hugart is coming to Dragon's End on the morrow," Xolan replied, "He is traveling with his Lady wife, five children and one hundred guards. I have told my servant to get the guest chambers ready, and was wondering were to put the guards?"

"See if there is room in the King's Guard Tower," the King suggested, "We will also need to let the cooks know for feast, and find extra servants for Lord Hugart and his family." The King thought a moment than said to his Queen "You will be able to entertain Lady Hugart I hope?"

"Of course I will be glad for the company."

"Did the message say how long he is planning on staying?" The King asked Xolan.

"No, Your Grace, but I would assume they will leave after the sacrifice."

"I am glad he is coming. His men can spread word to the southwest about what happens when you test my laws. Xolan, I will want you around the whole time Lord Hugart is here. You have a great gift for reading people and I need that," the King ordered.

"Yes, Your Grace, I will be your shadow," Xolan said.

"Very good, make sure everything is ready for their arrival," and with that the King turned his attention back to his wife. Xolan bowed and left the King.

Lord Raghu Hugart of Fire Harbor showed up at Dragon's End at midday. A massive host of one hundred guards surrounded a curtained wagon. Lord Hugart's banners swayed in the wind, orange flames on a black background. Lord Hugart and his sons, Ratan and Ratnam, were riding behind the first line of guards. His wife Lady Krishna and daughters Rashmi, Rati and Ratna rode in the curtained wagon. As the guests entered the gates of the capitol, the common folk scattered to get out of the way. Lord Hugart made his way up the road past the inn, brothel and market towards the castle. The King's Gate opened before his guests arrived and Xolan walked with the King out into the courtyard to meet their guests.

Twenty guards on horse came riding through the gate first, all in a bronze colored armor with half helms and black cloaks. The Guards on the end held the banner of House Hugart. Lord Hugart and his sons followed the first row of guards with five guards on either side of them. The curtained wagon followed surrounded by guards and the last twenty guards were behind it.

Lord Hugart dismounted his horse and helped his sons down from their horses, as Lady Hugart stepped out of the wagon with her daughters close behind. The King and Xolan walked up to greet them. As they approached, the guests got down on one knee and bowed.

"Your Grace," Lord Hugart said "My apologies for the short notice."

"Do not worry yourself with that, I am glad you came," the King replied.

"Your Grace, let me introduce my wife Lady Krishna, my eldest daughter Rashmi, my heir Ratan, my younger daughters Rati and Ratna and our youngest son Ratnam," Lord Hugart said as he pointed to each.

"Your Grace," they all said and bowed their head to their King.

"Lady Krishna, my wife is expecting you and the children, I am sure she has a busy day planned, if you would like."

"It would be an honor, Your Grace," she replied.

The King led his guests into the castle and Xolan made sure to keep close behind. The King was still a young man of five and thirty and Xolan was finding it hard to keep up. As they climbed the steps into the great castle. Xolan was looking up at the towers above. The castle was built of sandstone and had fifty steps leading up to it. Three massive towers reached into the sky. All with a huge stone dragon perched on the top. The doors entering the castle were oak doors ten feet tall and had a stone dragon on either side of them. Each stone dragon in the castle was different; some had wings stretched out, some on all fours, and some sitting.

They passed through the doors and headed to the throne room where the Queen and royal children were waiting. The throne room had two great yellow banners on both walls with giant red dragons embroidered on them. Dragon skulls from long ago were in all four corners of the room. The Queen sat on a cushioned stool next to the throne and the royal children were standing beside her. She stood and approached Lord Hugart's host. She was radiant today in a crimson silk gown that flowed to the floor, at her shoulders streams of yellow silk came down to her waist. Her belt was gold with tiny rubies that matched the ruby around her neck. She wore her red gold crown on top her head and her raven black hair had been curled.

Lord Hugart bowed and kissed the Queen's hand "Your Grace," he said as he stood. His wife did the same along with their children.

"I am so glad you could make it Lord Hugart," the Queen said with a lovely smile, "these are our children, Princess Kaja, Prince Akash, Princess Kali and Prince Akhil." Each child gave a friendly nod as their name was called. "I am sure they will have a gay time playing with your children," the Queen said to Lord Hugart.

"Kaja, why don't you show Lord Hugart's children around the castle," the Queen turned and said to her daughter. The Princess went down the steps and took the hand of Rashmi and headed out the door with all the other children following behind.

"Lady Krishna would you care to join me for some summer wine, and I have a singer that I absolutely adore waiting?" the Queen asked Lady Hugart.

"It would be an honor, Your Grace," the Lady answered and followed the Queen out the door.

After everyone had left except the King, Xolan and Lord Raghu Hugart, the King told the guards to wait outside the throne room. "Lord Hugart, we had the trial for the Bull the day before and he was charged with rape, theft, murder and treason. He will loose his manhood and right hand, and then he will meet the dragon on the morrow," the King said.

"My thanks for your justice, Your Grace. The Bull murdered my men as well when we tried to capture him." Said Lord Hugart, "He has made many widows, and most have to start anew with no man to care for them. I was wondering what you would suggest I do?"

"May haps you can use some extra servants in your castle," the King answered, "The women who have lost their husbands are sure to welcome that."

"A wonderful idea, Your Grace. I was also wondering once the dragon is done with the Bull if I could take whatever would remain to show the villagers that justice was done?" Lord Hugart asked.

"I think that would be good for the villagers to be reassured that I don't take likely to rapists and murderers." the King answered, "You shall have any remains."

"My thanks, Your Grace." Lord Hugart bowed.

"Might I see the dragon the Bull is to meet, Your Grace?" asked Lord Hugart with a smile.

"Why of course, I have two dragons but I do believe that I am going to give the Bull to the male. They are both cruel but the male is much meaner," the King said, "Come, we will see my beasts."

The King lead with Lord Hugart by his side and Xolan following. They went out the back of the throne room to the stairs that lead to the dungeon. The dungeon was three levels, the first was where all the beasts

on the die were keep. The second for prisoners with minor crimes that were
not sentenced to death. The third level was for prisoners sentenced to die.
The third level was the worst, full of cells so small that the prisoners could
neither stand nor lay down flat.

They walked down the stairs and found two of the King's Justice Guards
outside the door to the first level. "Your Grace," they said as they bowed
and stepped aside. All the beasts were kept in pits so you could see them
from above. The first pit was full of massive snakes as big around as a man's
leg and twenty feet long. When a prisoner rolled the snake they would be
squeezed until their bones were crushed and their eyes popped out of their
head. The second pit was four gators, five and ten feet long with massive jaws
that would rip a man apart. The third pit had three bears, one male and two
females. They had cubs every year and made a great profit for the crown. The
fourth pit had six lions, with one male. Usually the King would only put the
male up to face prisoners but occasionally he would put more than one. At
last, they came to the final pit. Which was as large as the throne room and so
deep it went all the way to the third floor. Two beautiful dragons lay asleep.
The male was an emerald green with a head as large as a wagon. His tail was
thirty feet long with a point like a spear at the end of it. When he stretched
out his wings they were as wide as he was long. The female was a purple
black color, she was quite smaller than the male. Her head and tail were half
the size as her partners.

"Xolan get me the horn," the King said. Xolan went to the wall and took
a bone horn down and handed it to the King. The King pressed his lips to
it and blew a big Ahhhhhooooooooooo. Both dragons' heads shot up and
looked right at the King. Their eyes were the colors of rubies glowing in a
flame. They both stood on hind legs and stretched their wings with heads
pointed toward the sky.

"Eaahoo," the King commanded in a loud firm voice, and the dragons
opened their mouths and bright flames came out and licked at the stone
walls of the pit.

"I am their father, they know and trust me. They only take commands
from myself and Xolan. No other man can control them," the King told Lord
Hugart.

Lord Hugart was both amazed and terrified. All the color had left his
skin, but he could not take his eyes off the dragons. Xolan knew that look,
he wants the dragons for himself he thought. Xolan concentrated and tried
to enter Lord Hugart's thoughts. Lord Hugart was picturing the power he
could have if he had a dragon.

"Your Grace, what do you do once the dragons breed? Do you sell the eggs?" Asked Lord Hugart, the question brought Xolan back.

"Dragons' eggs take years to hatch, when that happens I will keep any offspring. I would not allow anyone else to have a dragon," the King said. *The King knows Lord Hugart wants one*, Xolan thought.

The dragons had three eggs two years ago and the female had them under her right now, though you could not see. The King had been hoping they would hatch soon. These were the only dragons left in all the four kingdoms, all the rest had died or were killed. It is not an easy thing to kill a dragon, but it is possible.

"Come Lord Hugart, I am sure you are weary from your ride and wish to rest before we eat," the King said and turned to walk back toward the door.

Lord Hugart stayed and looked at the dragons until Xolan put his hand on his shoulder and said "My Lord." Then Lord Hugart come out of his dream and followed the King.

As they walked up the stairs the King said "Xolan would you be so kind as to show Lord Hugart to his chambers?"

"It would be my pleasure, Your Grace."

When they reached the top of the stairs the King went toward his own chambers and Xolan said "My Lord, I have chambers ready for you in the Guest tower. I am sure your Lady wife and children have already been showed the way. I will have a servant come and let you know when the feast is ready."

"Very good Xolan," Lord Hugart answered and followed Xolan up the stairs toward his chamber.

"Her Grace has had a wonderful feast prepared in your honor, My Lord and there will be jesters and singers also," Xolan was telling Lord Hugart, hoping to get his mind off the dragons. A man's desires could be a dangerous thing.

"That is very kind of the Queen to go through so much trouble."

As they reached the fifth floor of the tower Xolan said "This entire floor is for you and your family, My Lord. Your chamber is at the end of the hall and your children have the other chambers."

"My thanks Xolan. Will you be attending the feast?"

"Yes, My Lord."

"Then I will see you soon," Lord Hugart said and entered his chamber.

Xolan was to the right of the King in the great hall when Lord Hugart and his family arrived. Lord Hugart had changed into an orange tunic with a leather jerkin over it, black breeches and high boots. His black cloak with orange flames was fastened at his shoulder with a bronze brooch that had crystals embedded in it. Lady Hugart was in an orange silk gown that had black pearls sewn around the neck and sleeves. She was younger than Lord Hugart and very pretty. Her round face was surrounded by dark brown hair, and she did not have as dark of skin as most in the south. She had an hour glass shape; big breast, small waist, big hips. She was an average sized woman, not skinny but not fat. Their children followed behind Lady Hugart all in the black and orange of their house.

"Lord Hugart and Lady Hugart, will you join our table? The children may sit with my children," the King asked.

"You honor us, Your Grace," Lord Hugart answered and took a seat next to Xolan and Lady Hugart set next to the Queen. Prince Amar and his wife Lady Rachana entered the hall next with their children Abhilasha, Akanksha, Amit and Amrit. Prince Amar took a seat by Lord Hugart and his wife next to him while their children joined their cousins. Then the Queen's brother, Lord Rajesh Smeltzer, came and sat next to Lady Hugart. The rest of the King's Council and their wives had been seated at a table by the children's table. Toward the end of the hall were twenty tables that sat Lord Hugart's guards and the King's Guard.

"Let the feast begin," the King announced, and with that the singers started to play their instruments and the servants hurried in with flagons of wine to fill everyone's chalice. After the chalices were full the first course came out. It was a clam stew with black bread. Xolan enjoyed the creamy stew and the sweet summer wine, as the King talked over him to Lord Hugart about Fire Harbor and the docks. The second course arrived as the bowls from the first course were being taken away. It was gator rolled and baked in crushed nuts with a sweet mustard seed sauce poured over it. After the second course was served, flame throwers entered the hall and in the middle of the room lit torches and started to juggle the flames. The children seemed very entertained by the jugglers. The third course was white cheese served with different raw peppers of the south. The cheese helped put out the fire the peppers left on their tongues. Xolan liked spicy food. The cooks in the south always used hot peppers and spices. The fourth course came as the jesters were filing in. It was roasted swan with green vegetables. The jesters were doing simple tricks and making the children laugh until their eyes were watering. The swan was delicious, very tender and moist. The last course was sweet rolls covered with honey, it was obviously the children's favorite dish.

After all the plates were cleared the women excused themselves and took the children. The knights and guards left to go to their post, or to a brothel nearby. Now it was just the King, Xolan, Lord Hugart and the council members. The council members got up from their seats at their table and joined the King's table.

"The sacrifice will be at midday on the morrow, Dagda the Great God will be pleased," the King announced. "Lord Punit, did you bring what I asked?"

"Yes, Your Grace," Lord Punit said and handed a small chest to the King.

"Lord Hugart, I told you that you could have any parts of the Bull, so here is a start. Whatever is left on the morrow you shall have then," the King said and handed Lord Hugart the chest.

Lord Hugart opened the chest to find the Bull's right hand and shriveled cock, "My thanks, Your Grace," he said.

"Now if you would excuse me, I would like to be rested for the morrow. Xolan walk with me to my chamber," the King stood and said. Xolan got up and followed the King out of the great hall.

"Xolan, I would like you to check on the dragons tonight before the sacrifice. Make sure that you let the guards know that no one is to leave their post outside the door on the first level of the dungeon, and no one is to enter except you or me. Lord Hugart is interested in my dragons and I would not like him to do something stupid that would make me kill him," the King said to Xolan.

"I will go to the dungeons after I see you to your chambers, Your Grace."

"Does Lord Hugart know about the eggs?" The King asked.

"No, Your Grace. I read his thoughts and he has no idea. The female was hiding them well. Even if someone was to enter she would not let anyone but us near those eggs," Xolan assured the King.

"Very good, I don't want him or anyone else for that matter to know that I will soon have three more dragons. I am envied throughout the four kingdoms for my dragons. If people knew about the eggs there would be a lot of trouble," said the King.

"Yes, Your Grace. I agree completely," Xolan answered.

Once they reached the King's chambers the King said "My thanks, friend," and entered his chambers and shut the door. Xolan headed toward the dungeons. He climbed down the stairs to the first floor of the dungeon and found two guards standing outside the door.

"The King orders that two guards be placed outside this door at all times. No one is to leave their post, and no one is to enter except me or the King," Xolan told the guards.

"Yes, My Lord," the guard replied and let Xolan enter. He walked to the last pit and took the stairs that lead to the door of the dragon's pit. He went into where the dragons were lying. They greeted him kindly, the female nuzzled his shoulder and the male laid his head down so Xolan could run his hand over the top of his head. He walked around them to the belly of the female, where she kept her eggs. She let out a cry as he walked around. He put a hand on her hot belly; it was like touching an ember out of the hearth. He went toward her hind legs and looked to make sure the eggs were safe and warm. He didn't see the eggs; he walked down toward her tail. They weren't there either, *may haps she moved them* he thought. "Flaahh," Xolan commanded and both dragons took flight. They had a twenty foot chain around one hind leg so they could not fly out of their pit. Xolan walked around the pit, looking in every corner and cave of the pit. *Nothing, they are all gone. How can this be even if Lord Hugart got past the guards the dragons would of burnt him alive at first sight*, Xolan thought. Xolan put his hand where the eggs used to be and tried to see who was last to enter the pit. He concentrated hard trying to see who took the eggs and where they are now. *Nothing, my powers can't even sense the eggs*, Xolan thought puzzled. The Red Wizard could read thoughts, sense danger, control fire, and see the past and future; but nothing was coming to him. This had to be the work of another just as powerful. Lord Hugart had no power or Xolan would have sensed it.

Xolan hurried from the pit, and ran to the door. "Who was the last to enter!" he commanded of the guard.

"The King with you and Lord Huggart. No one has entered since, My Lord," the guard replied. Xolan pushed past him and ran up the stairs toward the King's chamber. He ran out the dungeon toward the tower where the King's chambers were. He ran up the stairs and toward the door where the guards stood.

"Stand aside, I have urgent matters for the King," Xolan ordered the guards and they moved away from the door. Xolan didn't bother to knock and rushed right into the room. The King was sitting on the balcony looking out to the bay. Xolan rushed to his side, "Your Grace, the eggs are gone!"

WEST WATCH

King Cynon McCue, the King of the West, woke next to his naked wife, Queen Aileen. She had her head on his shoulder and her arm across his chest. Cynon slowly moved his wife's arm and slipped out of bed careful not to wake his Queen. He walked to the privy to relieve himself, and found his ward Dermot McNeely, who was the Queen's nephew, sleeping in his bed.

Cynon shook his ward awake, "Get my clothes," he told his ward and walked back to his bed chamber. Cynon always woke before day break. Being a King was a lot of work and it seemed there weren't enough hours in the day to get everything done. Dermot entered the room with a grey tunic, black breeches and a black doublet. Dermot helped the King get dressed. Cynon put on his sword belt and placed his sword *Justice* in its scabbard, and then he placed a dagger on the right side of his belt and another dagger in his boot. Dermot fastened his cloak of dark and light blue with a red crown embroidered on it.

When Cynon left his chamber he found his cousin Ser Brady standing guard, "good morrow cousin," the King said.

"Your Grace, Lennox was just here asking if you were up. He said to inform you that he would be waiting for you in the library with a message," Ser Brady told the King.

Lennox was the West Wizard, and a loyal friend to the King. Wizard Keep sent one of the four most powerful wizards to every kingdom to serve the King, and Lennox served Cynon's father before him. Lennox was very powerful and knew things before they occurred. Cynon headed toward the library to see what message awaited him.

When he entered he found Lennox standing by the window looking out to the sea. "Lennox, you have returned quickly. Is that good or bad?" The King asked his wizard.

"It has been done, Your Grace," Lennox replied and nodded to a chest in the corner of the room. Cynon walked over to the oak chest and opened it. Inside were three eggs, each egg was emerald green with black speckles.

"How did you get them so quickly?" The King asked.

"The South was preparing for an execution and Lord Hugart had come to the castle to bare witness. Lord Hugart kept the King busy and with all his men about no one was curious about an unfamiliar face," Lennox replied. "I put the dragons in a trance and slipped in and out in the blink of an eye. I was gone before the Red Wizard even knew the eggs were gone."

"Do you think the Red Wizard will suspect us?"

"No, I placed a spell to block his vision. He will think it was Lord Hugart. I could not have shown up at a better time."

"Good, I don't want the South to know it was us until the dragons are hatched and grown. King Abhay thinks he is the most powerful and feared of the kingdoms because he has the only dragons. Well that will be the case no more, he has two dragons and I will have three," the King was pleased with the news.

Cynon had been planning this since Lennox informed him that Abhay's dragons laid eggs, but there was never a chance to try to get them without being suspected. The West and South were always fighting. The West had better soldiers by far but they were no match to dragons. Now the West will be the strongest.

"Lennox when will they hatch?"

"When I touched them I got a vision that they will hatch in days."

"Good, the sooner the better, may haps its better we did wait so long to take them," the King replied. Cynon picked one of the eggs up. It was scorching hot almost too hot to hold onto.

"Lennox, take them down to the dungeon in the dark cells were no one goes. We can't have anyone finding out that we have this and risk word getting to the South."

"Yes, Your Grace. Most are still in bed I will take them down before the castle wakes," and with that Lennox picked up the chest and left the room.

A couple seconds after Lennox left there came a knock at the door. "Enter," Cynon announced and two servants came in with a tray of food and honey mead. Cynon broke his fast on bacon fried crisp, eggs with peppers and cheese, a hard bread and honey mead. After the King's belly was full, he left to find his brother Prince Cadogan to see if there were any important matters that needed his attention. All royal messages went to Cadogan first to lighten the load for Cynon. If it was important the King would address it himself. Cynon left the library and headed down the stairs toward his brother's tower called Sword Tower. When he reached the stairs to Sword Tower, the King started the climb. The first floor was for Prince Cadogan's children, Barry and Bedelia. The second floor had a dinning hall and a smaller library. The third floor housed his brother's servants, and the fourth floor was where his brother's chambers were.

Cynon made it to the fourth floor and turned to the right. He found Ser Wallace McBride standing guard outside Cadogan's door. "Is the Prince still in his chambers?" The King asked the guard.

"Yes, Your Grace."

Cynon knocked on the door and entered before his brother could respond. Prince Cadogan was still in bed with his wife Lady Athne. Cadogan woke when the King entered. Cadogan looked a lot like the King, so much that people would mistake them for one another when they were children. His red hair was a mess from sleep, and his bright green eyes were half closed. Both Cadogan and Cynon had more freckles to count on their pail skin. They both had the same build, wide shoulders, muscular arms and legs, and they both stood six feet tall.

"Why knock if you are just going to walk right in?" Cadogan asked his brother.

"You expect me to wait outside your door?"

"The rest of the world likes sleep brother. Might be one day you won't wake me before the sun does. So to what do I owe the honor of your presence?"

"We need to talk where no ears can hear brother. Might we go somewhere?" Cynon waited as his brother stood from the bed. Cadogan was as naked as his name day, and Cynon turned until his brother had covered himself. Cadogan led Cynon to the next room and shut the door. "Lennox has recovered the eggs," the King told his brother.

"And he was not noticed at Dragon's End?"

"No, Lord Hugart was there and brought many men, so no one thought twice about a strange face. Lennox also placed a spell so the Red Wizard can't trace the eggs to us. The South won't know about the eggs until they are hatched and grown," Cynon replied.

"Good, how are you to keep dragons unknown?" Cadogan asked.

"They are in the black cells of the dungeon. No one goes there and we haven't had a prisoner down there in years. They will go unnoticed until it is time to reveal them," stated the King.

"I got a message the day before and was going to show you today. King Tristan wants to join our houses with the marriage of his eldest daughter

Margery to your Aidan. I was unsure about the match, but now it seems like a great idea. If you hold his daughter then if it came to war against the South the East would have to join us. We would have the biggest army any of the kingdoms have ever seen," Cadogan informed Cynon.

"Yes, this could not have come at a better time. With all the knights and soldiers of the West and East, and three dragons no one would be stupid enough to defy us," said Cynon. "I will speak to Aileen and Aidan and have you send the reply."

"There are three eggs brother, once they are hatched we need to start training them. I am giving one to you to train; Lennox will train one, and myself. We are the only three that know about them and I want to keep it that way. The less people that know the less likely word will reach the South. Not even our wife's are to know, women have loose tongues," Cynon told his brother.

"I agree, but how are we to explain our absence when we are with the dragons? Both of us always have guards around us and people always need us for something," asked Cadogan.

"We will have them believe we are not in the castle. If they think we are not here they won't look for us, besides no one will go down to the dark cells," answered Cynon. "Lennox says they should hatch in a couple days, until then we will not talk about it. The walls of this castle have ears," Cynon said. Cadogan gave a nod of agreement.

Cynon could not believe that everything was finally falling into place. His whole life he had been working towards having the strongest kingdom. If anyone was stupid enough to defy him he would crush them easily. It was like the gods wanted him to be the most powerful. Since he had come into his throne, the South has been testing his power, and hiding behind their dragons. But now their two dragons would be nothing to the power he would hold.

Cynon was almost bursting with excitement. He would be the most powerful in all the Four Kingdoms. The North has their giants and beasts, the East has their gold, the South has their dragons, and the West were fighters. But now, no one could match the West's strength. With the armies of the West and East and three dragons, no one could stop him.

"When will you talk to Aileen about the East Princess?" Cadogan asked.

The question had brought Cynon out of his thoughts. "I will go to her now," he replied. Cynon left his brother and headed down the stairs out of Sword Tower. When he reached the bottom of the tower that was connected to the rest of the castle he saw his three children playing with their dogs in the hall.

His children favored their mother; they had auburn colored hair instead of his bright red hair. They had the pail skin, but barley any freckles and his daughter and younger son had blue eyes instead of green.

"Good morrow father," his youngest daughter Ailis said as she ran into his arms.

"Good morrow, I trust you slept well last night sweetling," he said.

"Yes, I was having a great dream, then Princess jumped on my bed and woke me," she told her father. Princess was the name of her dog.

The dogs were large half wolf and half snow dog. On all fours their back came below the King's hip.

"Father, look at the trick I have taught Bow," Ailin called. Ailin was Cynon's middle son and Bow was the name of his dog.

Cynon watched as Ailin told the dog to roll over, "very good," he replied. Aidan his oldest son and heir to the throne headed toward him with his dog Killer.

Aidan, was six and ten and already as tall as his father. His auburn hair surrounded his round face, and he had his father's bright green eyes. He was muscular for his age, broad shoulders and strong arms. Black breeches covered his long legs and leather boots covered his feet. He was wearing the colors of his house, a red tunic and blue jerkin. His long sword *Death Bringer* was at his hip.

"Aidan, I was on my way to see your mother, will you join me? I have news for the both of you," Cynon said to his heir.

"Yes, father. Did you get a message from Uncle Cadogan?"

"I have, and for once it is good news," Cynon answered. Aidan and Killer followed him toward the Blood Tower. When they reached his chamber, the guards had switched and this time Ser Angus, the King's cousin, guarded the door. Ser Angus was the son of Lord Donal who was uncle to the King. He wore steel armor and a red and blue cloak.

"Good morrow cousin, have you seen my wife?" The King asked.

"No, Your Grace, she has not came out of her chamber as of yet," Ser Angus replied.

Cynon and Aidan walked into the bed chamber and found Queen Aileen sitting on a stool with her maids fixing her hair. The Queen wore a blue gown that made her blue eyes brighter, her auburn hair fell in ringlets down her back and braids pulled it away from her round face. She had big blue eyes and full lips that smiled at him when he walked in. She stood to great him and her dress fell down to the floor, the bell sleeves almost to her knees had white pearls sewn around them. The V neck of her gown showed the tops of her breasts.

"My loves, to what do I owe the pleasure?" She asked as she kissed him and then her son.

"Cadogan got a message yesterday from the East. King Tristan wishes to join our houses with the marriage of his eldest daughter Margery to Aidan," Cynon said. His wife's eyebrows went up and wrinkled her forehead.

"That would be proper to marry a Princess to a Prince, it is a better honor than a high born lady. What is your thought on it?" She asked her husband.

"I think it is an alliance that we could use," Cynon answered.

"I have heard that she has grown into a beauty, golden curls with eyes as blue as the sea. Tell me Aidan would you agree to this marriage and alliance of kingdoms?" Aileen asked her son.

"If father believes that it would be good for our kingdom for me to marry this princess then I will," Aidan answered. Cynon was proud of his son, he would make a great king one day. A king had to think of what would be best for his kingdom above all things.

"Then it is agreed? Should I send to King Tristan and tell him we accept?" Cynon asked his wife.

"Yes, if I remember correct they are having their annual tourney until the next full moon. Invite him and his family to join us in the celebration of the marriage and joining of kingdoms to be held after his tourney is at an end," the Queen answered. "I will start on the wedding preparations and invites. We shall invite the royals from the other kingdoms also and all highborn lords of the West. It will be a celebration everyone will remember and no one will be able to top."

"Very good. I will go let Cadogan know. My love I will see you at midday," Cynon said to his Queen and kissed her full on the lips.

When they left the chamber Aidan asked his father "So what good would it bring our kingdom to join with the East?"

"If there ever comes a time when we are at war, the joining would require the East to be on our side, which would double our forces. Plus the East has more gold than the North, South and West put together. If it were the North or South wanting to join houses I would think harder on it, but the East could be helpful to have on our side," Cynon explained to his son.

"Will I meet this princess before the wedding?" Aidan asked.

"Most likely not, may haps the day before," Cynon answered. Aidan nodded, he was deep in thought.

"May I be excused father? I was going to practice swords with Ser Braden before midday meal."

"Yes, I will see you soon," Cynon said to his son. Aidan turned and went toward the court yard with Killer at his heels.

When Cynon reached the base of Blood Tower Lennox was standing by the stairs. "Your Grace," Lennox bowed in greeting.

"Lennox, find my brother and you and him meet me at the stables," Cynon said to the wizard.

"Yes, Your Grace," as Lennox hurried to the Sword Tower. Cynon found his ward Dermot by the Throne Room and instructed him to have three horses saddled. The boy wanted to join and Cynon insisted that he stay behind. Cynon waited awhile before heading to the stables. When he got there Lennox and his brother were waiting.

"Where are we off to?" Prince Cadogan asked.

"Toward the forest," was all the King said as he climbed onto his horse and galloped out the gates.

ICESTORM CASTLE

Ser Florian Gaddy lay in bed, the Queen asleep on his shoulder. She was big with child, his child. The entire kingdom thought it to be the missing King's child, but he and Ana knew it was his. Ser Florian was Queen Ana's personal guard. He was with her twenty hours out of the day. His bedchamber was connected to hers' and to get to her, people had to go through his chamber first. He came to Icestorm when he was a boy of six and ten. He was squire to the King Conell's personal guard. After he was knighted at eight and ten, King Conell appointed him to become Ana's guard, since that day he has not left her side. She was just a child of seven at the time. He had been guarding her for thirteen years.

At first they were as close as siblings, and then when Ana was four and ten she kissed him for the first time. They had been lovers since. He was heart broken when King Conell ordered on his death bed for her to marry her cousin Finn. Deep down Florian knew he would never be allowed to marry Ana. He was not a lord from a highborn family, but the thought of another man touching her drove him mad. He and Ana had continued their affair after her marriage to Finn, but Finn had rights to her.

When King Finn went missing six months past, it was the happiest day of his life. As long as their child turned out to be a boy Ana would not have to marry again. Her council has already been pressuring her to take a new husband, but she would not let them talk about it until after the child is born. King Conell left no male heirs, his wife died giving birth to his younger daughter Arian. King Conell remarried and that wife died of fever, and passed the disease to the King. Ana was the heir, but she needed a king and a Mathis always had to sit the throne. So King Conell ordered her to marry her cousin Finn so her name would not change and a Mathis would be king.

King Finn got reports of villagers being killed six months past, and took a hunting party to find the beast responsible. He never returned, nor did any of the hunting party. No body had been recovered, but the chances that he was still alive after so long were impossible. The Queen sighed, and Florian put his arm around her. He prayed every day that the Queen would have a son and not be forced to marry another cousin. If she had a boy, he would be king when he got old enough. No one could say the baby wasn't Finn's, which would make the baby the heir.

There was only a couple hours left before sunrise, and Florian knew he would have to go to his own bed before Ana's maids came in. Florian laid the Queen's head on the feathered pillow and slipped out from underneath her arm trying not to wake her.

"My love, come back to bed with me. We still have time before sunrise and the door is locked. The maids will have to knock," she said sleepily to him, her eyes still closed.

"We can not take any chances love," he answered her and kissed her forehead before leaving. He would try to get a couple hours of sleep before sunrise. He went to the door and unlocked it. Slipped into a night shirt then climbed into his own bed and closed his eyes.

He woke startled by the maids entering with a tray of food for the Queen to break her fast before dressing. Itala and Clara, the Queen's maids, hurried into her bed chamber. Ser Florian stretched in bed then got up to dress. He put on his silver armor and light blue cloak with the white unicorn of house Mathis. He placed his long-sword *Ice* in its scabbard at his hip. A knock came at the door.

"Enter," Florian said. His squire Mario Yoke came in with a tray of bread and cheese.

Florian was breaking his fast when Cosmas the White Wizard of the North entered his chamber. "Has the Queen left her chambers yet?" Cosmas asked.

"I would not be here if she had, My Lord," Ser Florian answered.

"Do you mind if I sit with you until she does? I must speak to her," Cosmas did not wait for a reply and sat in a chair across from Florian. Cosmas was an old man but no one really knew how old. Some said he was over a hundred; it didn't seem like Cosmas even knew how old he was. His white hair and beard were grown long to his waist. He was wearing a light blue robe with a silver belt of chains around his waist.

Florian could not help noticing the wizard starring at him. "I trust you had a good night, ser," Cosmas said to him with a wicked looking smile.

"I slept well," Florian answered annoyed. Out of the whole kingdom if anyone knew of his affair with Ana it would be Cosmas, but neither Florian nor Ana would ever confirm it.

"Would you like me to let Itala or Clara inform the Queen that you are waiting for her?" Florian asked hoping to rid himself of the wizard's stair.

"No, let the Queen eat and dress in her own time. I am quit content waiting," Cosmas replied. Florian narrowed his eyes in announce at the wizard.

When Ana did finally emerge from her chambers she was breathtaking, even big with child she was the most beautiful woman Florian had ever seen. She wore a blue velvet gown that was tight at the sleeves and breast, and then flowed loosely down her belly. Her breasts were full of milk already and had doubled in size. Before she was with child she had small firm breast enough to fill his hand. She wore her honey brown hair down and it fell past her shoulders, her silver and diamond crown atop her head. Her big blue eyes meet Florian's and her full lips parted into a smile that melted his heart. She was still small and petite, only about five feet tall and skinny everywhere but her belly.

"Good morrow ser, I trust you slept well," she said to Florian.

"I did, Your Grace," he answered her. The sight of her had made him forget that Cosmas was standing there.

Until the Queen said to him, "Cosmas, to what do I owe the pleasure of your company so early?"

"Your Grace, we have villagers that have come and request you see them. There are five from the village between North Star and The Pine, and ten from the village between Icestorm and North Star. They are in the Throne Room," Cosmas answered.

"Are they here about more attacks?"

"Yes, Your Grace. Half of the village between us and North Star have been killed, and twenty from the other village," Cosmas said.

"I see, and what is it they want me to do?" The Queen asked.

"Help them, Your Grace."

"Take the villagers to the Small Hall and feed them well. Tell them that I need to meet with my council before I see them. Then summon my council to the Throne Room. I will meet you there," the Queen ordered of the wizard.

"Yes, Your Grace," Cosmas said as he bowed, then left the room.

As soon as the room was cleared Ana ran into Florian's arms. "I do not like waking to you not beside me," Ana said.

"We can not risk it love, plus how am I to protect you without sleep?" He said to his Queen.

"May haps I will give you a day off," Ana said with a playful smile.

"My heart could not bear to be away from you."

"Good. We best go meet the council," she said as she let him escort her out the room toward the Throne Room.

When they entered the Throne Room the Queen's Council stood below the dais that the throne was atop. Cosmas stood in the middle with Ser Fintan Landrum, Ser Ben Goldberg, and Ser Gawain Degoyler to his right. To his left stood Lord Cormac Mathis, the Queen's uncle and father to her late husband King Finn. Next to Lord Cormac were Ser Conair Gribbens, Ser Jake Wiker, Ser Bedwyn Schmitt and Lady Aoifa Perrenot.

"My Lords, Lady and Ser's forgive me for disturbing you, I require your council," Queen Ana said.

"The villages in my kingdom are still being attacked. At first it was said by bears, but now they say the beasts are huge wolves. Half of one village's people have been killed and many more from the other villages. Two villages have sent people to plea with me. I have a thought but wanted to pass it by you before I spoke to my visitors," the Queen addressed her council. "I think an order should go out that all villages go to the nearest city for shelter. My people need to be behind high walls to keep safe, until the wolf problem is resolved. I will send one thousand golden crowns to each high lord to help accommodate for all the villagers. I will also pay each family from the village one hundred silver stars for their home and land, to help them move and get started out at the cities. Does anyone have any objections or suggestions?" Ana asked when finished.

"Your Grace, an excellent idea, but might I suggest a couple things?" Cosmas asked.

"Of course Cosmas that is why you are here," the Queen said to the wizard.

"Your Grace, we lost fifty guards along with the King, plus we need men to hunt down these beasts. Might I suggest one son from every village family take arms and be trained to serve the city they will occupy with promise of knighthood," Cosmas suggested.

"That would help us out, Your Grace. And the families will not turn down the opportunity for their sons to become knights," Lord Cormac stated.

"Very well, what else do you suggest?" the Queen asked.

"That you order a curfew, Your Grace. No one outside city walls after sun down, as well as the gates ordered not to open after sun down," Cosmas suggested.

"Very well," the Queen nodded in agreement. "Any other suggestions from my council?" Ana asked. The council shook their heads.

"Very well, Cosmas get it written up and sent to the high lords. Ser Fintan, you will go to the nearest village and instruct them on my orders and escort them to North Star to your father. Ser Ben you will go to the village by the Lake of Winter and escort them to your father's city. Ser Gawain you will escort the village by Horseshoe Bay to Snowflake Landing. Ser Conair you will be staying here with me. I do not think it wise to transport villagers by ship. Ser Jake you will escort the village by the Northern Split to Rivercross. Ser Bedwyn you will escort the village by the east crossing to Thor. Lady Aoifa, I would have you write to your father to let him know that Ser Fergus will be going in your stead. Ser Fergus will take the village in the pines. Ser Eber will escort the village by the Great Lake here to Icestorm." The Queen commanded, "All of you will have one thousand golden crowns for the city lords and three thousand silver stars for the villagers. You will also have one hundred men for guard."

"Cosmas, the villagers that have come, you will inform them of my decision. Find them beds and food, they will leave when everyone else does. My knights of the council, you will set out in one week. Also, since I have you all here, I plan on promoting Ser Brian Mathis to Master-of-Arms, since Ser Miles was with my husband," continued the Queen. "I thank you for your council, you are dismissed." With that the Queen stood and started toward the door behind the throne.

Ser Florian stayed close behind her, when all of a sudden Queen Ana hunched over and cried in pain. She almost fell to the floor, but Florian grabbed her under her arms to hold her up.

"Your Grace, what is wrong? Are you hurt?" Florian asked.

"The baby," she whispered and grabbed her belly. Ser Florian put his arm behind her knees and picked her up.

"Get the midwife and Itala and Clara! Cosmas come with me I need to get her to her bed!" He yelled. He held the Queen close to him as he rushed out the door and towered her chambers.

"Hold on, the midwife is on her way and Cosmas is here, you will be fine," he whispered to her.

"The baby is coming Florian, it hurts so bad! Like a knife has been suck in my belly," she said in a weak voice.

"The pain will be over soon, and you will be holding your child," he forced himself to smile at her. He could not bear seeing her in pain. It was killing him that he could not stop the pain from hurting her.

They climbed up the stairs that lead to her chambers. Even big with child, the Queen only weighed a little over a hundred pounds. When he reached his door he kicked it open with his foot. He walked through his bed chamber and came to her door and kicked that open as well. Florian laid his queen down softly onto her feathered bed. When he removed his arm from under her legs he noticed there was blood that stained his sleeve. Cosmas came rushing in behind them.

"She is bleeding Cosmas! Help her!" Florian ordered the wizard.

"She is going to have a baby, bleeding is part of it. You should go Ser Florian, a birthing is no place for a knight," Cosmas said to Florian.

"Are you a fool? I am her sworn guard not to leave her side! And no one is going to make me!" Florian yelled at the White Wizard.

"Ser, you should wait in your chamber then. There is nothing for you to do here, no one to protect her from. She will be in good hands, you must leave," Cosmas tried again.

"No, Cosmas let him stay. Florian will stay out of the way, he won't cause any problems. Will you?" Ana said in a voice strained by pain.

"I will stay out of the way," Florian nodded to Cosmas.

"Your Grace, if he stays people will talk, and rumors will spread," Cosmas eyed Florian.

"Let them . . . talk," she said to her wizard, and reached up and grabbed Florian's hand. He held tight, he never imagined that birth was more frightening than battle. Ana sat up and let out a painful scream.

"Where is the midwife?" Florian said to the wizard, "Can't you do a spell, make a potion, something. Help her."

"Help me remove her gown, I will do what I can."

Florian and Cosmas gently removed Ana's gown, and Florian slipped a sleep shirt over her head to cover her nakedness. She was breathing fast and there was more blood on her thighs. She grabbed his arm and dug her nails deep in his arm and let out the worst scream he had heard.

"Cosmas is it time? Where are the midwife and bed maids? A knight and a wizard should not be the ones to deliver the child," Florian felt so helpless and he hated it.

After what seemed like a lifetime, the bed maids came running in with a flagon of water and the midwife at their heels.

"You can leave now ser, we will bring the baby," Itala said to Florian.

"I am staying! So is Cosmas," he said to the maid with a cold tone and she did not argue.

The midwife lifted the bottom of Ana's sleep shirt, "it is time to push, Your Grace." Clara came over and pushed Florian up toward the Queen's shoulder and sat down on the bed by Ana's legs. Cosmas was at the Queen's other shoulder.

"Now, Your Grace, Push!" The midwife said. Ana breathed deep and sat up, her face red from pushing. She laid back down on the pillow her eyes full of tears. "Good, Your Grace, Good. Another, Push," the midwife said again. Ana took another breath, held it sat up and grabbed her knees. This time she let out a scream when she released the air from her lungs. Florian looked down between her legs, and soon realized that was a mistake. He had seen a man cut open from collar bone to bowls and somehow this was worse. *How long can this go on*, he wondered. He had seen men pass out from less pain.

"I see the head, Your Grace, you are doing well, another push, Your Grace, another push," said the midwife. Florian dared another look, a bloody mat of hair stuck out of her. She let out a cry, and sat up to push. He thought surely she was going to pass out from holding her breath so long.

"One more push, Your Grace, one more," the midwife was saying. Ana's brown hair was sticking to her forehead from the sweat. Her face and eyes were red, and she was breathing short shallow breaths.

"One more, Your Grace, almost done, one more." Ana sat up, grabbed Florian's hand so hard he thought it might break, and let out a loud painful scream.

Than a gasp and a cry filled the room, not the Queen's, cry of a baby. The midwife took the child to a wash basin and started cleaning the infant off. Itala and Clara had wet rags and were wiping the blood off the Queen's thighs.

"Is it a boy," the Queen asked breathless.

"Yes, Your Grace, a beautiful healthy boy."

Ser Florian slept in his own bed that night, and left the Queen with the babe at her tit. When he woke the next morning, he entered her chamber. Ana was sitting up with the babe in her arms watching him as he slept.

"Did you think of a name?" Florian asked his lover.

"He will be Conell Mathis the third, that should please everyone. I thought about naming him after his father, but I fear that would raise suspicion," she said with a teasing smile.

"Are you feeling well? Are you in any pain?" Florian asked worried that the birth took its toll on her.

"I am fine, hardly any pain at all. Cosmas gave me a potion."

She looked great for just giving birth. She slimmed overnight with hardly any belly left to her.

"Would you like me to summon your bed maids to get you some food?"

"Later. Come sit with me and your son," Ana replied and pulled back the blanket on her bed.

"You can't be saying that. You don't know who is standing outside your door listening," Florian said in a whispered voice.

"They would have to have good ears to hear through your chamber to mine," she smiled at him again with that teasing smile. He wanted to take her right now; he could not help stiffening as she looked in her eyes.

"You are right, just be careful my love, you never know who you can trust," he cautioned.

"It is not fair that our son will have to grow up thinking his father is dead. I am Queen and should be able to take any man for a husband," she complained.

"The North will not honor a bastard from a low born knight as their king. They must think he is Finn's other wise you may lose your kingdom." He felt the same as her but knew the way of the world.

"I know, a Queen can dream can't she. Don't worry, I would not risk any harm coming to you or him," the smile had left her face when she said that.

"You and I know that he is mine, that is good enough," Florian put his arm around his Queen and kissed her forehead. "When will you present him to the court?"

"After midday, he was up a lot last night and I was hoping to rest a while."

"Let me take him to Clara for a while so you can rest. They will bring him when he is ready to eat, you can't rule a kingdom without sleep," Florian said.

"Very well, but tell them to wake me when he is hungry," she said and put the baby Conell in his arms.

"They will not let the King of the North starve," and with that he gave her one last kiss and left the room so she could rest.

Florian went through his chamber and crossed the hall to the bed maid's chambers. Itala and Clara's chamber was directly across the hall from his door. He entered the room to find Clara and Itala asleep in the bed they shared. It was common for maids and even ladies to share beds in the North, the body heat helped keep the cold away. Clara was curled up to Itala with her arm around her waist. Florian put his hand on Clara's shoulder and shook her awake. She rolled over with half closed eyes.

"Her Grace wishes you watch the babe so she can rest."

Clara sat up and the blanket fell from around her shoulders reveling her big plump breast. Clara was a younger woman, older than the Queen but not by much. She had brown hair and a common face. She was plump but not fat, a little meat on her bones helped keep her warm. Her breast where as big as small melons and her nipples dark round circles.

"Get dressed," Florian said to the chamber maid. She could be attractive he supposed but after having Ana no woman excited him but the Queen. Clara got out of bed and stretched and Florian could not help his eyes from lingering to the mound of hair between her legs. *She is not even half as beautiful as Ana* he thought. Clara slipped on a simple dress that tied in the back, and took the babe from Florian's arms.

Florian went back to his own chamber to dress for the day. He picked black breeches with his black leather boots. A quilted tunic under his chain mail and armor, and the light blue cloak with a white unicorn. He fastened *Ice* to his hip and slipped a dagger in his boot, then went to find his squire so he could break his fast. Mario's room was next to Itala and Clara's room. Florian went in as Mario was getting dressed. Mario wore brown breeches with brown boots, a simple blue tunic with a leather doublet over top.

"Good morrow ser, are you ready for your food?" Mario asked.

"Yes, run to the kitchens and fetch it. When you return be quiet, the Queen is sleeping. The babe kept her up last night," Florian said to his squire.

"Yes, Ser," the boy replied and hurried off.

Florian was breaking his fast on fried bread and eggs when Lord Cormac entered his chamber. Florian hurried to his feet, "My Lord," he said and gave a slight bow.

"How fairs my grandson and his mother?" Lord Cormac asked.

"The babe is strong. Her Grace named him Conell Mathis the third after your brother. He kept Her Grace up most of the night, so she is sleeping now and the babe is with Clara, My Lord."

"A fine name I am sure my son would of approved," Lord Cormac said. "When is Her Grace expecting to present the babe to court?"

"Midday, My Lord."

"Very good, I will see that preparations are made. I was hoping to see the child, can you take me to him?"

"Yes, My Lord," Florian said and lead Lord Cormac to the maids chambers.

Clara was sitting on the bed with Itala to her right, both women cooing over the baby. When they looked up and saw Lord Cormac they both sprung to their feet.

"My Lord," they said.

Lord Cormac gave a nod and walked over to the babe. He looked upon the child as if he were a lost treasure. Lord Cormac had a glow about him that Florian had never seen. Clara handed over the child and Lord Cormac held him in his arms.

"He looks like his mother did when she was a babe, same brown hair and blue eyes he even has her nose. I remember when she was born, she was not this big but other than that looked the same," Lord Cormac said. Florian wasn't sure if Lord Cormac was talking to him or himself.

"He will be a strong King, with two Mathis parents," Lord Cormac said and this time looked at Florian.

"Yes, My Lord, with his mothers beauty and his fathers strength," Florian answered.

Lord Cormac handed the babe back to Clara.

"Walk with me Ser Florian, might we talk back in your chamber?"

"Of course, My Lord," Florian answered and followed Lord Cormac across the hall. "Please My Lord, sit," Florian said and pointed at a chair at the table. After Lord Cormac took a seat Florian sat himself across the table. "What can I do for you? My Lord."

"This babe is my blood, his mother, my niece, and his father my son. He must not come to harm. He is the rightful King now and until he is a man he must be protected," Lord Cormac stated.

"Yes, My Lord, I agree. Do you think there will be attempts to harm the babe?"

"I know not. All I know is that he must be kept safe. You have done a fine job protecting the Queen and until the boy gets older, I will expect you do the same for him."

"Not to worry, My Lord, as long as I breathe no harm shall come to the Queen or her child, you have my word on that," Florian answered. "May haps my squire will be suited to guard the child when he is older," Florian suggested.

"May haps, but not now. I want my son Ser Ronan with the child when you and his mother are not," Lord Cormac said.

"I am sure Her Grace will have no problems with that, My Lord."

"Good, tell Her Grace I was here when she wakes," Lord Cormac said. Florian nodded and Lord Cormac stood up and left the room.

An hour past the Queen emerged from her chambers, "Florian, go fetch my maids and tell them I crave their presence," she said.

"Right away. Oh your uncle came to see the babe," he told her.

"What did he have to say?"

"He said the child looks like you did when you where a babe."

"Yes, I can't imagine why he looks nothing like Finn," she said with a wicked smile, "did you tell him I mean to present Conell at midday?"

"Yes, he said he would have everything ready. He also wants your cousin Ser Ronan to guard the child when the child is not with you and me," he answered.

"Very well, I see no harm in that. What do you think?"

"I think it would be wise," he agreed, "I will get your maids."

The maids came and went and came back with food. Florian was reading a book about creatures of the North while he was waiting on his queen. Ana finally emerged, with the babe in her arms rapped in a snow fox fur. She wore a white wool gown with big bell sleeves that had pearls sewn around the neck. She had a blue cloak with the same kind of white fox fur at the top of it. When the light hit the diamonds of her crown it reflected rainbows through the room.

"You look beautiful, Your Grace," he said to her.

"You are too kind Ser, shall we go present the King?" She asked and took his arm with her free hand. The babe was fast asleep.

They used the door behind the throne to enter the Throne Room. The Queen's Council stood at the front of the hall below the throne. Behind them stood knights of the Queen's Guard and Castle Watch, commons filled the rest of the hall.

"My people of the North I present to you King Conell Mathis the third, son of the late King Finn Mathis and Queen Ana Mathis, ruler of Icestorm Castle and the King of the North," Ana said in a loud voice that echoed off the walls of the room. "May his rein be long and peaceful." The crowd rejoiced and the hall filled with cheers. "Until such time that my son can rule I will rule in his steed as Protector of the Realm. Come and see your King."

The guards closed in and lined the people one by one to see the new born King. The Queen sat radiant on her silver throne. The throne was massive, the back of it reaching eight fight tall, and it had unicorns carved into the back and two big diamonds sitting on the top. The Queen held the babe King in her arms in a protective loving way as each person came up the steps to kneel before the throne and see the new King of the North. It was a long process, first the council members, then the commons. After the commons left the Throne Room, the knights came one by one. By the time the last man had knelt before the throne, the King was screaming with hunger. The walls of the room echoing his cry.

Florian escorted the Queen back to her chamber so she could feed the child without showing her kingdom her breast. Florian was waiting in his room when Cosmas entered with a rolled parchment in his hand.

"I have a message from the West for the Queen," he said and did not wait for a reply before he entered her chamber. Florian got up and followed behind the wizard.

"Your Grace," Cosmas said with a bow, "King Cynon McCue of the West request you join them in the marriage of their son Prince Aidan to Princess Margery Carrender of the East. They will join houses in one and a half moons."

"Joining houses? The West with the East?" she asked with her brow wrinkled with thought.

"Yes, Your Grace," Cosmas answered.

"Why would King Cynon marry his heir to the Princess of the East?"

"I know not, Your Grace," was all Cosmas had to say.

"The message also asks that if the child is born by then that you bring it as well."

"Well that is not going to happen. He is a babe and I would not risk him becoming ill on the journey west. But the royals of the kingdoms do always attend the marriages of the heirs. The McCue's were at my marriage, I have to return the favor," she said.

"Good news, Your Grace. King Cynon also states that there is a village after the Northern Split that he will clear the Inn for your stay on the way to West Watch. Once in West Watch he will have chambers made for you," Cosmas said.

"Very well, write back to the King of the West that I will attend the wedding and I will need that Inn as promised."

"Yes, Your Grace," Cosmas bowed.

"Also send word that I require a wet nurse and want to personally meet all that want the position," she ordered.

"At once, Your Grace."

"And get the council together I will meet with them in an hour," Ana said to her wizard.

"Yes, Your Grace," Cosmas bowed and left the room.

Florian walked his Queen back to the Throne Room to find her Council waiting. The Queen climbed the steps and sat on her throne.

"King Cynon is marrying his heir to the Princess of the East and I am required to attend this wedding. Most of you will be gone moving the villagers. I am leaving Lord Cormac Mathis to sit the throne in my leave. I am also leaving King Conell the third here at Icestorm to Ser Ronan's guard. Cosmas is searching a wet nurse to care for him. I have decided that I require Princess Arian, Lady Aoifa, Cosmas, Ser Florian, and my maids Itala and Clara to accompany me. Lord Arthur will stay behind to assist Lord Cormac. I will also be taking five hundred guards. I need all preparations made for me and my party to leave in one moon's turn."

ROSEGARDEN

Maggie sat in the King's pavilion waiting for the knights to show for the joust. Two more days remained of her father's annual tournament and Maggie was glad it was almost done. She sat on her stool to her father's left looking like the Princess she was suppose to be. After the tourney, her family and she would start the long journey west. Maggie was curious about the west and her husband to be. Her uncle Prince Alexander always said that the people of the west hair were red because of their fiery temper and thirst for blood. Everyone that was born in the west had some red in their hair. Bright cherry red, auburn, rusty, orange, brick colored or just plain red. Maggie wondered if her children would have red hair or her golden hair. One day her son would be King of the West and that was exciting.

Ser Clifford Turk of Dolphin Keep and the King's Guard rode up to the north end of the fence with the colors of his house on. Blue cloak with a grey dolphin embroidered in the middle of it and silver thread around the outside. His shield had the same blue background and a grey dolphin, and his black stallion matched his master. Ser Clifford put his bronze helm on that covered his face, and his squire handed him his lance. To the south end Ser Burke Stoddart of Lionsgate and the King's Guard rode up on his brown stallion. Ser Burke wore a green cloak with an orange lion on it and his stallion dressed the same. His squire handed him his big oak shield painted green and the lion on it was all scraped from all the blows the shield had taken. Ser Burke had a magnificent helm, a golden lion's head with razor sharp teeth.

King Tristan stood, "Good knights, we are down to the final days of my tournament. The winner of this match will have a chance to make it to the finals, the loser is done. Good knights of my King's Guard, lower your lances and start at will," the King announced and the crowd cheered.

Both knights lowered their lances and Ser Clifford was the one who started riding first. They rode toward each other. Then came the sound of lance hitting armor, Ser Burke had struck Ser Clifford. But not hard enough, Ser Clifford was still upon his horse. Both knights rode to the opposite end from which they had started, lowered their lances and started again.

This time it was Ser Clifford who struck Ser Burke, and he went flying from his horse to make a crashing sound when he hit the dirt. The crowd cheered and Ser Clifford rode to the center of the pavilion in front of where the King sat. Ser Burke's squire ran up to him and pulled him up of the ground. He had a nice dent in the breast plate of his armor where the lance had hit him.

"Ser Clifford of Dolphin Keep is the winner of this match. You are one step closer to the gold," Maggie's father announced. Ser Clifford bowed his head to the King then turned his horse and rode off.

Her father looked very kingly today, his golden hair pulled back and his crown of golden thorns atop his head. He wore a golden cloak with the red rose of their house embroidered on it. The cloak had golden beads sewn around the outside. He had dark brown breeches that matched his leather boots and a red tunic with a dark green jerkin over top with thorny vines sewn into it. Every other finger had a golden ring and he wore a large golden chain around his neck. His long-sword *Thorn* hung at his hip with a golden hilt that had a single rose on top. The scabbard for the sword was brown leather that had different gemstones on it; rubies, emeralds, amethyst and diamonds. King Tristan sat on a great oak chair that had big red cushions filled with feathers.

The crowd started booing as the next knight rode up and Maggie looked to see who it was. Ser Uduak Hizer from a lowborn family in the south rode to the north end on his red stallion. Ser Uduak picked a lizard for his sigil when he was knighted. It was a bright green lizard on black, his shield, cloak and horse to match. Ser Asher Merriman of Acorn Hill and the King's Guard rode up to the south end. He looked handsome in his dark green cloak with hundreds of acorns sewn into it. His armor reflected the sun and his bronze hair matched his bronze armor. Both knights lowered their helms on their heads and took up their lances.

"Begin at will, the winner has a chance at the gold," the King announced.

Ser Asher rode toward the southern lowborn, green and brown striped lance pointed and shield held up. Ser Uduak kicked his horse to a gallop and rode toward Ser Asher. Then they collided, Ser Asher's lance snapped when it hit Ser Uduaks armor and a cry of pain went over the lancing yard. Ser

Uduak fell from his horse with half of Ser Asher's lance sticking out of his shoulder. Maggie looked away at the sight of the blood pulsing out of Ser Uduak's wound. She glanced back to see Ser Uduak being carried by four men who held each arm and leg.

"Our winner Ser Asher of Acorn Hill and the King's Guard," her father announced and the crowd cheered loudly.

"Lancing is done for the day. We will start the archery tournament one hour after midday," the King said. He gave Maggie his hand and the Queen his other hand and escorted both ladies from the pavilion.

"What did you think of the lancing Maggie?" Her father asked.

"Very entertaining father," she lied. Maggie did not see the point of hitting one another with long sticks, but she knew her father enjoyed it and didn't want to disappoint him.

"We will eat before the archery Maggie I have had a golden rose made for the winner of the archery tourney and I was hoping that you would be the one to present it," King Tristan said to his daughter.

"I would be honored father, nothing would please me more," Maggie replied.

"This is the last my people will see their Princess and they are not happy about me marrying you to the west. They need to see that you are happy with the choice," he said.

"I am happy father. One day my son will be King. That is more than I would get if I married a Lord. I am just nervous about leaving my home and my family," she told her father.

"We will see each other. That I promise you," her father replied and led her and her mother toward the castle.

They entered the Small Hall to find the rest of her family already sitting at the table. King Tristan, Queen Helen and Maggie took their seats and the servants started to bring out the food.

"How did the lancing go? I want to know who I might be up against on the morrow," Prince Alexander asked. He had been undefeated in the lancing and was already in the championship tourney.

"Ser Clifford won the first match and Ser Asher won the second," her father answered.

"I would rather go up against Ser Clifford, Ser Asher will make me work for the title," Prince Alexander replied.

Maggie was eating roast duck smothered in honey when her father turned to her. "In two days we make our journey love. We will stay with Lord Herman Stoddart at Lionsgate. Then we cross the Great Lake which will take a day if not more. Then we stay with Lord Gwern McClure of Autumnway where King Cynon, Queen Aileen and Prince Aidan will meet us. Then we travel the royal road to a village Inn and onto West Watch Castle."

"So it will be a week or more before we reach it," she asked.

"Yes at the least, we are going to the other side of the kingdoms, but this is the shortest way, it would take longer going by ship," her father answered.

"Who all is coming with us?" she asked, her father kept changing his mind on who was going and who was staying behind.

"Your mother and I, your brothers and sister, Ser Jason, Ser Clifford, Ser Asher, Ser Byron, Ser Burke, Ser Clive, Pascal and Gabriel. Plus we will have about five hundred guards," the King answered.

Gabriel was called the Great Wizard and it did not surprise Maggie that her father would bring him. All the other Kings and Queens were sure to have their wizards too. Maggie wondered what the wedding would be like with all that royal blood in one hall. The Ice Queen of the North with her hard and hairy men, the Dragon King with his black haired wife and all the red heads of the West in one hall. *Well it won't be boring* she thought. Not to mention four great wizards who think their powers are the strongest.

"Who would like to join me for the archery tourney?" The King asked.

"I do father, I want to see who wins," Jon the heir said.

"Then come and watch with me, Maggie are you coming?" He asked.

"Yes, father," she said and got up from the table and followed her father out the Small Hall. Ser Jaron came after them. He was in the competition.

They climbed the pavilion steeps to their seats. The archery targets had been set up in long lines. All of the archers stood, bows in hand watching the King. Harding Carrender, son of Prince Teagan came walking up to her father with the long stem golden rose in his hand. He handed the rose to the King then ran back down the steps.

"Archers, you are competing for gold," the King announced and held the rose up for all to see. "The winner of this competition will received a golden rose from my beautiful daughter Princess Margery," the King continued and handed the rose to Maggie. She took the rose from her father and was surprised at how heavy it was *it must be worth a fortune* she thought as she held it in her hands.

"Archers, draw your arrows," the King said in a loud voice. The line of archers grabbed an arrow and strung it to their bows.

"Fire!" the King shouted.

The arrows let lose and rained into the targets. Calvan Hearon her uncle on her mother's side, was the judge. He walked down the line of targets and inspected all the arrows. Those that hit the middle circle stayed in the competition, those that didn't were eliminated. Only ten archers remained after the inspection.

"Move the targets back five feet," the King said, and servants ran to the targets and moved them back. After all the targets were moved and the servants out of the way, the King said, "Archers, draw your arrows." They did as commanded, "Fire!"

Down to six archers and the King had the targets moved back five more feet, and continued the competition. Ser Jaron, Alfred Manly and Roger Cedillo were the only ones remaining.

"Move the targets ten feet," the King commanded, and the servants did as ordered. "Archers, draw," he said, "Fire!"

Alfred's arrow hit the ground about five feet in front of the target. Ser Jaron hit the target but not in the middle. Roger victoriously hit just outside the middle circle. Three servants each picked up a target and carried them to the pavilion and set them in front of the King.

"Roger Cedillo you are my archery champion, come claim your prize," the King announced.

Roger walked up to the pavilion and Maggie stood to met him. He knelt down to the King, then took Maggie's hand and kissed it.

"Roger Cedillo you have won the title of champion of the archery competition and best archer in the East. I give you a golden rose as your prize," Maggie said to the man on his knees.

Roger stood and Maggie had to look up to see his face. It was a common face not handsome, but not ugly either. He had pox scares on his cheeks but that gave his face character. She met his grey eyes and handed him the rose.

"My thanks, Princess," he said and kissed her hand again. She nodded at him and he lifted his prize toward the crowd.

After the archery was sword fighting. The competitors were given blunt swords and a shield and would be judged by blows. If a man was knocked out he lost. Mostly knights competed in the sword fighting but once in awhile a common would try it, they never lasted long though. Maggie sat down and waited for the servants to finish setting up for the competition. A serving wench was going around with a flagon of wine and Maggie waved her over. The wench filled her chalice with sweet strawberry wine.

"Don't go far, I will want more soon," Maggie said to the girl.

"Yes, m'lady," the girl said and hurried off.

Maggie sipped at the sweet wine greedily. It was a wonderful day for wine, not a cloud in the sky, not hot but not cold and a gentle breeze was blowing from the west.

The servants were done setting up and the wench had been back twice to fill Maggie's cup when the knights finally started to arrive. Highborn knights and lowborn knights standing side by side waiting for their turn in the ring. You could tell the lowborn from the highborn, they had cheap looking armor and plain looking shields. Where as the highborn knights had elaborate cloaks and shields with armor that shimmered in the sun and helms in the shape of animal heads and decorated. Ser Adam and Ser Alex Manly were lowborn standing next to Ser Byron Chitwood of Golden Rock and the King's Guard. Maggie thought they looked funny standing next to each other, but that could have been from the wine.

The King had each knight place their sigil in a helm and the men did a blind draw to see who they would face in the ring. The King had the men draw numbers from another helm to see which order they would fight in. Every man would have at least two fights and the winners would move on. Ser Byron drew the number one and the sigil for Kimsey which was a lowborn house. Ser Byron stepped into the wooden ring followed by Ser Gilles Kimsey, both men with blunt sword and shield.

"Begin," the King announced, and the song of steel on steel began.

Ser Byron's blows were so hard that Ser Gilles stumbled every time he was struck, but Ser Gilles was faster so Ser Byron missed more that struck. Ser Gilles could not get a blow in and Ser Byron had already struck Ser Gilles at the least five times. Every time Ser Byron made contact Maggie blinked her eyes from the sound. Ser Byron finally knocked Ser Gilles down and the competition was over.

On and on it went, men hammering at each other with sword and shield. Maggie was bored and her ass was going numb from sitting so long. She spotted the serving wench and waved her over for the fifth time. By the time they were to the last fight, Maggie's head was swimming with wine and she feared having to stand up. She decided that she would look sisterly and put her arm around her brother for support, without making it obvious that she was drunk. She had no idea who had won the last fight and who would fight on the morrow. When her father stood she had a sudden rush of panic.

"Jon, you have to help me to the castle. I drank too much and I don't want to make a scene falling on my ass," Maggie leaned over and whispered to her brother.

"Don't drink so much then," he whispered back.

She almost slapped him but remembered where she was and stopped herself. "Please Jon," she said instead.

When it was time to leave the pavilion Jon stood and took Maggie's hand and walked her down the steps. She leaned toward him and had her arm wrapped in his, but it didn't seem like anyone noticed how drunk she was. They were walking behind their mother and father toward the castle when King Tristan stopped to talk to a knight. Maggie wasn't paying attention and ran right into the back of her father. He turned around with a wrinkled brow and lips pressed tight together.

"My apologies father, I was not watching where I was going," she said not meeting his eyes.

He turned back toward the knight and finished talking. *Bloody Hell, now he knows I am drunk*, she thought. They were so close to the castle she would have gotten away without notice once inside. Jon had a smile on his face and Maggie pinched him in the side.

When they reached the castle her father grabbed her by the arm and drug her up the stairs toward her chambers. When they reached her room he pushed her door open and shouted "OUT!" to Tansy and Violet. The bed maids hurried out the room without a word and shut the door behind them.

"Are you mad?" The King asked, but did not wait for an answer. "Do you think Prince Aidan wants a drunken fool for a wife, or that King Cynon wants a drunken fool to be Queen of his kingdom after he dies?"

"Prince Aidan and King Cynon are not here father," she said, and King Tristan slapped her hard on the face.

"You think people won't talk? You think none of the knights here are going to your wedding? What if King Cynon hears and changes his mind about marrying his heir to you?"

Maggie couldn't remember the last time he was this mad at her. "My apologies father, I did not realize how much wine I drank until I stood up," Maggie started to tear up.

"You are to act a proper lady like the Princess you are and the Queen you will be!" He said his face red with anger. "Well, I will not have you go back down and make a bigger fool of yourself, you will not be at the feast tonight! Sleep off the wine and rise anew for the last day of the tourney. No wine on the morrow Maggie, do you hear me?"

"Yes, Your Grace," Maggie said with her eyes lowered to the ground.

"This is the last time Maggie, no more. You are to go to West Watch and be a proper lady not a foolish drunk child!" And with that her father walked out and slammed the door behind him.

Tansy and Violet came back not long after her father had left. "I want a bath," Maggie said as she was sitting looking out her window at the Bay below.

"Yes, m'lady," Tansy said and left the room.

Violet came over and asked, "Would you like me to take your hair down and help you out of your gown, m'lady?"

"Yes Violet, my thanks."

Violet took the crown off of Maggie's head and pulled the pins and ribbons out of her hair, golden curls fell past Maggie's shoulders. Then Maggie stood so Violet could unlace the back of her gown. When Maggie was down to nothing but small clothes Tansy returned with hot water and started filling the tub. Steam was rising from the tub as her maids helped her step in. The water was scalding hot that it made her gasp when she sat down. The bath had not helped like Maggie thought it would and before long her head was spinning and her stomach was making terrible noises.

"Help me out, I do not feel well and need to go to bed," she said to her maids.

"Do I need to fetch Seer Pascal?" Tansy asked.

"No, I need sleep is all," Maggie replied and lifted herself from the tub with the maids help.

She went to her bed naked and dripping and fell into the feathered mattress. She grabbed a pillow and put it under her head, and her maids left the room. Sleep came quick, at first she was spinning but then the world was dark and she escaped to her dreams.

She awoke to the blinding sun and drums beating in her head. Maggie sat up to her head spinning and she was trying not to vomit. *Bloody wine*, she thought and stood to stretch out her cramps. Tansy and Violet came in with a tray of food and sat it on the table. Maggie looked at the food and the sight of it made her ill.

"Take it away, I am not hungry," she said to her maids, and Tansy grabbed the tray and left the room.

Violet helped her dress in a pink silk gown with big bell sleeves and white lace. Her golden curls was pinned on top of her head with her rose and ruby crown. Once finished dressing, she left her chambers to face the day.

Maggie went down the steps from the castle, through the court yard and toward the pavilion where her father would be waiting for the jousting to start. King Tristan was sitting in his big oak chair, his golden hair pulled back and his thorn crown sitting heavily on his brow. He had a stern face, and she wondered if he was still cross with her about the day before. When he turned his head and saw her, he rose from his chair. He was dressed in brown leather breeches that matched his boots, a simple white tunic with a leather jerkin overtop. The jerkin had golden roses sewn into it and went well with his cloak.

"Good morrow father," Maggie said and gave a little bow.

"Good morrow, did you sleep well?"

"I did," she answered, *a dead drunken sleep* she thought.

"Maggie, I fear I was too hard on you. You are a woman grown, and leaving me has me worried," he said.

"Worried? Why?"

"You will be on the other side of the country and I will not be there to watch out for you," the King had a sad look to him, and Maggie knew his words were true.

"Not to worry father, I will have a husband to look out for me. And one day I will be Queen of the West while Jon is King of the East, there is nothing to worry about," she said with a smile.

"You are right, still I apologize for last night."

"No need," Maggie said and took a seat on the oak stool to her father's left.

The rest of the day went by quickly. Prince Alexander was named champion of the joust. The other knights and commons that won titles for champion of the other games were given their gold, either in coin or roses. The music played and the commons danced and ate and celebrated. Next was the Ending Feast, all champions were seated at a table of honor next to the Royal Family. Then the high lords of the East, in the middle were the knights that had competed and lost, and at the end of the Great Hall the wealthier commons sat.

After everyone was seated in the Great Hall the Royal Family was presented. They stood outside the hall lined up and waited to be announced.

"All rise for King Tristan Carrender first of his name, ruler of Rosegarden and King of the East, and Queen Helen Carrender of House Hearon," the Paige shouted over the crowd. Everyone stood from their chair as her father and mother entered the Great Hall.

"Princess Margery Carrender, and Prince Jon Carrender, heir to the throne," Maggie took Jon's arm and they marched in the hall past the many tables and faces to the table at the front of the room. Her brother and sister came next. Then her uncles and their families, until they were all standing in the front of the hall.

"My loyal subjects, I invite you to join me in a feast to celebrate our champions!" King Tristan announced, and with that hundreds of servants hurried in the hall carrying flagons of wine and ale.

The first course was cheese and olives. White cheese, yellow cheese, sharp and mild, some with peppers, some plain, and black and green olives. The second course a creamy soup with clams, scalps, fish and crab served with garlic bread. The main course was roasted herring, roasted boar, venison and swan, served with carrots, peas and greens. After that different nuts and fruits, apples, pears, melons, oranges, and every berry you could think of. The sweet was tarts of different types, raspberry, blueberry, strawberry and blackberry.

By the time the feast was over Maggie was ready to burst, her stomach so full she was sure she could go days without eating. The men and knights were drunk off wine and ale and drowned out the music playing in the background. This was the last night in her kingdom and this would be her last memory and she was happy with that. People started dancing and everyone was laughing. Maggie had been drinking goat's milk instead of wine for fear that she would upset her father again. The milk only made her more full and she was tired from all the eating and the tourney.

"May I take my leave father?" She asked.

"You may," he said with a nod.

She got up from her seat kissed her father and her mother and headed toward her chambers. Once in her chambers, she quickly got ready for bed. Excited and nervous about the journey that will make her a wife and eventually a Queen, her full stomach put her to sleep. Usually these feelings would keep her up, but for the second night in a row, she quickly succumbed to her dreams.

The next day they left at day break with Lord Herman Stoddart of Lionsgate and his party. Queen Helen, Maggie and Kate rode with Lady Kacey Stoddart and her daughters Kalie and Kara in a curtained wagon surrounded by knights. King Tristan, Jon, Jason and the wizard Gabriel were on horse with Lord Stoddart and his son, Kayden, toward the front of the party. The wagon was comfortable but slow. Maggie, Kate, Kalie and Kara played different games to try and pass the time.

By the time the sun had started to set they reached the village between Rosegarden and Lionsgate. King Tristan was not pleased. He had hoped to reach Lionsgate in one day and would have been able to if not for the large party and wagons. The King paid the inn keeper for the whole Inn and any commons that would of stayed there he gave their money back out of his own pocket. It was a common inn and not what Maggie was use to staying at. The mattresses were stuffed with straw instead of feathers, though the inn keeper promised no fleas but Maggie was doubtful.

They were served a single course meal of mutton stew, bread and ale in the common room. Between the Royal Family, Lord Stoddart's family and their maids there were not enough rooms for the knights. So they had to set up tents around the inn. When Maggie entered her room after the meal, there was no privy just a chamber pot by the bed. She looked around and saw no tub, no chairs, no table, just a small straw stuffed bed in the corner. Maggie tried to make the best of it and had her maids help her change without a bath. Sleep did not come easy. The straw was hard and in some places stuck out from the mattress and poked her. She saw no fleas, but just the thought of them made her itch. *It's only for one night* she told herself and closed her eyes to try to sleep.

She woke the next morning stiff and sore. She tried to hold the urine but finally gave up and used the chamber pot. She had her maids dress her quickly and left the room as soon as possible. When she got to the bottom of the stairs where the common room was, her father and Lord Stoddart were sitting on one of the benches at a table. Her father stood to greet her.

"Good morrow Maggie, did you sleep well?" He asked.

"As well as could be expected," was the best answer she could give.

"Sit and break your fast with Lord Stoddart and myself. You are the first of the women to rise," her father said to her.

She took a seat on the bench next to her father and Lord Stoddart sat across from him. The King waved to the inn keeper and within a couple minutes they were served fried eggs and bread. Not much of a meal, but it filled her belly nonetheless.

By the time the party started moving it was midday. The Queen and Lady Stoddart took forever getting ready and then broke their fast slowly. They had to wait for the guards and knights to take the tents down and put them away. Maggie was as upset as her father about that because she had wanted to get away from that inn as soon as possible. The wagon crept on bit by bit. Maggie pushed the curtain back to watch the sun slowly moving across the sky. It was a nice day, the sky blue with not a cloud in sight. To the north was the Lion Woods and birds were singing in the trees and rabbits ran from the sound of their party approaching.

As the sky was turning purple they approached the walls of Lionsgate. Two massive marble lions stood on either side of the gate, they had to be at the least ten feet tall. The torches had already been lit even though it was still light enough to see. They passed through the city toward Lord Stoddart's castle. Whores were calling to the knights from a brothel's balcony. Some of the whores had the top half of their gowns down to their hips and their tits were out for all to see. Queen Helen reached over and closed the curtain and they rode the rest of the way blind.

When the curtain reopened it was her father to help her mother and Lady Stoddart from the wagon. When Maggie got out she looked up at Lord Stoddart's castle. It was not as big as Rosegarden, but elegant nonetheless. Four towers reached up to the sky made of red sand stone. Each step leading up to the doors of the castle had a marble lion sitting on it. The wall around the castle separating it from the rest of the city was iron, not stone and the commons were looking through to see the Royal Family. Kayden, Lord Stoddart's eldest son and heir, escorted Maggie into the castle while the knights and servants started to unload the wagons and care to their horses.

Plain gray stone floors lead throughout the castle. The dining hall had wooden pillars reaching up to the ceiling. A single table occupied the hall with at least fifty cushioned chairs surrounding it. Maggie sat next to her father. Lord Stoddart's servants had prepared a better feast than the Inn had provided, and Maggie was happily full when the final course arrived. Lady Stoddart showed Maggie where she would be staying for the night, and Tansy and Violet followed close behind. The room was massive, a feathered mattress bed big enough to sleep six people, a big oak desk, a balcony and her own privy with a marble bench and scented with a bowl of herbs.

"Shall I have our servants bring some hot water for a bath my lady?" Lady Stoddart asked.

"That would be much welcomed. My thanks," Maggie replied.

"Not a problem my lady, you are welcome to anything in our house," Lady Stoddart said and bowed before leaving the room.

While Maggie was soaking in the hot water and Violet was washing her back, her mother came into the room.

"Maggie you should sleep good tonight, you are going to need it. On the morrow we head toward the Great Lake and there take a ship across. Enjoy the comforts while you can, you will not have them on the ship," the Queen said.

"Yes mother, I plan to go to bed as soon as I am done."

"Once we reach the West your husband-to-be will meet you and you are to look and act your best."

"I will not disappoint you," Maggie promised, the Queen kissed her on the brow and left. Maggie got out of the bath and her maids dried her off and dressed her. She was tired from not getting sleep the night before, so as soon as her head hit that feathered pillow she fell into a deep dreamless sleep.

DRAGON'S END

Lord Raghu Hugart lay bound to the iron table on the third floor of the dungeons. Chains around his neck, wrist, waist and ankles. Jengo Kirsch who some men called the Butcher, was flaying the fingers on Lord Hugart's right hand.

"Where are the eggs," Xolan asked again.

"I doooo noooot kno . . . w of a . . . ny eggssss," Lord Hugart replied. He had been saying the same thing since he was arrested.

"So you would have me believe that the eggs just happened to disappear the day you show up?" Xolan asked, "Do you take me for a fool Lord Hugart? How did you get them? Who did you pay? Was it a wizard? WHERE ARE THEY?" Xolan asked again.

"I tttollld you mmm' lord . . . I I I don't knoww of any egg . . . ss," Lord Huggart replied again his eyes starting to roll in the back of his head.

"Jengo I don't think Lord Hugart is in a talkative mood, can you fix that for me?" Xolan said to the Butcher.

"I can make him sing if you want," Jengo said with a smile. Half of his teeth were gone or rotten and his skin was almost black from the dirt caked on it, but he did his job and no one cared what he looked like down here.

Jengo took a red hot iron poker from the brazier and laid it across Lord Hugart's left check. Lord Hugart let out a scream and tears started streaming down his face.

"I . . . I . . . I p . . . p . . . prrommise m . . . m . . . m'l . . . lor . . . rd I d . . . don't . . . t . . . knowww," he cried to Xolan.

"You are the only one who would! Did your brother Lord Raj tell you about them? Did he hire someone? Does he have them now? May haps I should have the guards bring him down to meet my friend Jengo hear," Xolan shouted.

"NO m'lord, NO," and with that Lord Hugart lost consciousness.

"Put him back in his cell, and tell him I will see him on the morrow," Xolan said to Jengo.

"Aye, m'lord," Jengo said and started removing the chains that bound Lord Hugart.

Xolan climbed the steps that lead out of the dungeon. Lord Hugart had been their guest now for a month. Same questions same answers daily, Xolan had enough questioning. He had to find another way to get Lord Hugart to confess, and tell him who he had hired. The day of the sacrifice while people were heading over to watch the Bull meet his fate; Xolan and fifty guards had captured Lord and Lady Hugart. Lady Hugart and her children were kept comfortably in the tower. Guards stood outside their door day and night, but every comfort was provided to them. *May haps if I threaten his wife he will tell me something,* Xolan thought.

Lord Raj Hugart had freedom of the castle but was not allowed to go outside. Lord Raj had also temporarily been removed from the Royal Council and the position for Commander of Docks was open for the moment. All of Lord Hugart's guards had been questioned and then killed. Anything that had been touched by Lord Hugart, his family, or his guards had been searched. They closed the gates to the capitol after the sacrifice, but the Capitol Guard had said some commons had left. Three ships had left Dragon's Bay the morning of the sacrifice. *The eggs could be any where,* Xolan thought, *even if we get the name of the man hired by Lord Hugart he could be across the Sea by now.*

Xolan reached the King's chambers, Ser Ime Merrion and Ser Thabo Andre were standing guard outside. Both men dressed in red gold armor and yellow cloaks with a red dragon. They had spears in hand and they made an X in front of the door.

"I need to speak to His Grace," Xolan said to the knights, they uncrossed their spears and Xolan knocked on the door and waited for and answer from within.

Many minutes later Xolan heard "Enter," in the King's voice. Xolan walked into the room to find King Abhay and Queen Kala sitting at the table on the balcony nibbling on cheese and peppers.

Xolan walked over to the King and Queen, "Your Grace, might we talk somewhere private, I have news and do not want to give the Queen night terrors," Xolan said to the King.

King Abhay looked up to his Red Wizard from his seat, "of course old friend, come," the King replied.

"Please excuse us My Queen, I will not keep him long," Xolan said and bowed to kiss the Queen's hand.

"Best not," Queen Kala replied with a friendly smile.

Xolan followed the King out of the room toward the library which was at the end of the hall. Ser Ime and Ser Thabo walking closely behind, when they entered the library the guards stayed outside the door.

"Has Lord Hugart told us anything?" King Abhay asked.

"No Your Grace, his right hand has been flayed, hot iron pokers applied to his skin, and he still says the same thing. May haps he is protecting someone. Would you turn in your own brother or your wife?" Xolan asked.

"But I have no proof, I can not arrest two lords and one lady on no proof or confession. You must get Lord Hugart to confess."

"I will do my best Your Grace, but I do not know how much questioning Lord Hugart can take. He is close to death," Xolan informed.

"Then let him die. We will say he confessed that Lord Raj informed him about the eggs, but died before naming the person he hired," the King suggested.

"May haps that will work, but do you really think that someone on your own council betrayed you?"

"Not purposely, I think Lord Raj told his brother about the eggs innocently not knowing his brother would be foolish enough to steal them," King Abhay answered, "a King can trust no one."

"You can always trust me, Your Grace."

"I know my friend. I meant a King can trust no man. You are not a man, you are the Red Wizard. We must think of something Xolan. Fire Harbor will start asking why their Lord has not returned to them. It can not be known that there are three dragons' eggs somewhere. If found they would be sold to the highest bidder," the King said to Xolan, "plus we will be leaving the South soon and this needs to be done before we leave."

"Leaving the South, Your Grace?" Xolan asked, this was new to him. He had been down in the dungeons most of the day.

"Yes, I received an invite from King Cynon. He is marrying his heir Prince Aidan to Princess Margery of the East and we are required to attend. I don't want to give him a reason to hate us more," the King informed Xolan.

"The West is joining houses with the East? If there is ever a war it would be two armies against one," Xolan said, he did not like this news. The West and South were always threatening war.

"Two armies is still no match to my army and two dragons," the King replied.

"That is true Your Grace, but do you think it wise to leave the South?"

"I have no choice Xolan, all the Royal Families always attend the weddings of heirs. I had to go to the frozen hell of the North to watch the Ice Bitch marry her cousin, it would be insulting if I did not go."

"We must start preparing to leave, I want Lord Hugart taken care of," the King commanded, "You have until midday, before the council meeting."

"Yes, Your Grace, Lord Hugart will be with the dead soon," Xolan answered and left the room.

Xolan headed back toward the dungeons to give Jengo the order. This was not like the King to put someone to death without proof or a confession and it had Xolan worried. He feared what the King would do if they didn't find the eggs soon. The King had been waiting two years for the eggs to hatch and now they were gone.

After making sure Lord Hugart was no longer among the living. Xolan set out to inform the King before the council meet. He found the King by the Throne Room talking to Lord Kalyan Brunson about goods from some ships at the docks.

"Beg pardons Your Grace, but may I have a word," Xolan said.

"Of course, please excuse me Lord Kalyan, I will see you in a minute at council," and with that the King left Lord Kalyan and walked with Xolan.

"It has been done Your Grace," Xolan informed the King.

"Good, at council I will go over what I plan to do next about the Hugart family." Xolan followed the King to the council room, all the council members were there and waiting.

"Members of my council I have been betrayed by one of the Lords of my Kingdom and possibly by one of my council members," the King informed the council. "Lord Raghu Hugart of Fire Harbor has betrayed my hospitality and stolen something very dear to me, and has endangered my kingdom," the King continued. "Unfortunately Lord Hugart has died during questioning before he could reveal any useful information. Therefore I am appointing my brother-in-law Lord Rajesh Smeltzer to Lord of Fire Harbor. Let it be written, I Abhay of House Cvetokovich, Lord of Dragons End, King of the South and protector of the realm, do here by strip all titles and rank, all land, income and holding to House Huggart." The King ordered.

"There has been no proof that Lady Krishna Hugart had any part in her husband's treachery, she will be returned to her brother, Lord Kalidas Brunson of Gator Swamp. Her sons Ratan and Ratnam will be ward and squire to Lord Rajesh in hopes of future knighthood. Her daughters Rashmi, Rati and Ratna will be Queen Kala's ladies, and be married to suitable husbands when the time comes. Lord Hugart did not deny his brother's part in his treachery, therefore Lord Raj Hugart is hereby banished from the South and if returned, will be put to death." The King continued.

"Your Grace, what has Lord Hugart stolen?" Asked Lord Kalyan, who was brother to Lady Krishna.

"It is not safe to say, if it is known to the world nothing good could come from it," the King replied.

"Your Grace, people will ask why the Hugart's titles and claims have been removed," Lord Aravind stated.

"Let them ask, do you doubt your King Ser?" The King asked.

"No Your Grace," replied Lord Aravind.

"All the people of my kingdom need to know is that Lord Hugart has betrayed my hospitality and is a traitor to the South. It is done, I will hear no more of it," and with that the King stood and left the room.

Xolan rushed after the King, "Your Grace, you did not mention anything about traveling to the West."

"Bloody hell Xolan I forgot completely. I will bring it up on the morrow after this Hugart thing has been taken care of. Xolan I want you to secure passage for Lady Krishna to Gator Swamp. I also want you to give Lord Raj some golden crowns and find him a ship at the docks to leave the South for good."

"Right away, Your Grace, how many guards would you like to accompany Lady Krishna?"

"As many as you see fit," the King answered, and entered the next room he came to and shut the door.

Xolan found Raj Hugart in his chambers. "The King has made his decision," he told Raj.

"What has His Grace decided?"

"You have been banished from the South with a punishment of death shall you return. I will give you enough golden crowns to get you going, I will also pay passage for you from a ship of your choosing to whatever destination you desire," Xolan replied.

"And what are my crimes Xolan?"

"Your brother did not deny your assistance with his treason."

"And what treason is that? This is nonsense I have been nothing but loyal to the King. Where am I to go?"

"Your brother abused the hospitality of the King and stole from him. And it is because of that loyalty that you have only been banished and not received the same fate as your brother."

"What of his children and wife? What will become of them?"

"There is no proof of Lady Krishna assisting her husband, she will return to her brother in Gator Swamp. The boys will become ward and squire to Lord Rajesh with hopes of knighthood, and the girls will be the Queen's ladies and married to suitable husbands when the time comes," informed Xolan.

"And my brother, what fate did he meet?" Raj asked.

"Raghu died during questioning," said Xolan, he had always liked Raj and did not think he had any part in Lord Hugart stealing the eggs. But Xolan was wise enough not to say that to Raj himself.

"Can I have some time to gather my things?"

"I will be back in an hour, will that be time enough?"

"I suppose it will," Raj said and turned his back on the Red Wizard.

That would give Xolan enough time to inform Lady Krishna. He found the guards standing outside her chambers and told them to step aside. When he entered the chambers, Lady Krishna was working on embroidery and the children were playing on the floor beside her. She sat down her needle and rose from her chair.

"Lord Xolan, to what do I owe your company?" she asked. She was still very courteous despite all that had happened.

"Lady Krishna, may I speak to you privately? We can use the room across the hall?"

"Why of course Xolan," she replied her face showed no emotion.

Xolan led her across the hall the guards watched but did not question the wizard. Lady Krishna held a straight face until she was safely away from her children. Xolan realized she was being strong for their sake. As soon as Xolan shut the door Lady Krishna eyes started to tear and her brow wrinkled.

"What has become of my husband?"

"Lord Hugart has died My Lady, I am sorry for your loss," Xolan said in a sympathetic tone.

"Do not lie about being sorry when chances are he died from your own hand," she said and started to sob. "So what is to become of my children and myself?" She asked, her face had turned red and splotchy, not the stone hard face she had in the other room.

"Your sons will be ward and squire to Lord Rajesh with hopes of knighthood one day. And your daughters will become the Queen's ladies, and be married to suitable husbands when ready. You, My Lady, will go back home to Gator Swamp to your brother, and I will arrange you safe passage," Xolan informed Lady Hugart.

"The King expects me to leave my children with the brother and wife of the man that killed their father? Xolan you cannot expect me to just leave them. Why can't they come with me? My brother will take them in and they will be raised up right and will be loyal to the King. Please Xolan let me take my children. Please," she pleaded.

"I am sorry My Lady, the King has ordered. Your sons will be knights and your daughters married to lords, you can not hope for more. They will be taken care of, I promise."

"As well taken care of as my husband was?" She spat back at him, the tears with flowing from her eyes in streams and her nose had started to run.

"It is done, My Lady. The King has ordered and you will not be able to change his mind. You will have the rest of the day to say your farewells to your children and pack. On the morrow you will leave for Gator Swamp," Xolan said with his voice cold and sharp.

"What could my husband of done for the King to be so harsh towards innocent people?" Lady Krishna wanted to know.

"He committed treason in the Kings own castle."

"And what is treason Xolan? Anything the King wants it to be," she said, "give me a minute, before you take me back. I do not want my children to see me like this."

"As you wish, My Lady, take as long as you need." As Xolan left the room he instructed the guard to let Lady Krishna have some time alone before being taken back to her children.

Xolan made his way back toward Lord Raj's chambers. When he reached the room he found Lord Raj sitting on his bed with three trunks in front of him.

"Are you ready?"

"Yes, Xolan," Lord Raj answered and stood.

Xolan had servants carry the trunks and brought ten guards with him just in case Lord Raj decided to do anything stupid. They walked side by side toward the docks. When they reached the docks, thirty ships waited in the bay.

"Do you know where you are planning to go?" Xolan asked.

"Any ship will do. I have never known anything but the South. I will just make do."

They walked up to the first ship and asked for the captain. The ship was named *Sea Goddess* and the captain was a heavy man, with a peppered beard and ragged clothes.

"Where are you off to?" Xolan asked.

"West, I hear there t' be a weddin. I was gonna try t' sell some o' my gems," the captain answered in a thick accent.

"I don't think the West is the place for an exiled southern lord," Lord Raj answered. Xolan was glad about that, the King would be going west for the wedding and he didn't need to run into Lord Raj.

They moved on from ship to ship. Three more ships were going west for the wedding and two were going up to The Horseshoe. Lord Raj didn't fancy freezing either. The sixth ship they climbed on was the *Sweet Leann*. The crew was very dark, skin of ebony. The captain had the same dark skin, his hair all gray and frizzy. Xolan thought him to be about forty, may haps a little older but not much. The captain's arms where very muscular and his chest broad. He was sailing to the Islands of Azica to the east, which was where he was from. Lord Raj thought a different country might be the best choice, where no one knew his name. Xolan agreed and paid the captain for passage, he gave Lord Raj enough gold to last a poor man a year and waited on the docks until the ship sailed.

At day break, Lady Krishna Hugart left Dragon's End with one hundred guards and tears in her eyes. The Hugart children were crying for their mother to stay. Xolan had to have guards hold them back from running after the wagon that their mother was in. Xolan delivered the boys to Lord Rajesh Smeltzer and the girls to the Queen's ladies. After a busy morning with not even enough time to eat, Xolan hurried to the Council Room. His stomach rumbling and his silk red robes sticking to his skin Xolan entered the room red faced and out of breath.

"Xolan good of you to make it," the King replied when Xolan entered the room.

"Beg pardons, Your Grace, I was making sure all the Hugarts were taken care of and where they need to be," Xolan answered and bowed his head.

"Not to worry, I was just giving you hell. Sit," the King said with a smile. The King seemed like he was in a better mood today. Xolan took his seat next to his King and the King began, "I must travel West. King Cynon is marrying his son and heir Prince Aidan to Princess Margery of the East."

"Your Grace, the West is joining kingdoms with the East?" Prince Amar seemed shocked by the news. "That beast of a King in the West is always threatening war. With the armies of the East on his side what is to stop him from going through with his threat?" The Prince asked the King.

"My dragons are what will stop him. Two armies still can not beat one army with two dragons, King Cynon knows that," the King replied.

"Anyway, it is happening and I can't do anything about it. What do you want me to do, break up the wedding? That would guarantee war. No I am not going to worry about King Cynon's and King Tristan's armies. I doubt King Tristan would even know how to fight a war, he is too busy smelling roses in his garden," said the King and every council member laughed out loud. "I have not known anyone to die of a thorn prick," the King told his brother with a smile.

"You will not be smiling when you have two armies at your gates brother," the Prince said back.

"I will not talk about it more, the wedding is happening and I am required to attend," the King ended the conversation there.

"Now, back to me going West. I will be leaving with Lord Rajesh toward Fire Harbor. I will stay there a night then make my way to Autumn Way. Lord McClure has offered his hospitality for the night. King Cynon has cleared an Inn in a village halfway from Autumn Way and West Watch. And on to West Watch and this wedding," the King stated his plans. "I will need a gift for the happy couple. I have heard the Princess loves animals and the King likes beast so I plan on giving them one of my lions. It would be a pity if one of them got mauled," the King said with a laugh. "I will also be bringing some of our summer wine which is a lot better than the horse piss they drink, and some peppers. My Queen is giving the Princess silk and lace as well."

"Prince Amar, you will sit the throne when I am away," the King turned to his brother and said. "I will be taking Queen Kala and my children. Along with Zuri, Xolan, my King's Guard and five hundred additional knights. The rest of my council will stay here and help my brother run my kingdom," the King instructed. "Lord Rajesh will be taking the Smeltzer guards with him to Fire Harbor, so with Lord Rajesh and I gone, Dragons End will be down seven hundred guards," the King informed.

"We can have the Castle Guard do double shifts until you return, Your Grace," Lord Punit suggested.

"Very well," the King agreed.

"We also will have two open seats at council. Lord Rajesh is to stay at Fire Harbor and keep the peace. So we require a new Master of Coin and Commander of the Docks. Any suggestions?" the King asked his council.

"Rama Maillett is heir to the Vipers and can fill in until he is needed to take over for his father," suggested Lord Rajesh.

"Lord Rajender, would your brother want this task, it would be temporary until he is needed back at the Vipers?" the King asked.

"I thank you, Your Grace, but my family has two islands to control and my brother rules one and my father the other. I can write him, but I doubt he would take the honor," Lord Rajender answered.

"That is fine, we will think of someone," the King replied. "I think that is all I have for the day, I would like to leave in one week and need all preparations taken care of. Council dismissed, my thanks," the King said and stood to leave.

AUTUMN WAY

Maggie could see land! It had been hell on the boat from Lionsgate across the Great Lake. The first day the moving of the ship beneath her feet had made Maggie sick, and she was stuck in bed vomiting in a basin. She felt better today but her stomach was weak, and she had not dared to eat anything. But now she could see land, she was ready to get off the *Lions Tooth*. It was Lord Stoddart's boat, and her father had paid Lord Stoddart enough to buy him a new boat. The sun was high in the pail blue sky, big fluffy clouds floated past. To the north Maggie could see Wizard Keep and to the west she could see green land. Her stomach gave a rumble and she thought she might vomit again, not knowing if it was nerves or the boat. She kept her eyes toward the west and watched the land slowly creep closer.

"Maggie do you have everything in order?" Her mother asked.

"Tansy and Violet are making sure of it. Mother, will the King and Prince be there when we dock?"

"I know not, all I know is they are planning on meeting us at Autumn Way."

"I hope they are not there until later. I know I look terrible. I don't want the Prince to see me looking like this," Maggie said.

She was excited to finally meet her Prince. She would have two and a half weeks to get to know him before the wedding. She was afraid she would not meet him until the wedding day, but her father left early so she could.

Three hours later they were almost to the shore, Maggie could see knights and wagons and people standing watching the boat approach. She couldn't make out faces, the only thing that gave away the knights was their armor reflecting the sun. The boat crept closer, inch by inch, until Maggie could make out women from men. Finally, the boat could not move forward anymore without getting stuck. Small row boats were lowered and her family was the first to go to shore. King Tristan went down first, then the Queen and then the children. Two sailors were in the boat to row them to shore. It seemed the row boat moved faster than the larger one. Before long they were on land.

Servants waded in the water up to their knees and walked out to carry them to shore so they would not get wet. Her father refused to *"be carried like a maid"* but her mother gladly let the servants carry her. When a big man with fire red hair and skin white as snow came up to Maggie, she wrapped her arms around his neck and he bent down to put his arms behind her back and under her knees. The man's neck was very muscular and Maggie thought he had to be a smith or a builder with muscles like that. When they were safe from the water the big man sat Maggie gently on the grass. She thanked him, he nodded and hurried away.

Lady Fiona McClure walked over to Maggie and knelt down in the grass and kissed her left hand. Lady Fiona was shorter, about Maggie's height with strawberry blond hair and beautiful sea blue eyes. Her hair was down and flowed past her hips. She had an hourglass shape to her, big breast, small waist, big hips. Lady Fiona was not skinny but not fat, average sized.

"My Princess, you honor us with you company," Lady Fiona said.

"It is you that honor me. I thank you for your hospitality," Maggie answered.

"No trouble at all. You are always welcome at Autumn Way."

Maggie was happy she was so welcomed. She had feared she might be seen as an outsider and not be loved by the people of the West. But if everyone welcomed her like Lady Fiona she would not have a problem.

Next Lord Gwern McClure came over and bowed and kissed her hand as well. "My Princess, welcome to the West," he said.

Lord Gwern was a heavy man with a big belly and two chins, hidden by his beard. He had rusty colored hair, with light skin and many freckles. His bushy eyebrows took away from his bright green eyes. The buttons on his doublet looked like they would pop off at any moment.

"You are too kind, Lord McClure. My thanks for letting us stay the night," she replied with a smile. He smiled back and nodded, then walked over to her father and started talking to him.

Her mother and Lady McClure walked over in her direction with Kate following close behind. "We have a wagon ready to take us to Autumn Way. Will you honor me with your presence Princess?" Lady McClure asked.

Maggie gave a nod and followed her to the wagon. The big man that had carried her ashore helped her in the wagon than climbed up top to steer the horses. The wagon was very nice. With cushioned benches and blue silk curtains that were pulled back to let the sun in. There was a table built into the middle that held sweet honey rolls and honey wine. Honey and steel was the West's main trade. Maggie had heard that something with honey was served with every meal. She was fine with that, she loved honey. Better than peppers, which is what the South had with every meal.

The wagon crept on, the thunder bolt sigil of House McClure flying on all four corners. All the men rode horseback and flanked the wagon on all sides.

"King Cynon and Prince Aidan should be arriving at night fall. We are to have a great feast," Lady Fiona said, "that should give you time to freshen up."

"Yes, a bath would be most welcome. I am afraid I was not built for boats."

"No woman is built for a boat, you are not alone trust me," Lady Fiona replied. "Queen Helen, how long are you planning on staying after the wedding?" Lady Fiona asked.

"Not long I'm afraid, my husband must return to his kingdom," her mother had been cold ever since they left Lionsgate.

As they were approaching Autumn Way, Maggie could see the grey stone wall that was built around the city. Two guards stood at the oak and iron gate and nodded up top for the gate to open when the wagon got close. They entered the city from the east. Apartments that were four stories high, were built of the same gray stone the wall was built from. People stood from the balconies to watch as the party crept by. They cheered and threw flowers down. They passed several apartments before they came upon the market of the city, where men were selling their goods from tables. Maggie saw jewelry, weapons, furs, fruits and vegetables, fabrics and much more. After the market they passed three inns, and one brothel. Finally they came upon the gate to the McClure castle. It had iron gates surrounding it similar to Lionsgate. The grey and yellow thunderbolt of the house flew on banners on the gate and towers. Maggie saw another banner mixed in amongst the thunderbolt, the blue and red crown of the king.

The women waited in the wagon until all the men had dismounted their horses. Servants rushed over to help them out. On the steps that lead up to the castle, four boys waited. Maggie guessed them to be McClure's also by the way they were dressed. Each boy wore brown breeches with a grey tunic under a leather doublet and a grey cloak from their shoulders. The tallest boy had a long sword at his hip. All boys had the rusty colored hair of their father. King Tristan and Lord McClure climbed the steps first, followed by

Queen Helen and Lady Fiona. Maggie and Jon went next with her other brother and sister behind, followed by Tansy and Violet, and the King's Guard. The servants were caring to the horses and unloading the wagons. The four boys knelt as the party approached them.

"Let me introduce my sons. Fergual my oldest and my heir, Fergus, Finley and Finnan," Lord Gwern announced, each boy stood after their name was called and gave a dutiful bow.

They entered the doors into a great hall, grey stone floors and walls made the room dark. The thunderbolt was hung upon the wall along with the red and blue crown.

"My sons will show you to your chambers. I have servants waiting to get you anything you desire. Fergal, would you be so kind as to show Princess Margery to her chambers? Fergus, you show Prince Jon; Finley, show Princess Kate and Finnan, you can show Prince Jason to his chambers. King Tristan and Queen Helen, I will have the honor of showing you to your chambers. If you would follow me," Lord Gwern said.

"Very well, Ser Asher, go with Maggie, Ser Jaron with Jon, Ser Clifford with Jason, and Ser Byron with Kate. Ser Burke and Ser Clive with me," the King said.

Maggie's father had been having Ser Asher with Maggie a lot lately, and she wondered if there was a reason for that. Maggie, Tansy, Violet and Ser Asher followed Fergal. They made a right turn then a left turn, came to a stair, climbed four stories, turned right again and he opened the fourth door on the left. Maggie hoped Ser Asher was paying attention to all the turns, she was likely to forget how to get back. Maggie walked into the room and found a large canopy bed, big enough to sleep at the least four people. A looking glass that was taller than her and fitted in gold. A big oak desk with a cushioned chair, and her own privy. Maggie was very pleased with her room.

Two servants waited in the room, both middle aged women with common faces and red hair. Fergal left her to get ready for the feast.

"Can we get you anything m'lady?" one of the servants asked.

"Yes, I would very much like a bath," Maggie said, and both servants hurried off. "Ser Asher would you be so kind as to stand outside the room while I get ready?" she said to the knight.

"Yes my Princess," he said with a bow and stepped outside the room and shut the door behind him.

"Tansy and Violet help me get out of these clothes," Maggie said to her bed maids, and they hurried to obey.

Lord Gwern's servants came back with hot water and filled the tub. While Maggie was taking her bath she asked them to go and find her trunks, and they did as they were told.

Violet was just finishing Maggie's hair when trumpets sounded. Ser Asher came in the door and said, "My Princess, the Prince has arrived we must go down to meet him."

"Yes, I just finished getting ready," Maggie replied and followed the knight out of the room.

Ser Asher remembered how to get back to the great hall at the front of the castle. Ser Asher was at the least a foot taller than Maggie and had longer legs, so she had to almost run to keep up with him. They reached the hall just when the doors were being opened.

"Maggie you almost missed your prince," the King said with a smile.

Maggie smiled back at him while she was trying to catch her breath. She stood to her father's left and her mother was to his right. Her brothers and sister stood behind them. The McClure family had gone out to meet the King of the West.

Maggie could hear footsteps coming up the stairs to the castle and all of a sudden her stomach was in knots. Her breathing became short and shallow and she could feel the blood rushing to her cheeks. She didn't think she would have been this nervous to meet the Prince. The first people through the door were a very tall muscular man, and a tall and slender woman. The man had big broad shoulders and a stern round face covered by a red beard. He had a crown on his head and was exquisitely dressed. Maggie figured out quickly that was the King. The woman had auburn hair pulled back on the sides with braids. The hair in the back flowed down almost to her hip. She had a kind smile and large almond shaped eyes. Her gown was deep blue with elegant bell sleeves and lots of lace. She had to be the Queen.

Her father stepped forward and went up to the man and clasped him on the forearm, which soon turned into a hug. "Cynon old man, it has been too long. Where is this son that is to marry my daughter?"

"Aidan is on his way up. How was your journey?" King Cynon asked.

"Fine, fine. Let me introduce my beautiful daughter Princess Margery, and of course you remember my wife Helen."

"Why of course, Helen it is great to see you again. And Princess Margery we have heard rumors of your beauty, and they turn out to be true."

Maggie blushed and bowed her head, somehow she had forgotten how to speak, words would not come to her. Then when she looked back up there was a very hansom man. Auburn hair down to his shoulders, green eyes you could lose yourself in. He wore silver armor, and a blue cloak was over his broad shoulders. He was much more attractive than his father was.

"Aidan, this is Princess Margery," King Cynon said to his son.

Then the Prince came over and got down on one knee, he took Maggie's right hand and kissed it gently. Maggie could feel herself blush and her head was dizzy.

"My Princess, your beauty is a legend and it would give me great honor to be your husband."

She didn't know what to say, she couldn't think, just his presence was intoxicating. Finally after what seemed like forever the words came to her lips, "You are too kind, the honor is mine," she said. She was very happy with herself, her voice didn't squeak or crack.

Next thing she knew everyone was gone except Ser Asher, Prince Aidan and herself.

"Where did everybody go?" she asked Ser Asher.

"They went to the dinning hall My Princess, they asked you to join them but you didn't answer," he replied.

She looked at her Prince and he said, "I didn't hear them either. Shall we join them?"

"Yes," was all she could say.

He held out his arm and she took it gratefully. Ser Asher led the way and they fallowed. Maggie could feel the muscles of his arm through his chain mail and it made her blush again. She could not keep her eyes off him, he just wasn't what she expected at all. Her uncle had always said that men of the West were short and stout with red hair, freckles and a bad attitude. Prince Aidan didn't seem like he had a bad attitude, he didn't have the cold stern face that his father had.

When they entered the dining hall, King Cynon said very loudly, "looks like the love birds decided to join us," and gave his son a look.

Maggie didn't know if it was a good look or a bad look. Prince Aidan did have the same color eyes as his father, but his father's eyes were cold and Aidan's eyes were full of feeling.

"Beg pardons father," Aidan said.

"Well sit, so we can start this feast. Bring your pretty bride here," King Cynon replied.

King Cynon and King Tristan had two empty chairs between them and their Queens sat by their husbands. Maggie took the chair next to King Cynon and Aidan took the chair next to her father. The feast began.

The servants came in with flagons, one in each hand. "Have you ever had honey mead Princess Margery?" King Cynon asked.

"No Your Grace, I have not, and please call me Maggie."

"You have to try it, strong and sweet."

When the servants approached her and asked "mead or wine?"

"I'll try the mead," Maggie said to the servant.

The servant filled Maggie's chalice. Maggie put the chalice to her lips and tried the mead. Just like the King described sweet and strong, a little too strong. Maggie would not be able to drink more than a cup.

"What do you think?" Prince Aidan asked.

"Good, a little strong, but good," she said.

The first course came in, a cream soup with chunks of clams, muscles, crab and fish. Maggie tried it and it was heavy and very filling. The second course was lamprey pie. Then cabbage smothered in butter and venison roasted tender, also a warm wheat bread with honey butter. Maggie tried a couple bites of each course, but Prince Aidan gobbled up all of the food put in front of him. Next came a salad of pears, walnuts, grapes and apples.

"We will leave on the morrow, tis three days to West Watch," Aidan said in between bites, "you can ride in my mothers wagon if you like. I am sure it is a lot more comfortable than a horse."

"Three days, really. I thought it was closer," Maggie said.

"It would be faster without the wagons, but three days isn't that long. At the village we stay at on the morrow there is an inn that is very nice. My father has already assured all the feather beds will be ready and that there will be enough for all of the Royals. At the village after that one, the inn is nicer and much bigger, then on to the castle," Aidan answered.

The last course was custard with blueberries in it. It was very good and Maggie gobbled it up. They had been through all the courses and Maggie still hadn't emptied her chalice, but she was already tipsy. King Tristan and King Cynon were trying to talk to each other over Maggie and Aidan.

"Will you dance with me, My Princess?" Aidan asked.

"Why of course I will," Maggie answered and gave Aidan her hand.

Prince Aidan led her to the middle of the dining hall, he put one hand on the small of her back and took her other hand. He spun her around and started leading her around the middle of the floor. He was very graceful even in his armor. Before long her mother and father joined in, and Lord and Lady McClure. Then Finnan the McClure's youngest started dancing with Kate. Aidan kept them in the middle of the crowd, and they danced song after song after song. When the music finally stopped the moon was high in the sky.

King Cynon was drunk on mead and laughing with his wife. It was the first time Maggie could see any feeling in his face. When the King did smile he had crows feet on the corners of his eyes. Queen Aileen had a beautiful laugh, almost musical. King Tristan and her mother had sat back down in their seats, but Aidan and Maggie walked around the dining hall visiting. Maggie was starting to get tired it had been a long day, and she was still wheezy from the boat. Before long she was fighting back yawns and wanting to close her eyes.

"My Prince it has been a long and tiring day, I must bid you good night so I will be ready for our trip on the morrow. Would you excuse me?"

"Why of course my Princess, go get some rest and I will see you on the morrow. Dream about me tonight?"

"There is no one else I would dream of," she said with a smile.

He kissed her on the cheek and led her to the door. Ser Asher was standing there watching.

"Should I escort you to your room Princess?" he asked Maggie.

"No need, Ser Asher will do that, my thanks," she replied. Maggie looked at Ser Asher and nodded and he followed her out the door as she left her prince.

When Maggie woke the next morning she was lying in between Tansy and Violet. Both of her maids were still asleep, Maggie slipped from her bed and went to the windows and opened the shutters. Toward the east the sky was pink, that turned to purple, dark blue and grey as the sky reached up.

She was still looking out the window when Violet came up behind her and asked, "would you like to get dressed, m'lady?"

"Yes, I want the pink silk gown with the pink pearls," she said back to her maid. After the gown was tightly laced, Tansy started piling Maggie's golden curls on the top of her head, and placed her rose crown in front.

When she opened the door to her room she found Ser Asher sleeping on a cot right outside her door. This was new, she had never had guards sleep outside her door before. Was there danger that she did not know about, or was her father just being careful. Ser Asher was still in the armor he was wearing last night and he was snoring loudly.

Maggie put her hand on his arm, "Ser Asher?" she said. Ser Asher let out a snort and opened his eyes, "Princess?" he said with eyes half closed.

"Yes, I want to go down to break my fast but you are in my way, I cannot leave my room with your cot right there," she said.

"Beg pardons Princess, I will take you down," he said and hurried out of the cot and pushed it out of the way.

When she entered the dining hall King Cynon was sitting with Lord McClure talking about the wedding plans.

"Princess Maggie, come break your fast with us," the King said to her and pushed the chair next to him back.

Lord McClure waved at one of the servants and by the time Maggie sat down the servant was back with a bowl of porridge with a saucer of milk and a jar of honey. "Would you like ale to wash it down, m'lady?" she servant asked.

"No ale thank you, do you have any milk?" she said.

"Yes m'lady, would you like honey in it to sweeten it?" the servant replied.

"Yes, that would be fine," she said back to the servant, and he hurried away to the kitchens.

Maggie was pouring honey in her porridge when Lord McClure asked, "Did you sleep well my Princess? Did my servants take care of you?"

"Yes, the bed was very comfortable and your servants did everything I asked of them," she answered Lord McClure.

"Maggie, we have a little over two weeks before you wed my son. When we reach West Watch I will have my Queen go over the wedding plans with you, I think she has enjoyed planning this wedding. The Royal family from the South is coming and the Ice Queen will be there as well. Have you ever seen a unicorn Maggie?" King Cynon said to her.

"No, Your Grace," Maggie replied.

"People say the Ice Queen has her wagon pulled by unicorns. I saw a few myself when I went up North for her wedding. The people of the North don't like riding them, but they use them to pull wagons," the King said.

"I would very much like to see a unicorn, I have heard they are beautiful creatures," Maggie said.

"That they are, much larger than regular horses and they have thicker hair. Their hair is as white as snow and their ivory horns are swirled with silver," the King told her. "And in the South the King has dragons. He won't be bringing them though, he keeps them hidden away until he has a sacrifice," the King continued.

Maggie had heard of the sacrifices, instead of regular executions like the rest of the kingdoms where you just hang a criminal or cut off his head. In the South the King would feed criminals to his beast and call it a sacrifice to his gods.

"I would much rather see a unicorns than a dragon, Your Grace," Maggie said and the King chuckled.

Maggie had finished her porridge and was getting ready to excuse herself when Prince Aidan walked into the hall. Today he had his hair pulled away from his face with a leather strip. He wore his silver armor with black breeches and black boots, his blue cloak hanging from his shoulders like a waterfall.

"My Princess you wake early, have you already broke your fast?" he said to her.

"Yes, your father and Lord McClure were keeping me company," she replied.

"And now you have my son to keep you company," the King said, "come Lord McClure lets have the servants start getting everything ready to leave." The King and Lord McClure got up and left Aidan and Maggie in the dining hall alone.

The servants brought Aidan his porridge and ale.

"I hope you will like your new home, once we get to West Watch. My father is giving you an entire floor of Hammer Tower. You have a bed chamber, your own privy, rooms for your guard and servants, and a library. After we are married you will move into my chambers. I have the whole top floor of the Spear Tower," Aidan said.

"I am sure it is beautiful."

"Not as beautiful as what you are use to I am sure. I have heard your father's castle shines like gold when the sun hits it and reaches up to the clouds."

"Yes, it shines, but my mother, father and uncles have the best towers. I only had a bedchamber and privy," Maggie told her prince. "Your castle must be bigger than mine if it is going to house all the Royals and Lords."

"It has enough rooms for the Royals and Lords, but all the knights and guards have to sleep in tents that my mother had set up. The knights, guards and commons will also dine in tents. We don't have the room for everyone in the Great Hall," Aidan explained. "By the time we get back, the servants will probably have all the banners flying, and flowers everywhere and who knows what else my mother has them doing for the wedding. My mother keeps saying it will be the biggest wedding that no one can top," Aidan continued.

"I am sure it will be. I can't wait. But I am glad I got to meet you before our wedding day," Maggie confessed.

"Me as well, I was afraid of the same thing," Aidan told her. "Shall we go out in the yard and see how everything is going?" Aidan said after his bowl was empty, "I can show you my horse."

"I would like that."

The Prince took her hand and led her out of the hall, Ser Asher following close behind.

When they got to the stables the stable boys were rushing around trying to get the horses ready. They walked to the last horse on the left, a big black stallion with a long mane and tail. A boy who was nicely dressed was trying to saddle the horse, but the horse was not having it.

"Maggie let me introduce my squire, Rory McDaniel," Aidan said to her.

The boy bowed his head and said, "He won't let me saddle him m'lord."

"I've told you Rory, you have to approach him from the front, so he can see you," Aidan replied.

The boy took the saddle and came at the horse from the front and was able to get the saddle on. When Rory tried to bridle the horse though he got bit on the hand, hard enough to draw blood. Aidan laughed and took the bridle from the boy, and put it on the horse himself.

"Maggie, this is Night Terror."

Snow Cap Mountains

The snow was falling in sheets outside. Beneath the Snow Caps it was always warmer, the heat from the earth rose and the walls of the mountains blocked the cold wind. Gundahar, the Leader of the Dark Dwarfs of Snow Cap, was looking over the silver and gems that had been dug up, when he heard what sounded like a horse whining.

"What was that sound?" Gundahar asked Wodan.

"The wind blowing through the mountains, what else would it be? Who would try to come through the mountains during a snow storm?" Wodan replied.

"No that was not the wind. Get Weland and Etzel we will go see what that was," Gundahar said.

The Dark Dwarfs were dwarfs of the mountains, abandoned and exiled by man. They were considered evil from birth because of their disfiguration, a curse from the gods. The dwarfs had the same size head and torso of a man, but stunted arms and legs and little stubby fingers. But thanks to man the dwarfs were tough, they could survive where other men could not. They lived hidden in caves of the mountains and dug silver and gems for the Ice Queen, and the King before her, and the King before him. For hundreds of years they have been digging.

And they were surviving, but for half a year they have been plaqued by wolves along with men. These were not normal wolves, these wolves were as big as a horse. They tried to chase the dwarfs out of their caves, and failed. So the wolves finally gave up and went to terrorize men. Once in awhile the wolves would come back and try again, but the dwarfs killed them with their axes and used their skins for warmth.

Gundahar had his great axe in hand, the staff was taller than him and the blade was as wide as he was. Wodan, Weland and Etzel came to the entrance of the cave with their axes and they set out. White blankets of snow covered the mountains, with a grey sky overhead. The dwarfs started to climb up the outside of the mountain to get farther up to see if someone or something was approaching. The good thing about being a dwarf was the small hands and feet, they didn't need big steps or hand holes to pull themselves up. They climbed a good twenty feet or so, not even a quarter of the way up the mountain, but high enough to see. Gundahar looked to the southwest and saw silver men surrounding villagers. He squinted and saw four blue banners. Queen's knights, but what were they doing with the villagers in his mountains?

"I will go down to meet these knights to know their business. You stay hidden. I do not want them to feel threatened. They out number all our men five to one," Gundahar said to the men that came with him.

Wodan nodded and Weland and Etzel made their way to stay hidden before the knights spotted them. Gundahar made his way down. It was always easier going up than going down. His stunted legs wouldn't move fast enough, then his left foot caught a patch of ice and he slid the rest of the way down the mountain on his ass. By the time he reached the bottom of the mountain, all his wolf skin clothes were covered in snow.

Gundahar was ok with the snow covering him, the knights would not see his approach. Gundahar waddled toward the knights through what brush there was at the foot of the mountain. He could hear their approach, they were not traveling quietly. Gundahar stayed behind a bush to watch and make sure there was no danger. The knight riding in the front of the party had a black cloak with a silver eight pointed star, the sigil of North Star. Gundahar took him for one of Lord Landrum's knights. The knights face was covered by his helm. Gundahar slowly stepped out from behind the bush holding his axe up as to not pose a threat.

"What is your business in my mountains?" Gundahar said to the knight at the front.

"Last I checked they were my Lord Father's mountains that he lets you live in," the knight replied. That meant the knight was either Finlan or Ser Fintan.

"Who are you Ser?" Gundahar asked.

"Ser Fintan of the Queen's Council and North Star," the knight replied.

Lord Landrum and the Queen were the only people who showed the dwarfs some kindness, but still looked down on them like everyone else.

"I am glad you came out of your cave Gundahar, I have questions for you."

"What kind of questions?"

"Might we talk out of this snow storm? Would you give us shelter?" the knight asked.

Gundahar thought on that, his people would not be happy with man in their cave, but if he offended Lord Landrum's son that could bring death to his people.

"Very well, come with me. But you leave as soon as the storm is gone. Your people show no kindness to dwarfs, but I am not as cruel as your fellow man," Gundahar replied and led the party toward the cave.

He was not happy about it, the village people were always hunting in the mountains and taking their game. Then when they traveled to Icestorm to trade with the Queen the villagers would try to steal their gems. But he was out numbered and had little choice. There had to be at the least one hundred knights with Ser Fintan let alone the men of the village.

When he got to the entrance of the cave he stopped and said to the knight, "If you want shelter leave your weapons here, I will not have you bringing pain to my people."

The knight talked to the knight beside him and finally gave a nod.

"Oh and if anyone tries to touch our silver or gems, remember we are the only ones with weapons and you will not have shelter for long," Gundahar said to Ser Fintan.

"Never thought I'd be taken orders from a dwarf."

Gundahar waited outside the cave until everyone was ready. Ser Fintan left ten knights outside with the horses and weapons, the rest came into the cave. When they entered the cave there wasn't a dwarf in sight. Gundahar knew they heard him outside and they were hiding in the shadows.

"Come," Gundahar said and led the knights and villagers down a narrow passage. Everyone besides Gundahar had to duck their heads to pass through. When they came out of the passage they entered a big cavern. There was a fire burning in the middle, with tree trunks set around for the dwarfs to sit upon.

"Your knights and villagers may stay in here. Don't go wondering around!" Gundahar said, "Ser Fintan come with me so we can talk."

They took the passage to the left, the dwarfs had torches in the wall lighting most of the passages. Finally they came upon the cavern that Gundahar and his family lived and slept. His wife Brunhild was sitting on the bed mending some of Gundahar's breeches. She looked up expecting to see Gundahar or one of their sons, but her eyes fixed on Ser Fintan and the anger showed across her face.

"Gundahar what have you done! Showing him where we live, betraying your people. He'll run home to his Lord and we will be smoked out then robbed," his wife yelled at him.

"Ser Fintan needs to speak to me, and he and his party needed shelter from the storm. They left their weapons outside, and will not betray our hospitality. Isn't that right Ser Fintan?" Gundahar said.

"Yes, m'lady no harm will come to your people," Ser Fintan answered.

"Do I look like a lady to you Ser?" his wife spat back at the knight. The knight did not answer.

"Brunhild would you excuse us, so we can talk," Gundahar asked his wife.

"Be careful Gundahar, men are the reason we live in a mountain. Remember that," and with that is wife waddled off. Her grey stringy hair matched the grey wolf fur she wore.

Ser Fintan had removed his helmet and Gundahar was surprised the helmet had not frozen to his face. Ser Fintan stood stiffly, it was obvious he was more uncomfortable in the cave than the dwarf was around men.

"So Ser Fintan, what is it that you need to talk to the leader of the Dark Dwarfs about?" Gundahar asked the knight.

"There have been wolf attacks throughout the villages. The Queen has ordered that we move everyone to the cities behind walls. Have you seen these wolves?" Ser Fintan replied.

"We have, they try to come into our caves, but don't live long enough to get comfortable," Gundahar replied.

"Have you lost any of your people to these wolves?"

"One or two, not many. Why?"

"You are part of the Queen's people, if you want you can have shelter behind my father's walls. The Queen has ordered all that seek shelter be given it," the knight continued.

"Trust me Ser, my people face a greater threat than wolves behind your father's walls. No, we will stay here. I think our chances are better with the wolves," Gundahar replied.

"Have it your way. I offered as I was required to do," the knight said. "How big are these wolves? I have heard they are as big as horses," the knight continued.

"Aye, huge beast, but vulnerable during the day. Night is when they pose a threat, it seems there strength grows with the moon," Gundahar informed the knight.

"And you have slayed them?" the knight doubted.

"Aye, it took all my men, we kept the pelts. I could show you," Gundahar waddled over to the bed and pulled the big skin off and handed it to the knight.

The knight inspected the pelt with a wrinkled brow. "The Queen wants to put a hunting party together, would you want to join them?"

"I think not, if we hunted wolves we could not dig up the Queen's silver and gems," Gundahar replied.

"Well she is offering a reward for every wolf killed. Bring the heads when you bring the silver and you will be paid for both," the knight continued.

"May haps I will."

Gundahar led the knight back to the large cavern the other men were in and went off to find Wodan, Weland and Etzel. Gundahar had known all three his whole life, they grew up together in the mountains. Wodan was a chubby fellow, three feet tall, two chins that were covered by his peppered shaggy beard, and a big gut. Weland was the smallest, not even three feet tall. His crow black beard stretching down past his waist, and very skinny for a dwarf. Etzel had a snow white beard like Gundahar's, he had a thin face with sunken eye sockets and high cheek bones.

They were all three by the entrance watching the knights that were left outside with the horses.

"What is going on Gundahar?" Wodan asked.

"The Queen has ordered all villagers be moved to cities to be behind walls so the wolves will not get to them. Ser Fintan has also offered for us to go behind his father's walls, I refused him," Gundahar answered.

"How long are they going to stay?" Etzel asked.

"Until the storm passes," said Gundahar.

"That could be days!" Weland squeaked.

"I know how long a snow storm last in the mountains! They had women and children and it was Lord Landrum's son who led them. If I refused then we could face Lord Landrum's wrath," Gundahar replied.

"We don't have the food," Etzel said.

Gundahar thought on that, "may haps they do, I gave them shelter they could give us food." "What about the gems? A man's greed can be dangerous," Wodan warned.

"Their weapons are with the horses, and they have been warned," Gundahar answered. "Come with me, it will be dark in hours and we need to talk to Ser Fintan," Gundahar said to his friends.

They entered the great cavern were the villagers and knights were, the dwarfs called it the *meeting hall*. Ser Fintan and about ten other knights were over in the corner talking, while the rest of the knights stood at each tunnel entrance and the villagers were gathered round the fire. Gundahar, Wodan, Weland and Etzel approached Ser Fintan.

"It will be dark in hours, you need to try and get your horses sheltered and your knights in. We seal the entrance at nightfall," Gundahar informed the knight.

"What shelter for the horses? They won't make it through that passage," Ser Fintan replied.

"We do not have horses so I do not know what to tell you. I do know come night fall the entrance is sealed and not reopened until morning," said Gundahar. "Also, do you have supplies? Food?" he asked the knight.

"The villagers brought what food they could carry. Why?" Ser Fintan replied.

"We don't have much food to feed all of you and keep ourselves fed. We will combine food and eat well tonight," Gundahar said.

Fifty knights tried to quickly build a sort-of shelter out of tree branches for the horses. They tied all the horses up and brought all their supplies in the cave. Gundahar had Wodan, Weland and Etzel take the weapons and put them somewhere safe, the knights did not like that. The snow was still falling heavily and the sky was almost black by the time the knights were done. The dwarfs helped carry the supplies to the meeting hall. Once in the hall they split up the supplies, clothes, furs, food. There were twenty loafs of bread, ten onions, three bushels of carrots, two bags of apples, and salted meat. There was about fifty skins of wine.

Gundahar left to find his wife so they could start preparing the food. She was in their cavern talking to their son Alberic.

"Brunhild, get some o' that wolf meat and salt and the big pot. Bring it to the meeting hall. Alberic go spread the word that we will have a great feast tonight and everyone is to be there in the hour," said Gundahar. His son ran off, but his wife gave him a look that sent a chill up his spine.

"You are going to feed them our meat?" she said.

"Trust me, we get the better deal. They got bread and onions and carrots and wine, lots of wine," Gundahar replied.

"I still don't know 'bout this Gundahar," she said.

"Trust me, now go get the pot."

The supper was interesting, all dwarfs on the east side of the hall, all knights and villagers on the west side. The children who had never seen a dwarf before or the dwarf children that have never seen a man tried to mingle, but were quickly carried off by their parents. They had used all the meat from a wolf, one onion, three carrots, and ten loafs of bread and ten skins of wine. The dwarfs drank seven of the skins. Even the wine had not brought them together though. As soon as the stew was gone, the dwarfs hurried down the tunnels and passages to their caverns.

Gundahar looked up and saw he was the only dwarf left in the hall. He went over to Ser Fintan, "Do you require anything before I retire?"

"I think we have everything, unless you can stop the snow," the knight replied.

"We are dwarfs, not elves," Gundahar replied and went toward his cavern.

His sons and wife were already in bed, and only a single candle burned in the dark. Gundahar got undressed and slipped in his bed next to his wife.

Gundahar woke to the loud voices of men. He got out of his bed and his wife shivered and said something he did not understand. He put on his wolf skin breeches and doublet then threw a wolf skin cloak over his shoulders. He slipped on his leather boots that he had stolen from a man he killed five years ago and made his way toward the hall.

Ser Fintan was the one who approached him, "when will you move that damned boulder?" the knight asked all little too harsh for Gundahars liking.

"At day break," Gundahar replied.

"How the bloody hell do you know when it is day break inside a mountain?" the knight asked annoyed.

"We will know," Gundahar said and walked away back towards his cavern.

The knights had lost five horses to the snow that night. The sky was grey and the snow falling harder than it had the day before.

"I don't think you are leaving today," Gundahar said to one of the knights.

The knight kicked the snow and went stomping back into the cave. By midday the snow had fallen another two feet and was almost blocking the entrance to the cave. Knights tried to dig some of the snow out of the way, but the snow was falling so hard it made no difference.

The dwarfs helped the knights cut the meat from the dead horses. Ser Fintan no longer had knights standing guard outside because of the snow, so everyone was crammed back in the hall. When they ate at midday they had the horses meat, Gundahar was glad that dwarfs did not have horses, he was not fond of the meat. After the meal the dwarfs left to go work the mines, and the villagers and knights stayed in the hall, Gundahar stayed behind.

"What is your father going to do with all these villagers?" Gundahar asked Ser Fintan.

"The Queen is paying him to accommodate everyone, plus he will get a son from every family to be trained for his guard," Ser Fintan answered. "Once the wolves are taken care of they will be free to go back to their villages if they wish," he continued.

"How long do you think this storm will last? My father is expecting us and I am afraid he will send a party out to find us if we are delayed much longer," Ser Fintan said to the dwarf.

"It is hard to say, in the mountains it could snow for weeks at a time, or it could end on the morrow," Gundahar replied, "if the snow does continue I do not know how long your horses will last, you might be walking the rest of the way."

"Aye, if only there was a way to bring them in, is there no other entrance?" said Ser Fintan.

"Not in this mountain, there are other caves though, but to be that far from your horses I am afraid the threat would be worse. The mountain lions, bears, wolves and other beast would find them soon," Gundahar answered.

Ser Fintan grew quiet for awhile. Gundahar looked around at the villagers, they were starting to get restless. The children crying the men arguing.

"They need to stay calm, we can't have them fighting amongst themselves. The sooner we can get moving again the better," Ser Fintan said.

"I agree, men were not made to live under a mountain as dwarfs were," said Gundahar. "If I give your knights back their weapons they will not betray my hospitality I trust?"

"That would help us keep the peace, I will personally guarantee no harm will come to your people," Ser Fintan replied.

Gundahar left and when he returned he was pushing a cart full of all the weapons he made the knights give up. Ser Fintan gave a grateful nod.

"I need to leave for awhile, no one is to leave the hall except to go outside. People could get lost in the mountain if they are not familiar with the tunnels," Gundahar said to Ser Fintan.

The knight gave a nod, and Gundahar headed off down the passage to the left. The dwarfs were working deep into the mountain, it took Gundahar over an hour to reach them. Over a hundred small carts were filled with different gems and silver. Gundahar walked down the carts and inspected all of them, at the end Wodan was standing supervising the dwarfs work.

Gundahar stood by Wodan and watched his dwarfs at work. The picks and hammers echoed off the walls with every blow, it was quit loud. "The villagers are getting restless, I had to give the knights back their weapons so they could keep the peace," Gundahar shouted to Wodan.

"Do you think that wise?" he shouted back.

"I told them I would give them shelter, it is up to the knights to control the villagers if they want to stay," Gundahar replied.

Wodan gave a nod.

When Gundahar returned to the hall after a long day in the mines he found two men tied up in the corner. "I see you had a good day," he said to the knight.

The knight gave a shrug, "they got into a fight and it took four of my knights to pull them apart."

"Tell the villagers that the next ones to fight will be with the horses," Gundahar said.

"I am in charge of them, not you," Ser Fintan replied.

"And they are in my mountain, they need to respect my home," Gundahar said.

The knight gave an annoyed look but did not argue.

That night the dwarfs did not eat with the men. The villagers and knights stayed in the hall, and the dwarfs dined in their own caverns. If the villagers were fighting amongst themselves Gundahar did not want to risk them fighting with the dwarfs. Gundahar dined with his family on salted venison and ale. The ale was strong, they had bought it last time they went to trade their silver with Lord Landrum. His family was quiet, they were not comfortable with the men still staying in the mountain. Gundahar did not want to push the matter, so he dined in silence and went to bed as soon as his horn of ale was empty. That night they slept to the sound of wolves howling in the mountains.

The next morning when the bolder was removed from the entrance they found the horses torn apart and pieces of them strung on the ground. Every horse was dead.

"What happened? How could something kill ninety five horses?" Ser Fintan yelled.

"A big pack of wolves," Gundahar said, "good thing we block the entrance during the night."

"What are we going to do now? We had a two day ride on horseback until we reached my father's city, now with no horses and all this snow it will take us five," Ser Fintan was still yelling.

"At least the snow has stopped, all your villagers were traveling on foot, why can't you?" Gundahar replied.

Ser Fintan spun around and smashed a mailed fist in Gundahar's face. Gundahar went down hard in the snow. His mouth was full of blood, when he stood up he spat out half of a tooth.

"Now you have no choice but to walk. You are no longer welcome here Ser. I said I would give you shelter from the storm and I have done so, the storm is done. Leave," Gundahar said in a stern voice.

"This is your fault Gundahar! I told you we needed to bring the horses in," the knight spat back at him.

"Don't blame me for your horses, if not for me the wolves would have taken you and your villagers instead. Gather your things and your people, I want you away from my mountain by midday," Gundahar said back to him, and waddled inside the cave.

When he entered his cavern his wife looked up at him and her mouth fell open.

"Gundahar what happened to your face?" Brunhild asked her husband.

"The wolves killed all the horses, so Ser Fintan thought to blame me for it. Not to worry they will be gone by midday, the storm is over," he replied.

His wife soaked a rag in some water, rang it out and came over to him and started dabbing the blood from his lip.

"I warned you Gundahar. Men cannot be trusted," she said.

"It has nothing to do with trust. He hit me because he can't control his anger," he said back.

She brought him a horn of ale and said, "Rinse your mouth with this," and she turned and went back to her sewing.

The ale burned, but Gundahar did as told. His front tooth had been broken in half by the blow, and his top lip had split. He swished the ale in his mouth and spat it out in a basin by the bed.

By midday all the villagers were gathered outside the cave. All the supplies that the horses had carried were split up amongst the knights and carried in sacks across their backs. Ser Fintan was barking commands and everyone was rushing to get out of his way as he came towards Gundahar.

"You owe me ninety five horses Gundahar," the knight said.

"The wolves owe you ninety five horses. You owe me thanks for sheltering you," Gundahar said back calmly.

Ser Fintan grabbed the hilt of his sword. The blade sung as it was being pulled from the scabbard. The sun hit the steel blade and reflected onto Gundahar's face.

Ser Fintan held the sword up and said, "I'll say it one more time Gundahar you owe me for ninety five horses!"

"I owe you nothing," the dwarf said and stared back at the knight with cold eyes.

Ser Fintan moved in and the tip of the sword was pressed against the middle of the dwarf's throat. "Are you sure?" the knight said.

Gundahar just looked at the knight and said nothing. Ser Fintan's lips were pushed together so tight you could not tell one from the other.

"You damned dark dwarfs are a waste of good air," the knight said and turned to walk away.

"And you damned knights have shit for honor and piss for brains," Gundahar yelled back after the knight had turned around.

Ser Fintan spun, blade in hand. Gundahar watched as the steel blade came down and gave the death kiss across his throat. Gundahar looked down before he fell to see his white wolf skin clothes turn to red. He fell to his knees and gasped for a breath, but it made no difference. Then he was on his face in the cold snow with the warmth of blood around him and it went dark.

ELF FOREST

The air was clouded by grey smoke, blocking the sun. The forest was ablaze, every tree around the village was kissed by fire. Animals fleeing from the forest, some already caught on fire. She heard screams of pain, and crying. She stood in the middle of the burning village and saw women holding onto their bloody and dying husbands. Children with ragged clothes trying to wake their dead parents. She tried to stop the flames from spreading but her powers did not work, she tried again, nothing. Warm salty tears were falling down her cheeks, the smoke burning her eyes. She saw his house, the roof was ablaze, orange and yellow flames licking at the sky. She walked towards it, winding through the people running around her. The door was closed, she pushed it open and smoke drifted out.

An older man, fifty years of age lay face down in a pool of blood. His grey beard turned red. She went to the next room, his brother sprawled on the bed, his belly full of holes from a blade. All his clothes soaked red. She looked at his bed, he was not there. She left the room and went to the kitchen, no one. She opened the back door and stepped outside. Bodies covered the ground, dead or dying. She walked past each one, he is not here. She looked up and saw something hanging in a burning tree. She walked over to it. He was hanging by a hemp rope. He had been beaten so badly he was almost unrecognizable, her lover was dead.

Aldreda woke with tears in her eyes, her breathing was quick and shallow, and her heart was racing. *Just a dream* she thought, *I have time to stop it.*

Aldreda was the daughter of Bronimir, the leader of the elves; her family has the gift of prophecy. Though sometimes, it seemed more a curse than a gift. They could see things in their dreams before they happened, and sometimes change it. *The future can always be changed, you just have to find a way to change it,* her father always said. She just had to think. The dreams never had a time or date, so it was almost impossible to know exactly when it was going to happen.

She tried to think back to the dream, *the air was chilly, but the leaves were green.* She didn't have much time. The elves had already celebrated Mabon, Autumn Equinox. The leaves would start to change soon. *This had to be the work of man, elves would not destroy the forest,* she thought. She got up from her bed, her silver hair falling in her face and her gown flowing to the floor. She got dressed quickly, she braided her silver hair so it would stay out of her face. And she put on a simple green wool dress with her leather belt. She had to see her father.

The sun had not broken through the trees yet, it was near dawn. Her family lived in the Great Willow, a tree that had lived thousands of years. The trunk of it was so big that fifty men could not stretch around it. In the trunk, rooms were hollowed out, leading all the way to the top. She stepped out and grabbed the branch above her and started her climb.

Her mother and father slept towards the top. She walked the massive branch that led to their room. When she entered they were still sleeping in their moss bed. Aldreda walk quietly over to her parents and shook her father gently. Bronimir opened his violet eyes.

"What is it?" he said to his daughter.

"I had a dream father, I must speak to you," Aldreda replied.

Bronimir stood from the bed. His silver hair flowed past his waist, and was tucked behind his pointed ears. He wore a simple grey wool sleeping shirt that went down to his knees.

"I will get dressed and be down soon," he said.

Aldreda left her father and started climbing down the tree to wait for him at the bottom. When Bronimir appeared he wore brown wool breeches, with a green wool tunic and a leather belt and shoes. He had pulled his silver hair back behind his pointed ears. Though her father was two hundred and fifty years of age he had no lines on his face. Elves could live hundreds of years longer than humans. His smooth cream skin looked as young as a human child. His high cheek bones made his face look long and his thin lips were straight. His violet eyes were full of worry.

"What worries you my child?" her father asked in a caring voice.

"I had a dream that the Blair's village was ablaze, along with the forest around it. Houses burning, everyone dead or dying. Julian, they beat him and hung him in a burning tree. We must stop this father, we must," she said through the tears.

"What was the weather like?"

"Cool, but the leaves on the trees were still green."

"Then this will happen soon. How are we to stop this? We should not get involved in the troubles of men Aldreda."

"Father, I will not let Julian die," she said sternly.

"I warned you what would happen Aldreda, I told you it is not safe to love a human. You did not listen. You will lose him, if not now then years from now, but you will. Elves live hundreds of years and don't age, humans get old and broken then die in less than a hundred. You can not stop death," Bronimir said to his daughter.

"I cannot stop natural death, but I will stop him being killed," she said. "Please father, think on it. Talk to the wise ones. Try, for me," she pleaded.

"I will try, but I cannot guarantee," he answered. "Go to him, but do not tell him. Keep him near to you."

Aldreda went back to her room grabbed her bow and arrows and threw them over her shoulder. She stood on the branch and whistled. A chestnut colored mare with a black mane and tail and a white diamond on her forehead trotted up under the branch. Aldreda dropped down to her back and grabbed her mane, she pushed her heels into the mare's side and galloped off. Elves did not use saddles like humans did, they rode their horses bareback and wild, a human would not be able to ride an elf's horse. She raced towards the village deep into the forest.

She came to the edge of the forest, the village was on the other side of the trees. Aldreda dismounted her mare, and the horse ran off back into the forest. She entered the village, a woman and her three children were fetching water from the well. Aldreda recognized one of the children from her dream, and it sent a chill up her spine. She walked on towards his house, she closed her eyes and saw the flames licking the roof. The villagers were staring at her, every eye following her to his house. The villages in the forest learned to tolerate the elves, but they did not trust them.

She came to the door and knocked. A big man about fifty with a shaggy grey beard opened the door.

"Good morrow Justin, I need to speak with Julian, where is he?" Aldreda asked the big man.

"Tendin' the fields. We gotta pay our due to Lord Mullen or face his men. They came by da other night n' said if we don't pay, there'll be hell," Justin answered, "he can't go runin off wit you today."

"I just need a word with him is all, thank you," she replied and left towards the field.

Men were working the fields with big bags strung across their shoulders to put the crop in. They all looked up and watched Aldreda walk by. Ludwig came running up to her, he was Julian's brother.

"Aldreda, we gotta work today, Lord Mullen is cross with the village," Ludwig said.

"Yes your father told me. Where is Julian?"

"All the way at the end," he replied, and went back to picking.

She walked to the end of the field, it was close to the forest so she would be able to sneak him off easily. He looked up at her as she was approaching, and gave a heart melting smile. His dark brown beard had been trimmed short around his square chin, and his curly hair reached his shoulders. His smile made two dimples in his cheeks. His hazel eyes seemed to look right into her soul. She smiled back at him, and grabbed his hand and led him towards the nearest tree. The men were still watching so she kept him insight.

"What are you doing here?" he said in his deep voice.

"I could not bear to be away from you, I had to feel the touch of your skin on mine," she answered with a teasing smile.

"I can't get away today. Lord Mullen wants his due," he replied.

"I know, I won't keep you long. My heart aches without you. Do you wish for me to be in pain?" she gave a playful frown.

"Of course not, ok but not long," and he snuck off into the woods when no one was looking.

Julian was five and twenty and still blessed with youth and strength. His tunic was tight around his wide shoulders and muscular arms. He was thin, as most poor villagers were. She took his hand and led him towards the river. She looked up and smiled at him, he was at the least half a foot taller than she was. He bent down and gave her a gentle kiss, and slid his arms around her waist. She put her arms around his neck and pulled him closer, his mouth opened and she slipped her tongue inside. The kiss soon became more intense and before long she jumped in his arms and wrapped her legs around his waist.

Holding her up, he stopped the kiss and said, "You missed me that much?" with a smile.

"I cannot live without you, every time we are apart I feel like I am dying inside," she replied.

He looked deep into her eyes, and she wanted him to take her then, but she knew they had to get farther away from the village. So she pushed herself down out of his arms, and grabbed his hand.

"Come," she said.

When they reached the river bank she sat down on the pebbles and he took a seat beside her.

"Don't leave me ever, I really can not live without you," she said.

He leaned close and kissed her again, "why would I ever leave."

"Then come with me, back to the Willow. Be my partner for life, my father could perform the ritual. I could give you many children. And we would be together, no more sneaking around."

"What about my family Aldreda? And live with the elves? Would they want a human living amongst them? Everybody says we should not be together," he replied.

"Who cares what everybody says. Do you love me?"

"You know I do."

"Then that is all that matters. Come with me, live with me, be with me."

Julian cupped her face in his hand and pressed his mouth to hers. Aldreda started unlacing the top of his tunic, while she kissed him back. She pulled the tunic over his head to reveal his course dark brown hair on his chest, she gave his nipples a squeeze and he laid her down on the river rock. He didn't even bother with removing her dress, he just ran his hand down her thigh and slowly slipped a finger in her. Aldreda let out a moan of pleasure, and squeezed Julian's nipples harder. She ran her hands down his sides, grabbed his ass, then moved to the front of his breeches and grabbed his hard cock. She fumbled to unlace his breeches and pulled his cock out. She still had his cock in her hands as she slipped it inside her.

He pushed deep as she wrapped her legs around his waist. The rocks she was laying on were digging into her back, but she barley noticed. She grabbed a handful of hair and pulled his mouth to hers. She kissed him hard and fierce, arching her back to push him deeper. His hand went up and gave her right breast a squeeze through her dress. She squeezed her thighs and rolled. Then she was on top riding him, he was starring deep into her eyes. Her braid was coming loose and strands of silver hair were falling in her face. He grabbed her hips and held them down to him and let out a moan. She could feel him spill his seed inside her. She rolled off him and laid down next to him and put her head on his bare chest.

"Is that a yes?" she said breathless.

He kissed her forehead he was breathing hard and said through breaths "after the harvest."

That was not what she wanted to hear, her dream would come true very soon, and possibly before the harvest is done she had to think of a way to make him stay. She did not give a reply, just laid there on his chest and listened to his heart beating fast.

"Would your people be fine with me living amongst them?" Julian asked after awhile.

"I am the daughter of Bronimir, leader of the elves, they will not refuse," she replied. "My people are more peaceful than man, Lord Mullen will not bother us. The forest is ours, it has been for a thousand years, and will be for a thousand more," she continued.

"I cannot say I would miss seeing Lord Mullen. May haps you are right, I need to get away. But I cannot leave when my family needs my help. Yes, after the harvest we will be together always," he said.

Then they heard the scream. Aldreda knew it was time, her dream was coming true.

Julian sat up, "what was that."

"I know not," she said.

Julian got to his feet and pulled his tunic over his head and started lacing up his breeches. "It came from my village, I have to go back."

"It was probably nothing, do not leave me yet. Stay," she said in a hopeful voice.

Julian looked to the south toward his village. Then the smoke started rising in the sky. "There is a fire! I have to go Aldreda," he said and pulled her to her feet.

Aldreda started to panic, she did not know what to do she just knew she could not let him go back to his village. Julian's eyes grew big and he turned his back to go. Aldreda looked down and saw a rock the size of her hand, she bent down and picked it up.

She held it behind her back, he turned to face her "go back home Aldreda, I will see what is happening and come to you later."

He turned again and headed towards his village, she followed. When she got close enough to him she raised the rock and brought it down on the back of his head.

Julian fell to the river bank, "I am sorry my love, if you go you will not return to me. I had no choice," she whispered.

She checked him to make sure she had not hit him to hard. He would be out for a couple of hours, and have a nice bump, but would be alive. She gave a whistle and her chestnut mare came before long. She hauled Julian over the mares back like an animal she had killed in a hunt. She mounted her mare and headed toward the Willow.

She rode as fast as she dared with Julian on the back of her mare. When she reached the Great Willow elves were gathered around talking to her father. Her brother Elis and his friend Noll came up to her and helped get Julian off the back of the horse and laid him on the ground.

She pushed her way to her father, "It has begun. The village is burning. We need to send the wind elves to try and stop the fire from spreading through the trees," she said to her father.

"We need to stay away until it is over, I don't want our people being attacked as well. What did you do to Julian?" he said back to her.

"I knocked him in the head, I had no choice, he was going back. I could not loose him," she replied.

"And what about his people? How do you think he will be when he finds out they are dead?" he asked her.

"I could not save the village, but I could not let him die either," Aldreda said.

"This was not wise getting involved Aldreda. But it is done, we can do nothing about it. What do you plan to do with him?" Bronimir asked his daughter.

"Why would we have the gift of prophecy if not to use it? He will stay here with us, with me," she said back.

"You are asking for me to let a human live amongst us?" he replied.

"Yes father, I love him," she said back in a whisper.

"Very well, but we are not getting involved with Lord Mullen," Bronimir said and went back to talking to the other elves.

Elis and Noll carried Julian to Aldreda's room and laid him on her bed and left. Aldreda was sitting on the bed next to him when Julian woke. "How are you my love?" she asked him.

Julian blinked a couple times and looked around and said, "What happened? Where am I?"

"You slipped on the river rocks and fell and hit your head, it knocked you out. So I brought you back to the Willow," she answered.

Julian sat up and felt the back of his head, "I don't remember slipping," he said.

Aldreda gave a shrug.

He sat there for a minute rubbing his head then said, "My village, I saw smoke, heard screaming, what happened?"

"I know not, when you fell I brought you back here," she replied.

"I have to go. I have to see what happened," Julian said and stood from the bed. He wobbled and sat back down on the bed.

"You cannot go now Julian. You hit your head, you need to rest."

"I am fine I need to go to my village Aldreda, what would you do if it was your family?" he asked her, his forehead wrinkled and his eyes full of worry.

"If you go, I go with you," she replied, she would not let him face his village alone.

Aldreda's mare would not let Julian near her, the horse was more cautious with him awake. So they had to walk to his village, Aldreda was happy with that. The longer it took them to reach the village the better. They walked side by side quietly. By the time they reached Julian's village the sun was setting in the sky, turning it to a mixture of purple and pink.

Some of the trees and houses had a flame left to them, but most of the village was ash and smoke. Bodies lay on the ground bloody and disfigured. Those who were not dead cried out in pain, they would most likely not live long. Aldreda looked over to Julian, his hazel eyes watery and his cheeks and forehead red.

"My house," was all he said as he walked over to where his house once stood. All that was left was some smoldering beams and black ash. Julian walked through the rubble, kicking over any wooden beams that were in his way. "Aldreda," he said and knelt down in the ash, his brown curls covering his face as he looked down at the ash.

She went over to him and looked at what he saw. A hand was sticking out of the ash. Nothing left to it but some scorched flesh stuck to the bone, Aldreada guessed it to be Ludwig Julian's brother.

"My family is gone. My home is gone. My village gone," he said down at the hand, tears creeping down his cheeks.

"Come my love, there is nothing left here but pain," Aldreda said to him.

She bent down and pulled on his arm until he looked up at her. The pain in his eyes was almost too much for her to bear. He got up quietly and walked with her out of the ash that once was his house.

His pain soon turned into anger, "The Mullen's will pay for this. I will make him pay for what he did," Julian said to himself.

"What do you mean to do?" Aldreda asked.

"I will do to him what he has done to them," he said and pointed at the bodies.

"My love, I understand why you want Mullen to pay, but there are other ways to try first. Bring this matter to the King, let him strike Mullen with force. Surly the King will not stand for his people being butchered so," she said while looking him deep in the eyes.

"May haps, but if the King does nothing, I will Aldreda," Julian said sternly.

"Then you will not do it alone. Come, we can leave on the morrow," she replied.

Julian woke many times in the night, sitting up instantly forgetting where he was. Aldreda woke every time he did and held him until he was asleep again. About the eighth time Julian woke Aldreda gave up on going back to sleep and just lay awake with her head on his chest. By day break Aldreda's head and eyes hurt from lack of sleep and she was sore from the day before. She got dressed quietly trying not to wake Julian and went to find her father. When she emerged from her room she found her father was already up and at the foot of the Willow.

She climbed down to him, "Father I wish to travel with Julian to Rosegarden. He wants to address the King and plea for justice to be done. I feel I should go with him," she asked her father.

He looked at her with displeasure, "Aldreda you look awful, did you not sleep at all?" he said.

"Not much, Julian was up a lot last night. Do I have your leave to go to Rosegarden?" she said to her father.

"And if I said no, would you listen? Aldreda you and I both know that no matter what I say, you will go where Julian goes," he replied.

She gave a nod, he was right.

"Elves are not safe out of the forest and on the road. You will need to take precautions as to not reveal your true self. Go to your mother, she will help die your hair a human color, brown perhaps. You must also wear blue clothes, it will make your violet eyes look blue. And always keep your hair down and your hood up," he said with a frown.

Aldreda got on her tiptoes and gave her father a kiss on the cheek and climbed up to find her mother.

When Aldreda emerged from her mother's chambers she did not look like the woman that had entered. Her light silver hair had been died a dull brown that looked the color of mud, and was left down to cover her ears. She wore a light blue wool dress with sleeves that were tight down to her wrist and a dark blue hooded cloak.

She entered her room and Julian looked at her a blinked in shock, "Aldreda? What have you done?" he said with surprise in his voice.

"I am not safe as an elf outside of the forest, so I will travel a human," she said with a smile, "do you still want me? Even like this," she continued pointing at her hair.

"I would want you even if you were bald and had no hair," he smiled back at her, and pulled her close and kissed her lips.

"How are you love?" she asked more seriously.

"I am doing well. Lord Mullen will pay for what he did, by the King's hand or my own. Then my family can be in peace in the otherworld," Julian replied.

"What about your other brother Ser Kevin where is he?" she asked.

"He has been at Crystal Keep since I was a boy. He only visited about every five years or so," he answered.

"Mayhaps we should go there first, he could try to get Crystal Keep the Queen's house on our side," Aldreda suggested.

"Yes, he should know what has happened to father and Ludwig," Julian said.

Aldreda could see he was not as well as he clamed, his eyes were red and had dark bags under them.

"We should get ready," he said.

They packed a satchel each with two extra outfits and food. Aldreda had given Julian some of her brother Elis's clothes until they could buy new. Her father had given her two golden crowns, fifty silver stars and some coppers to help them on their trip. Aldreda grabbed her bow and arrows, and Julian had two daggers. Vasco, an animal elf, had found three horses that had escaped the village, still saddled and rained. Aldreda would have to ride one of them instead of her wild mare, so as to not attract attention to them. They tied their satchels to their horses and were ready to set off.

Bronimir came over to them as they had finished loading the horses, "Julian you take care of my daughter, she must not be revealed as an elf," her father said.

"She will be safe with me. I promise I won't let any harm come to her," Julian replied and clasped her father on the forearm.

Bronimir than came over to Aldreda and kissed her on the forehead, "Be safe, and come back soon."

"I will father," she replied and hugged him goodbye.

They mounted up on their horses and set off toward Crystal Keep.

SOUTHERN SEA

The *Sweet Leann* rocked with the waves of the Southern Sea. Raj Hugart stood at the front of the starboard side of the ship, watching the oars move up and down, to move the ship forward. The dark captain Kaleo, was the only one on the ship that spoke the tongue of the Kingdoms, which made for a lonely voyage. Raj had found out that Kaleo was the captain of the magister of Azec's personal fleet. Kaleo told Raj that the magister Kimo Xenos would surely welcome a lord from the Kingdoms, and Raj hoped he was right. The Islands of Azica were not ruled by anyone in the Kingdoms, instead each city had a magister.

Raj stood watching the oars and thinking about what he would do once he arrived at Azec. May haps he would travel to the biggest of the Islands. It had eight cities and was as big as the Eastern Kingdom he was told. He would first see Azec, and whatever else there was to see. Raj had been on the *Sweet Leann* for a week now and was not found of the company it kept. The sailors were rough and looked at him with cold dark eyes. Below deck was full of slaves rowing the oars. The captain was the only one kind to him and that was because he was getting paid.

The dark skinned sailors wore only breeches with no shirt or shoes, and carried whips to beat the slaves with. Raj made sure not to stare at them, he did not want to offend someone. He looked down at the ocean, three dolphins were swimming alongside the ship and jumping with the waves.

The captain Kaleo approached him and said, "We reach Azec by sun up," and walked away.

That was talkative for the captain. *One more day, and then I start a new life* he thought, but he didn't want a new life. Raj left the side of the ship and went below to where his cabin was. He passed the slaves rowing to the beat of the drums and the sound of the whip cracking against their backs. When he entered his simple cabin and shut the door he could still hear the drums as if they were right next to him. He lay on the cot that was hanging in the corner of the room and closed his eyes to try to sleep. Sleep did not come easily. Between him trying to figure out what he would do next, and the beating of the drums.

After hours of drifting in and out of sleep Raj gave up and left the cabin to find some wine. Wine was not popular on this ship. The sailors drank a dark liquor that burnt your mouth. He went to the back of the ship where they kept all the supplies and started his search. He came upon some summer wine from the South in a clay pot and snatched it up. When Raj returned to his cabin he had no cups, so he drank the wine out of the jug. After the jug was empty, and his eyes grew heavy, Raj finally found sleep.

"We there lord," said Kaleo as he shook Raj awake.

Raj opened his eyes and looked around confused, "What?"

"We at Azec, bout to dock," Kaleo answered.

Raj sat up and rubbed the sleep from his eyes. "My thanks Kaleo, I will be up on deck shortly," he told the captain.

Kaleo gave a nod, his grey fuzzy beard brushing his chest.

Raj stood up and dressed in his nicest clothes to meet the magister. A white tunic with a leather jerkin that had golden flames embroidered on it, and his black cloak with the flames was clasped to his shoulder by a gold and ruby brooch. He slid on his sword belt and slipped the long sword through the scabbard, and slid a dagger in his right boot.

When Raj emerged from below deck the ship had been docked and the sailors and slaves had started unloading the goods. Raj looked around the docks, there where at the least thirty ships docked and trading. Farther on the Island all he could see were strange trees, with rough trunks and big wide leaves.

"I will bring you to magister after all is unloaded," Kaleo came up behind Raj and said.

"Very good, my thanks," Raj said with a friendly smile and a nod, and left the ship to wait.

The wealthy people of the Island were walking from ship to ship viewing the goods. They wore white linen chitons wrapped around them that flowed down to their ankles, with colorful peplos wrapped over top and leather sandals. Most had slaves around them caring umbrellas to shade them from the sun. The slave men wore only breech clothes and the slave women wore simple chitons that you could see their breast through. Only the sailors from the ships wore breeches. All their skin a different shade. There were wealthy men with skin of ebony holding onto their wife's that had skin of cream.

Some even had the olive-toned skin like the people in the south. And some skin was a copper tone.

The slaves were marked differently also, the women were tattooed on their face or shoulder, the men branded, and some wore collars. They hurried after their masters and loaded up all the goods that were purchased. Some of the masters had whips, others had knights in armor behind them carrying the whips. They all rushed from ship to ship haggling with the captains. Some spook the tongue of the Kingdoms and some and strange tongue like the sailors on the *Sweet Leann*. Raj sat on a crate that had been unloaded and watched and waited.

After an hour or so Kaleo came up to him, "you should get magister Kimo a present, it is custom," he said to Raj.

"What do you get a magister of Azec?"

"The better the gift the more he likes you," the dark captain answered.

Raj walked around the other ships, there was elegant dinning wear, weapons, fabrics of all kinds, gold and silver statues of foreign gods, and food and wine. *What do I get a magister of an Island I know nothing about?* Raj thought on that as he walked around. He watched the wealthy people of the Island and what they looked interested in.

He came across a big fur that was striped black and white, he had never seen an animal with such fur. "What did this come off of?" he asked the captain.

"This Zebra, like horse from Kingdoms wit stripes," Kaleo answered.

"Would the magister like a pelt like this?" Raj asked.

"Lots of Zebras on big island to the east, very common," answered the captain.

Raj thought about buying the pelt for himself, but decided against it. Then he came across a golden bird with different colored jewels encrusted in the wings and tail.

"What bird is this?" he asked the man.

The man said something that Raj did not understand.

"That parrot, you will see in trees," Kaleo said.

"How much," Raj replied.

Kaleo spoke to the man selling the parrot for awhile arguing back and forth, and then said "ten gold dalla's."

"How many crowns of the Kingdoms equal a dalla?" Raj asked.

"They the same, different marking, same weight," Kaleo answered.

Raj counted ten golden crowns and handed them to the man. The man bit each coin, and then handed the bird to Raj.

"Now what?" Raj asked the captain.

"Now we go," Kaleo answered and lead Raj towards the trees.

Once they left the dock elephants were tied up everywhere. Dwarf elephants with carts, and massive grown elephants with seats on top of them.

"Which would you like?" Kaleo asked.

"The cart," Raj answered, Kaleo gave a nod and walked over to the man with the elephant and haggled over a price.

Kaleo walked back over and said, "One silver."

Raj only had the gold that Xolan had given him. So he gave Kaleo a gold coin and the captain brought him back nine and ten silvers.

Raj and the captain got in the cart, and the man climbed on top of the elephant. The elephant was not as quick as a horse, and the cart rocked and bumped with every step. They entered the trees, and it became so loud it was impossible to speak to Kaleo who was sitting right next to him. Raj looked up and saw the trees alive, monkeys swinging from branch to branch yelling at them as they passed. Magnificent birds of every color sat at the top of the trees, flapping their wings and screaming. He saw creatures he didn't know even existed, some scurrying across the ground and some climbing in the trees like the monkeys. Great green snakes hung down from the branches, their back end curled around the tree.

The elephant trumpeted and the forest grew quiet for half a second, then yelled back. They crept on down the narrow road that was cleared through the forest. He had seen many creatures living at Dragons End but never creatures like what he saw in the forest. They came upon the clearing, shacks and hutches were built out of wood and the great leafs on the trees. Peasants were in the front of their homes working, chopping at these big nuts that when broke open spilled a white liquid. Some were skinning an animal from a hunt and pulling the organs from its belly, the fur was spotted. He had never seen a fur like it before in his life.

The peasants wore scraps of fur, barley enough to cover their sex. The younger women had their breast bare and the older ones had a strip of fur to cover them. They had the bright colored feathers of the strange bird, braided in their hair. They had painted their faces with different colored stripes.

"Rainbow Bird Tribe," the captain said to him.

Raj gave a nod. The peasants did not even look up at them riding past, they just continued on with their work.

After passing about twenty hutches the cart entered the forest again. The animals greeted them with shouts and screams. The elephant screamed back. By the time they reached the wall of the city the sun was in the middle of the blue sky. The wall was made of wooden spikes, unlike the stone walls of the Kingdoms. Soldiers wearing breastplates, helms and leather skirts walked the walls with spears and bows in hand.

"Capitol of Azec," Kaleo said when he saw Raj looking at the wall. The gates were open and the elephant passed through, and entered the city.

The buildings were made of a red stone and had thin pieces of slate layering slanted roofs. The rich rode past on litters carried by their slaves. Some rode carts like the one he was in, pulled by a dwarf elephant. And some walked, being shaded by their slaves. They wore white linen chitons with different colored peplos over top. Some had a girdle around their waist, some a sash of bright colored fabric. The masters had leather sandals covering their feet, and their slaves had no shoes at all.

They passed a brothel and the whores were outside naked trying to get the men to come in. Each whore had a tattoo on her right cheek and golden rings through their nipples. They called at the cart as it passed and he could not help stealing a look at one of the girls. Slaves were running around the road shoveling elephant droppings into a pail. One master was having his slave beaten by a soldier. The slave had been whipped so badly, no skin remained on his back.

When they reached the center of the city a great fountain stood with a strange statue of some beast. The statue had the body of a naked man, the head of some kind of cat, and wings of a bird.

"What is that?" Raj asked the captain.

"That Great God Killi," the captain answered in a rough accent.

The cart turned right at the fountain and followed the road until it ended.

They approached the gates of the biggest building in the city.

"Magister Kimo Xenos home," Kaleo said and pointed to the big house.

It was made of the same red stone as the rest of the buildings in the city. At the least six stories tall. It was built in a rectangle shape and had black slate slabs layered on the roof that slanted towards the front. Great balconies emerged from every window that was shaded by the roof. Many colored banners flew from the wall, plain with no sigil.

The captain got out of the cart and walked up to one of the soldiers at the gate. One tall dark man with a bronze breastplate, leather skirt and a half helm with a big spike atop it. Kaleo talked to the guard and pointed at Raj, the guard looked and finally gave a nod and Kaleo waved Raj over. Raj climbed from the cart and thanked the driver, then walked over to Kaleo with the golden bird in his arms.

"The guard will announce you," the captain said and led the way.

Once through the gate Raj saw that there were many gardens in front of the magister's house. Orange and lemon trees were to the east, to the west were grape vines. Twenty stone steps led up to the great door of the house, two slaves stood waiting on them.

They said something to Kaleo and he replied, then one of the slaves said, "You are welcome my lord, the magister is always happy to see a lord from the Kingdoms."

"My thanks," Raj replied and followed the slave inside the house.

Once inside, the house opened up to a great staircase, large enough for ten men to walk side by side up it.

"I will leave you here," Kaleo announced and stayed by the door.

The slave that had greeted them turned to the right of the staircase and Raj fallowed. They walked down a large hallway, all down the hallway stone carved likenesses of men sat on pedestals.

"Who are these men?" Raj asked the slave that was leading him.

"Those magister's that have served before Kimo," the slave answered in a heavy accent.

Raj guessed the woman slave to be about twenty, her olive-toned skin was rubbed with oil and shined in the sun. She wore a simple white chiton that was pinned at the shoulders by a copper clasp. He could see her dark nipples and the mound of hair between her legs through the chiton. She had a KX tattooed on her right cheek and wore a golden collar around her neck. She always looked at the floor and made sure not to make eye contact with him.

Once at the end of the hallway they entered a great hall with a cushioned bench at the far end by the wall. There where also rows of benches along the sides of the hall. Great pillars made of red stone reached up to the ceiling, strange animals of all kinds were carved into them. Towards the top were birds like the one Raj had purchased, in the middle were monkeys, and at the bottom were spotted cats, striped horses and elephants. The floor was made of slate tiles each had a different animal upon it.

"Magister be with you shortly, wait," the slave said to him.

Raj gave a nod, but doubted that she saw it, seems how she would not look at him. While he waited on the magister Raj looked at all the animals carved throughout the room, some he recognized and some he had never seen before.

"My Lord what do I owe the pleasure?" came a voice from behind him.

Raj turned startled, a chubby, short, bald man stood at the door. His skin was the color of cream, and his head and face were shaved smooth. He wore a white linen chiton with two golden feathers clasped at the shoulders, to hold it up. Over that he had a rainbow peplos, with a leather belt around his big belly. He walked over to Raj his leather strapped sandals making a swishing sound as he walked.

"Forgive me for startling you, I am Magister Kimo Xenos," the man said with a bow.

"Thank you for seeing me magister, I am Lord Raj Hugart of Fire Harbor of the South," Raj answered.

"And what is a Lord of the South wanting with the Magister of Azec?" the magister asked.

"Fighting slaves and a ship, if you please," Raj answered bluntly.

"You have come to the wrong place for fighting slaves, here at Azec we do not train slaves to fight. If you want fighters you need to travel to Xicalli. But a ship I might be able to help you with, what kind of ship would you need?" said the chubby magister, his chins jiggled as he talked.

"A war ship."

"Is the South at war? I have not heard that report."

"Not as of yet, but soon. And I need to defend my land. Do you have a ship I can purchase?"

"Again Xicalli would be a better place to purchase a fighting ship, Azec trades, and we do not fight. But I can arrange passage for you to Xicalli, if you can pay the price," said the magister.

"I can," Raj replied.

"Good I will have Kaleo sail that way in one week, until then please accept the hospitality of my house," Magister Kimo said with a smile.

"My thanks magister, I have brought you a gift for seeing me," Raj said and pulled the golden bird out and handed it to the magister.

"This is very nice, must of cost a lot. Yes, stay. You are welcome to anything in my home," he seemed very pleased with the bird.

The same slave girl came to him in the hall not long after the magister had left. "Magister say you stay, I show you room," she said heavily and lead him back toward the stairs.

Raj fallowed the slave up to the second floor then she turned left.

"At end of hall," she pointed.

She opened the door to revile a nicer room than what he had at Dragons End. A big feathered canopy bed with silk of blue and purple stood in the middle of the room. A big wooden desk in the corner, and a huge balcony. Even his own privy.

"Magister ask you eat with him, I have slaves give you bath," the slave girl said to him.

"My trunks?" Raj asked.

"Kaleo brought them, I have them bring up," she replied and left.

Raj was standing on the balcony looked at the grape vines when six slaves entered his room. Three big men carrying his trunks and three women carrying steaming water. The men sat down the trunks and left the room without a word. The women who had a pail in each hand filled the tub half way, then came over to him. Two of the girls were white with sun kissed skin, the other was as dark as Kaleo. One had blond hair so light it was almost white, the other had auburn hair that shone red in the sun, and the third had black fuzzy hair that surrounded her face. The blond reached up and undid the brooch that held his cloak to his shoulders.

"Thank you, but I can undress myself," Raj said.

The girl said something quickly in the tongue of Azec, a rough language that didn't sound pretty.

"I do not understand," Raj said back to her.

She said something else in the same language, and Raj gave up.

The girls stripped him down and pointed at the tub of steaming water. Raj climbed in. The slave with the auburn hair then removed her chiton and climbed in with him, while the other two started scrubbing him with sea sponges and soap. Raj could not help starring at the naked slave in the tub with him. She had a common face, round with a round nose and blue eyes. She was thin and young, her breast plump and perky. She straddled him and started washing his chest and shoulders. Her nipples were just above the water and when she leaned close to scrub him they brushed up against his chest. He tried to control his cock from responding, but it was becoming difficult. Her mound of hair between her legs was brushing up against his thigh.

He could not control it any longer and his cock grew. The girl felt it on her stomach as she was washing his chest. She looked at his face for the first time, smiled and said one word in that strange tongue.

"I do not know what you are saying," Raj said back with a smile.

She crinkled her forehead and cocked her head, like a dog when you speak to them. Raj shrugged his shoulders to try and show her that he didn't know what she said. The girl took it the wrong way and grabbed his cock, which startled him so much he jumped. She squeezed and started moving her hand up and down.

Raj sat up more, "No," he said.

The slave girl giggled and repeated "No," but did not stop.

His breathing was coming quicker, "stop," he said and grabbed her hand.

She pushed his hand away, smiled and said "stop," than sat on top of him guiding his cock inside her.

She moaned and grabbed a hold of his shoulders. The two girls on the outside of the tub were rubbing his chest and pinching his nipples and giggling.

Raj grabbed her hips and stopped them from moving, "you don't have to do this," he said in a kind gentle voice.

She smiled back at him, she would be pretty if not for the tattoo on her cheek. "No, stop," she said and started ridding him again.

Raj gave up and let her finish him off.

After his interesting bath the slaves dressed him in clothes he pulled from his trunk, and then they left. Awhile later a knock came at the door, before Raj could say anything, the slave woman that had showed him to his room entered.

"Magister ready for you to eat," she said to the floor.

"My thanks, what is your name?" Raj said to her.

"No name, slave do not have name," she said and waited for him. She led the way to a great dinning hall on the first floor.

The magister was sitting at the head of a long table, "Lord Raj come sit by me," he said.

Raj walked down the table and took the empty seat to the magister's right.

"Lord Raj this is my wife Kilikina and my children Kiana, Konani, Keoni and Kekoa," the magister said and pointed to each as he said their name.

"It is very nice to meet you, thank you for your hospitality," Raj replied.

"We don't often have visitors from the Kingdoms, the pleasure is ours," Kilikina replied almost without an accent. She was a dark skinned beauty, with her hair braided to her head. She wore a thin chiton and pink peplos. Their children had light brown skin which came from mixing their cream colored father to their dark skinned mother.

Magister Kimo raised his hand and the feast began. The first course was boiled monkey brains that were placed back in the skulls after they were cooked. A slave brought Raj his monkey skull on a golden plate, and Raj tried to hide his disgust. A slave filled his chalice with wine that was so dark it was almost black. Raj took a big gulp of sour wine with every bite on monkey brain.

"So Lord Raj, it is not often that we have lords from the Kingdoms, but when we do they never arrive alone. Why have you not brought any guards or knights?" the magister asked.

"They are needed in the south more than they are needed here," Raj answered bluntly, he did not want the magister to know he was a banished lord.

The second course was strange fruit that Raj had never tasted, orange and red and white.

"What are these fruits? They are very tasty," Raj said to the magister.

"The orange one is mango, the red papaya, and the white is coconut, they all grow in the jungle around us," the magister answered.

Raj enjoyed the fruit a lot more than the brains.

"I will send a letter with you for Magister Olujimi of Xicalli, letting him know what you seek. The letter should help you see him quicker than without one. You will learn Magister Olujimi is not as kind as I am. Which is probably why his slaves are so fearsome," said the magister.

"That would be much appreciated my thanks. Do you know how much a fighting slave goes for?"

"I do not, most slaves are sold at auction," answered Magister Kimo.

The third course was a massive roasted snake, as big around as a mans thigh. The snake still had the head and skin on it, and Raj felt like retching. He took another deep gulp of sour wine, the wine here was about as good as the food. *I will starve to death staying here for a week*, he thought. The slaves carved the snake and Raj saw the snake had not been gutted before being cooked. He soon learned that they eat the guts and all of a snake.

"It will be a five day voyage to Xicalli from here. Would you agree to two of your golden crowns for the passage," said the magister while chewing on snake guts.

"That would be fine. Do you want payment now or then?"

"Then would be fine. I trust my slaves have been good to you."

"Too good."

"If you require company tonight, any slave you like will not refuse you, you have my word on that," said the cubby magister between bites.

Raj gave a nod, the girl in the tub was enough for him.

After the feast Raj returned to his room, nauseous and tired. He undressed and climbed into the feather bed naked. Sleep came quick and before long he drifted off in darkness.

The next morning Raj woke to the three slave girls that had given him a bath the day before. They were filling the tub with steaming water and scented oil. Raj got out of the bed and went to the privy. When he emerged from the privy the girls were holding their sponges and waiting on him to get in the tub. Raj got in and this time the blond got naked and climbed in with him. The bath turned out the same as it had the day before, except this time Raj just let it happen without trying to stop the girl.

Thankfully he did not break his fast on any strange organs. The slaves brought him fruit, eggs, and a dark brown bread. He ate all of it, not knowing what they would serve at midday. After he ate he went down to the gardens to have a look around. He was walking amongst the citrus trees when the magister popped out from behind one.

Raj jumped and his heart skipped a beat. "Beg pardons magister you startled me," he said annoyed.

"Not at all I am sorry I scared you," the bald chubby man said with a smile. The magister weaved his chubby fingers through each other and said, "I was thinking since you will be with us for a week, may haps you would like to see our island."

"I would like that very much," Raj answered.

The magister led Raj to a large elephant with a seat on top, a rope ladder hung down so the men could climb into the seat. The magister went up first and Raj fallowed. When they reached the top of the ladder two slave girls were sitting there with their breast bared.

"I thought company would be nice for the trip," the magister said with a wicked looking smile.

Raj sat at the end, with the two girls in the middle.

"Would you care for some wine Lord Raj?" one of the slaves asked in the tongue of the Kingdoms.

He gave a nod and she grabbed up a chalice and filled it to the top. The slave was cream colored with golden hair that shone in the sun. She had her golden collar around her neck and below the color her breasts were white and plump with round pink nipples. Raj looked at her face, she had the same KX tattooed on her right cheek and a scare over her right eye. Her eyes were green, like the grass. She would not look at his face, she kept her eyes down.

The elephant started to move and the cushioned seat rocked back and forth with every steep the elephant took. They entered the jungle and were greeted with the yells of monkeys and the cries of birds.

"The jungle is very loud," Raj shouted to the magister, who was fumbling the slave girl's breast.

"The animals don't like intruders," the magister replied and gave the girls nipple a squeeze and she gasp in pain.

Raj didn't know if the magister meant the comment to be an insult, so he did not reply. They rocked on, he could see far up into the trees. He liked this view better than the view from the cart that he had the day before.

Magister Kimo took Raj to where the strange fruits mango and papayas grew. He showed him the different types of monkeys that lived in the jungle. One group of monkeys was bigger than a man and beat on their chest when they spotted the elephant. They saw spotted cats and cats as black as night. He saw more kinds of birds then he thought existed. And hundreds of snakes, brown and green with different patterns on their backs.

They ate at midday by a waterfall, some more fruit and a white cheese that was very dry. And some meat that was stringy and chewy. Raj had no idea what kind of meat it was and didn't want to know. The magister was nice and drunk by then and passed out not long after they ate. Raj ventured through the forest on foot for a couple hours.

The bugs were even strange here bright colored blue and green and red. He saw a frog with big red eyes hanging on a tree. The slave girl that spoke the same tongue as him came along with him, walking at least five steps behind him the whole way. Every once in awhile he would ask her the name of this bug or that, she would answer but say no more. It was very lonely here, the slaves were bad company.

When they made it back to the waterfall the magister had woke up. "Did you enjoy the jungle?" the magister said with a sly smile.

"Yes, there are many creatures I have never seen before," Raj answered.

"Yes, the Kingdoms do not have the beautiful creatures we do. Shall we head back?" the magister replied.

Raj gave a nod and walked over to the elephant and started climbing up the ladder. After the elephant had started moving the magister fell back asleep snoring loudly all the way back.

WEST WATCH

The rain trickled down from the grey sky; it was a chilly autumn day, with the sun hidden from all the clouds. Maggie stood by the window looking out at the grey world. It was the day before her wedding. On the morrow she would be Princess Margery McCue future Queen of the West. Aidan was everything she could have hoped for, but she was worried she would not please him. Her mother had talked to her many times about the wedding night since they arrived at West Watch, but Maggie wasn't sure she would live up to the Prince's standards in bed. She had barley slept in a week and it was starting to show, she had dark rings under her eyes. *On the morrow I will be married to my Prince*, she thought with a smile, but the doubt was still there.

A knock at the door brought Maggie out of her thoughts, "Enter," she said.

Her maids Tansy and Violet came into the room, "M'lady you must get ready, the celebration is starting soon and you are required in the Throne Room," Violet said.

Maggie gave a nod and came away from the window. Today she and Prince Aidan would be presented with gifts, then have a great feast and celebration for their last night before marriage. Violet removed Maggie's sleeping shirt and Tansy brought a red silk gown over. Maggie slipped on the gown and Violet laced up the bodice. The gown was rose red and had white lace around the bottom, the sleeves were great bell sleeves that reached almost to the floor and golden beads had been sewn around the seams. After Maggie was dressed she sat down and let Tansy fix her hair. Tansy brushed out Maggie's curls and started pinning them on top of her head, then weaved red ribbons into her hair.

Ser Asher came into the room, he was wearing his bronze armor and the green cloak with the acorns of his house. He had his long-sword at his hip and his hand on its hilt. "Are you ready to head down my Princess?" he asked.

"Yes, Ser," Maggie said to the knight and let him lead the way.

His armor clinked as he walked down the hall and his boots echoed off the floor. Maggie tried her best to keep up, her legs were shorter and her gown did not allow her to take large steps.

"Your father has instructed that I stay with you at West Watch after the wedding and be your personal guard, my Princess," Ser Asher said to Maggie as they walked toward the Throne Room.

"I thought he would, he has been having you guard me a lot since we left Rosegarden. Are you happy about staying and being so far from home, Ser?" Maggie replied.

"I do as my King commands, I am happy with anything he orders me to do," the knight said back to her.

Ser Asher lead her to the back of the Throne Room, her and Aidan would be using the King's door to enter. King Cynon, her father, and Aidan were standing at the door waiting on her arrival.

"Beg pardons, I did not know I was running late, Your Grace," Maggie said and bowed her head toward the Kings.

"Not at all child, your father and I were just going over everything, and Aidan just arrived," King Cynon said with an expressionless face.

"You look so beautiful, it's going to be a long day, are you ready Maggie?" her father said with a loving smile.

"Yes, father," Maggie said back and gave her father a kiss on the cheek.

"Princess Margery, you will be sitting in my wife's throne today and Aidan will sit in my own throne. You are the ones being honored. You will take the role as the King and Queen for the next two days, enter last, leave first. Speak loud and clear and do not bow or curtsy. Nod and make eye contact with the people who are presenting the gifts. Any questions?" King Cynon said.

"No, Your Grace," Maggie replied.

"Good, then let's get started."

King Tristan and King Cynon left to enter the hall through the front like the rest of the guest.

"Are you all right? You have turned white," Aidan said to her.

"Just nerves, I am fine," Maggie said with a forced smile, she had not had time to eat and her stomach was rumbling and in knots.

Aidan put his hand under her chin and lifted her face so their eyes met, "You will be fine, one day you will be queen, this is practice for that day," he said and kissed her lightly on the lips.

Maggie could feel herself blush.

"Now you have your color back," Aidan said with a kind smile. He held out his arm and she took it. She could feel his muscles through his leather doublet.

"All rise for Prince Aidan, first of his noble name, heir to West Watch Castle, future King of the West and protector of the realm, and his bride to be Princess Margery of Rosegarden," announced the herald.

Prince Aidan led Maggie through the door into the Throne Room. Maggie kept her eyes up, the room was packed full of royalty and highborn lords and ladies. Two great thrones sat on top the dais, one slightly smaller than the other. The thrones were iron. The back of the thrones were giant shields with the sigil of house McCue carved into them. Behind the shield stuck out the hilt of a sword and a battle axe. The cushions where half blue velvet and half red velvet and stuffed with feathers. Aidan led Maggie to the smaller of the thrones; she waited for him to sit in his father's before she took a seat herself. The room itself was made of grey stone and had six pillars reaching to the ceiling. The floor was made of grey and white swirled marble that reflected the light from the chandeliers. Oak chairs had been set up for all the guest, and grey stone benches were along the walls.

"We will begin the gift presentation. Comes now King Cynon McCue, first of his name, ruler of West Watch, King of the West and protector of the realm, and the lovely Queen Aileen, along with Prince Ailin and Princess Ailis," the herald announced.

King Cynon and Queen Aileen came forward both with a cushion in their hands that was covered by a piece of silk, their children following behind. King Cynon wore a white tunic with a brown leather doublet overtop, golden broaches in the shape of crowns pinned his blue cloak to his broad shoulders. His red hair fell down to his chin with his golden crown atop his head.

The Queen wore a blue silk gown that had rubies sewn into it and sparkled as she walked. Her auburn hair flowed down to her hips and was pulled back at the front by two braids. Her smaller crown sparkled with rubies and sapphires as the candle light hit them.

"You will rule my kingdom when I am gone, and a queen and king need a proper crown," King Cynon said and with that he and his wife removed the silk fabric covering the pillows.

King Cynon held a large golden crown; the band of the crown was embedded with hundreds of rubies and sapphires and at the tip of each point on the crown a diamond was placed. The crown the Queen held was identical but smaller and made for a woman. King Cynon handed the pillow to Ailin and climbed the steeps of the dais and placed the crown on Aidan's head. After he climbed down the Queen then handed her pillow to Ailis and climbed to place her crown on Maggie.

"It is very beautiful," Maggie said as the Queen was placing the crown on her head.

"So are you love," the Queen replied. Then the royal McCue family went and took a seat in the front row of the chairs.

"Now comes King Tristan Carrender, first of his name, ruler of Rosegarden, King of the East, King of man and elf, and protector of the realm. With the beautiful Queen Helen and their children Prince Jon, heir to the throne, Prince Jason and Princess Katlynn," announced the herald.

Her family stood and came forth; through the doors eight knights entered caring trunks. They placed four trunks in front of the dais and left the hall.

"To rule a kingdom you must have the means to pay for it, I bring you the gold of the East," her father announced and opened the huge trunks. Each trunk was full to the top with golden crowns enough to last a lifetime.

"My thanks, King Tristan, it is an honor to join houses with your own," Aidan said in a loud voice.

Maggie smiled at her family and her father gave her a wink. They went and sat next to the McCue's, and servants came up and carried off the trunks of gold.

"Comes now Queen Ana, first of her name, ruler of Icestorm, Queen of the North, Queen of men, giants and dwarfs, and protector of the realm," the herald called.

The Ice Queen came forward, she was very young. She wore a light blue velvet gown with pearls sewn around the neck and down the front. Her cloak was lined with white fur and reached down to the floor and swooshed as she walked. Her honey colored hair was left down and flowed to her hips, atop her head she had a silver crown that looked like icicles, with diamonds that sparkled in the light. She was no taller than Maggie and her pail skin was the color of snow. Her large eyes matched the color of her gown, and seemed cold when she looked upon Maggie.

The doors opened to the hall and four knights dressed in silver armor and silver helmets came into the hall. They wore the same kind of cloak the Queen wore except less elegant. They carried two trunks and came up and placed them at the dais.

"I have brought you the treasures of the North," the Queen said and the knights opened up the trunks.

One trunk was full of chunks of silver, and the other had gems of different sizes and colors. The Queen gave a smile at her and Aidan, and Maggie smiled back.

"My thanks for your gifts, beautiful Queen," Aidan said and Maggie gave a nod.

The Queen turned and took a seat in the front row on the opposite side of Maggie's family, her gown sweeping the floor as she walked.

"Comes now King Abhay Cvetkovich, first of his name, ruler of Dragons End, King of the South, and protector of the realm. With him the lovely Queen Kala and their children Prince Akash, heir to the throne, Princess Kaja, Princess Kali, and Prince Akhil," announced the herald.

The southern royals stood and came forward. All with raven black hair and all except the Queen had olive-toned skin. The King wore a red silk tunic with a jerkin made of skin Maggie had never seen before, he had black breeches and black boots and a yellow cloak with a red dragon pinned to his shoulders. The Queen was very beautiful, tall and slender with strait hair that flowed past her waist. She wore a red silk gown with no sleeves, and had yellow silk streaming from her shoulders and waist. Both the King and Queen had red gold crowns that looked like flames from a fire. The children all wore red and yellow silk and their hair tied back.

Maggie could not help but notice the hate in King Cynon's eyes as he watched the King of the South walk toward the dais.

"I have brought you one of mine own prizes," the King announced and with that the doors to the room opened and twenty knights carried in a caged lioness.

The lioness was not happy, growling and clawing at the cage. The knights sat down the cage and Maggie pushed herself as far back in her seat as possible.

"This is one of the beasts from my dungeons, I have always loved them and hope you will as well," the King said with a wicked smile.

"You are kind to bring us one of your own personal beasts," Aidan said to the King. The King gave a nod and his long black hair fell over his shoulder.

"My Queen has brought you a gift as well Princess," the King said to Maggie.

Two knights carried in two small trunks and laid them down in front of the Queen and opened them. "Precious silks and laces from the Islands of Azica. You can have many beautiful gowns made," the Queen said with a kind smile.

"My thanks, they are very beautiful," Maggie replied with a nod. She would have got up and looked at the fabric, but she did not want to go near the lioness.

"We have also brought summer wine and fire peppers," the Queen said to the couple. The royal family of the South walked away and took a seat by the Ice Queen. Servants came and took the trunks, then tried to move the lion cage but it took them many attempts.

On and on it went, Lord Pattrick McNeely and Lady Evelyn of The Sword brought them beautiful chalices. Davin McNeely heir to The Sword and his wife Darcy McNeely brought matching daggers with golden hilts. Lord Forbai McCorkle and Lady Enya of Forest End brought them a pair of hunting falcons. Lord Galahad McCowan and Lady Eve of Eagle Nest brought the couple casks of honey wine. Lord Gwern McClure and Lady Fiona of Autumn Way brought old books of the history of the West Kingdom that were elegantly decorated and bond. Lord Irnan McMahon and Lady Maeve of Leaf Landing brought Maggie a beautiful golden brush and hand held looking glass, and Aidan a great battle axe that he seemed very happy about.

Then came the rich commons and knights. From them the couple received great furs for their bed, two saddles made of brown leather and silver, and many jugs of honey. Aidan received a new oak shield painted blue with the red crown of his house, a new bow and arrow set, two spears that were taller than he was with leaf shaped points, and a very nice crowned helmet. Maggie received some rare perfumes, five necklaces, three rings and two arm golden arm bands.

The gift giving went on until an hour after midday. Then the Throne Room was cleared and everyone went to the Great Dinning Hall to start the feast. Aidan and Maggie waited outside the dinning hall until everyone had been seated.

"Did you like all the gifts?" Aidan asked her and gave her hand a squeeze.

"Yes they were all very beautiful, but what are we to do with a lioness?"

"That is just the King of the South's way," Aidan answered; Maggie could see that Aidan didn't care for the King of the South. "Shall we join our feast?"

"Yes," and with that Aidan escorted her into the dinning hall. Everyone rose from their seats when the couple entered. Maggie looked around and saw a lot of red hair and smiles, everyone seemed so happy for them. Aidan led her to the seat of honor at the table on a raised dais, the table only had two chairs.

"My Prince and Princess the Great Wizards of the Kingdoms have prepared a special treat for the two of you," King Cynon announced in a booming voice.

A very old man with white hair and beard that went down past his waist walked to the middle of the hall. He wore a blue wool robe that swallowed him up, and in his hand was on his great staff that had a huge crystal atop.

"May I present Cosmas, the White Wizard of the North," the herald announced.

The White Wizard gave a nod to Maggie and Aidan. Then the crystal on his staff lit up like lightning, the hall went quiet not a person made a sound. The wizard gave his staff a wave and the ceiling of the hall turned into the sky above. You could see the sun peaking out from behind a grey cloud in the dark grey sky. Then all of a sudden thunder clapped, and clouds rolled across the ceiling. The room lit up with a loud crack of lightning, Maggie closed her eyes. When she opened them the hall was back to normal.

She clapped her hand and laughed, "that was very impressive my lord," she said through laughs.

Next came someone Maggie knew well, Gabriel her fathers wizard. "May I present Gabriel the Great Wizard of the East," said the herald.

Gabriel was old, not as old as the White Wizard but still old. His pail skin hung loosely on his bones and he had wrinkles on his forehead and around his eyes. His grey beard went down over his golden silk robe that was tied with a red silk sash. His great staff in his right hand with the crystal that pulsed as he walked. The Great Wizard of the East gave a bow and tapped his staff on the floor three times. Roses started to rain down on her and Aidan. Red, pink, yellow, and white some still blooming as they fell. Maggie snatched a pink rose out of the air and it glowed when she touched it. She had not been this happy since she was a child sitting cross legged on the floor watching the wizard do tricks, this trick was always her favorite one. Maggie looked up and a rainbow had stretched across the hall.

"That has always been my favorite, my thanks Gabriel I shall never forget you," Maggie said. The wizard climbed the steps of the dais and gave Maggie's hand a kiss.

"May I present Xolan the Red Wizard of the South," the herald announced.

A tall tan skinned man, with a long peppered beard and black eyes came forward. He was wearing a red silk robe that left his shoulders bare, and had his great wooden staff in his right hand. He bowed to the couple atop the dais, and then raised his staff high in the air. Fire shot out of the crystal and swirled up towards the ceiling, red and orange flames dancing in the air. Then the fire took shape, a dragon came from the flames. The dragon flew the dining hall, wings stretched out and tail whipping side to side. It did a flip in the air and when it was up right again it opened it huge mouth and flames came shooting out towards the dais. Maggie was so scared she grabbed Aidan's knee under the table and squeezed, Aidan put his hand on hers and gave it a comforting squeeze back. Then the dragon was shrinking back into the crystal of the Red Wizard's staff, and before long it was nothing but a small flame. The wizard blew the flame out and bowed. The room was quiet; everyone had been frightened by the trick, but before long cries and cheers filled the room.

"That was a very good trick," Aidan said with a nod, the wizard nodded back then went back to his seat.

"Last comes Lennox the West Wizard," the herald said.

Lennox steeped forward, he was a tall man and younger than the other great wizards. He wore a simple grey wool robe with a leather belt at his waist. His red hair was cropped at the shoulders and his red beard was in a braid, his hair had streaks of silver in it and blended in with his grey robe. He had his great staff in his right hand and lifted it off the ground when he walked.

Lennox bowed in front of the dais, "My Prince I have known you all your life and I look forward to getting to know you better My Princess, today I give you the gift of prophecy, a glimpse of your life to come," he said to her and Aidan.

The crystal on his staff lit up and then her and Aidan were standing before them, except Maggie was big with child and Aidan was dressed in armor. He hugged Maggie and they kissed then he mounted his horse Night Terror and turned into mist. Then Aidan was fighting a great battle and killing anyone who came close to him.

Maggie sat scared in her chair on the dais, she didn't know if she wanted to see the future. The battle died away and the image floated off. Aidan was entering the gates of West Watch and Maggie greeted him with a babe in her arms. The next image Maggie and Aidan were being crowned King and Queen, the image turned to smoke and drifted away in the air. Then she and Aidan appeared much older, two boys standing by Aidan and two girls stood by Maggie and she had a babe in her arms. Three of the children had Aidan's auburn hair and two had golden curls. The next image was

Aidan and Maggie both with grey hair and loose wrinkled skin, then that disappeared as well.

"The future tells of many battles that you will live through. You will have five children together, three with auburn hair two with golden curls. You will rule long and live to and old age together," Lennox said to them.

"My thanks friend, I could not have asked for a better gift," Aidan replied. The wizard gave a bow, and walked towards the end of the hall.

"Did you enjoy our gifts?" Aidan leaned over and whispered in her ear.

"Very much, the wizard's powers are very strong," she whispered back with a smile.

Then the feast began. They had six courses, each course bigger than the last. Lots of honey wine, honey mead, ale, and summer wine from the south. There were fools dancing and singing and jugglers with flames twirling in the air. After the feast was over the music began and the guest danced for hours. Maggie danced with at the least twenty different lords. When Aidan took her hand to dance her legs were sore and stiff. The feast continued on until dark and by the time the candles were lit Maggie was exhausted. The guest were getting loud from the alcohol and laughing and shouting over the music. By the time Maggie retired to her room she could see the moon high in the sky. Sleep came quick, as soon as she hit the pillow.

The next morning Maggie awoke to a cool autumn breeze coming from her window. She shivered as she climbed out of her feather bed and walked quickly to the window, and closed the shutters. Tansy and Violet were entering the room as Maggie emerged from the privy chamber. Tansy had a tray in her hand and laid it on the table. Maggie sat down and broke her fast on dried fruit and nuts, wheat bread and warmed goat's milk. While she was eating, her maids filled her tub with steaming water. The water was still hot by the time Maggie slipped naked into the tub. Her maids scrubbed her with a sponge until her skin was pink and shinning. They dried her off then Maggie picked out one of the perfumes she had received as a gift, Violet dabbed perfume under both arms, both breast, between Maggie's legs and on her neck. The perfume was cold and Maggie's skin had bumps from the chill.

Maggie dressed in elegant virgin robes that were white silk the color of fresh fallen snow, and had baby pearls sewn around the bodice and sleeves. A lace sash was tied at her waist to show her curves better. She left her hair down, and her golden curls fell down her back to her waist. Violet slipped white rabbit skinned slippers on Maggie's feet that made her feet nice and warm. Then a white cloak with white fur at the top was fastened to her shoulders by a rose broach.

When Maggie emerged from the castle a great crowd had gathered to watch the royal couple leave for the temple. Aidan walked up to her with a big grin on his face. He wore a white leather doublet with the crown of his house embroidered over the heart and brown leather breeches that had his great sword hanging from the belt at his hip. His auburn hair had been tied back with a leather strap. His bright green eyes looked into hers and all of a sudden Maggie's nerves were calmed. He took her hand in his and led her toward a two person coach that was parked at the bottom of the steps. Aidan helped Maggie into the coach, and then climbed in after her. The coach had feather stuffed cushions of blue velvet and lace curtains. Maggie was looking out at the crowd as the coach started moving forward.

"Are all these people going to be at the temple?" she asked Aidan.

"Most, the royals and lords and ladies will be inside the temple with us, but the commons will wait outside," Aidan answered in a kind voice. "Are you scared?"

"No, I am glad that today and every day after I will be your wife," she answered sternly.

He leaned over and kissed her gently on the lips and her heart fluttered.

The coach came to a stop right in front of the temple; Maggie looked out the lace curtain and saw commons gathered as far as she could see.

"Everyone in the capitol has come to see the golden princess," Aidan said with a smile.

Maggie gave a nervous smile back. Aidan stepped out of the coach and took her hand to help her down. All the commons started cheering as she emerged from the coach. Aidan led her up the grey marble steps of the temple.

The temple was dome shaped, made of grey marble with a glass roof to let the sun in through the top. Two great wooden doors stood open to the temple, each door had three faces carved into it.

Maggie looked up to Aidan, "what are the faces carved into the doors?"

"Each face represents one of our gods, so they can look out to the world from their temple," he explained.

They were the first ones to enter the temple with the exception of the priest and priestesses. White marble statues in the likeness of women and men stood on both sides of the temple. The first statue on the right was carved in the likeness of a man, slender and bearded with a flowing robe. He stood next to a white marble hill that had a well on the top of it.

"This is Nechtan, our water god. He guards the holy well that holds the water of knowledge," Aidan said to her.

They walked across to the other side of the temple. This god was obviously a smith, he had a great hammer in his hand and in the other hand was a sword laid across an anvil.

"This is our smith god Goidhniu, he makes all the other gods and goddess's armor and weapons. He is the best craftsman there is and no sword can withstand a sword that he has forged," Aidan explained to her.

The god next to the smith held a chalice in one hand and the other hand was reaching out. The likeness of this god was a bearded middle aged man, and he wore robes that flowed all the way to the floor.

"This is Dian, the god of healing. He guards the sacred spring of health, when you drink the water from his chalice it can cure any illness and even bring back the dead," Aidan explained in a gentle voice.

They walked across the floor to the goddess that stood by the water god. She hand a common and kind face, long flowing hair and robes. In her arms was an infant and she was looking down at the babe with a caring smile.

"This is Ceridwen the goddess of fertility. She helps women conceive and have a healthy pregnancy and safe birth. You should pray to her after we are wed for healthy and strong children," Aidan said with a smile. Maggie gave a nervous smile back.

The last statue at the right hand side of the temple was of a woman. She was very beautiful and had long flowing hair. Her hands were stretched out with the palms of her hands facing up. She had a smile on her face and her eyes looked down upon you.

"This is Brigantia our queen goddess. She is the daughter of your mother goddess Anu. She will help those loyal to her with voyages, war, healing and prosperity. You must always pray to her first before addressing the other gods so you do not offend her," Aidan explained.

The statue opposite of the queen goddess was of an old bearded man with three hounds at his feet.

"This is Arawn the leader of the otherworld, and his hell hounds at his feet. If you please Arawn then his hounds will lead you to an otherworld that is a paradise of peace and plenty," Aidan said to her.

Maggie did not like the hounds, they frightened her with their teeth bared.

By the time Aidan was finished explaining the West's gods to her the temple was half full of royals and highborn families. Maggie looked around the temple and saw her family and Aidan's family in the front row, of the right side of the temple. The royals of the North and South in the front row of the left side. She gave a nervous smile to her father and he returned the smile and gave her a nod. When she turned back around toward the front of the temple an old, fat, bald man stood in front of her. He was wearing a simple brown wool robe that was tied at the waist, and had an iron chain around his neck.

"My Princess this is Peter our high priest," Aidan introduced her to the fat man.

The priest bowed down and kissed her hand, "it is an honor to marry you to our Prince, Princess."

"The honor is mine," she said back politely.

"We will start the ceremony shortly as soon as all the people have arrived," the priest said to her and Aidan then walked to the front of the temple. Aidan and Maggie followed the priest to a velvet cushion in between Arawn and Brigantia.

Before long the temple was packed full, everyone was standing shoulder to shoulder and the crowd went all the way to the doors. The priest gave a nod and two priestesses shut the big wooden doors and the temple grew quiet.

"You have come to witness the marriage of Prince Aidan McCue and Princess Margery Carrender. They have come to this holy place to take their vows before gods and men. Prince Aidan and Princess Margery will you please kneel before the gods," the priest started the ceremony.

Aidan and Maggie knelt on the velvet cushion before the priest. The priest then took a rope that was made of golden thread and braided then tied into a knot, and placed the rope around both of them.

"This sacred braid represents the life that these two people will have together, and it is bond as their marriage will be. You knelt as two people but when you rise you will be one. Do you vow before man and gods to serve the other and give them your loyalty?" the priest said to the couple kneeling before him.

Both Aidan and Maggie said "yes," at the same time.

"I now ask the gods to bless this marriage, may Nechtan bless you with knowledge that you must have to live a happy life with each other. May Goidhniu forge an armor around this marriage so no mortal can come between it. May Dian bless you with health. May Ceridwen bless you with many children to carry on your name. May Arawn see you together to the otherworld to live in paradise together. And may Brigantia bless you with everything else you need for a successful marriage." The priest bent down and kissed Aidan on the forehead than kissed Maggie on her forehead. "Now rise as husband and wife," the priest said to them.

Aidan gave Maggie his hand and helped her off her knees; once they were standing he bent down and kissed her intensely on the lips. Everyone gathered in the temple cried out with joy, and Maggie could feel her face getting red.

With the golden rope still around their shoulders Aidan grabbed Maggie's hand and led her out the temple. When they emerged all the commons cheered and cried out at them. Aidan walked quickly down the steps of the temple towards the coach. Maggie was having a hard time keeping up with his long legs. They reached the coach and Aidan gave Maggie a lift into it. The commons made a path as the coach began to creep forward.

"Was that like the weddings in the East?"

"The weddings in the East are very similar, they use crowns of woven flowers instead of the rope and we worship different gods," Maggie answered.

"Now you are a Princess of the West and will worship our gods," Aidan replied.

Maggie didn't have a response for that, she hadn't really thought about it. She guessed it made since though, if she was to be the Queen of the West she needed to have the gods of the West on her side. So she smiled back at Aidan and he bent down and kissed her again.

Commons were gathered from the temple to the castle, which made the way back slower than the way there.

"So what happens now?" Maggie said innocently, she was hoping that she would have some more time before they had to consummate their marriage.

"While we were at the temple I instructed the servants to move your belongings into my chambers, so when we return to the castle we can go up and change before the feast. Then all of our guest will great us and we will have a great celebration," Aidan replied. "After the celebration you will return to my chambers and hopefully tonight we will make a son," he continued with a smile.

Maggie gave a nervous grin.

"Do not worry, I know it is your first time, I promise I will be gentle with you," he said to her. He must have seen how nervous she was.

When they returned to the castle Aidan walked her up the steeps and led her towards Spear Tower. When they entered his chambers together the bed had been made up with curtains flowing from the canopy and six big feathered pillows were at the head of the bed. Blue and red quilts sat on top of the mattress and reached down to the floor. Just looking at the massive bed made Maggie nervous. Her mother had explained her duties to her but she wasn't sure she would be able to satisfy her husband. Maggie looked around the room, it was a lot bigger than the room that she had been staying in. It looked like it had at the least four connecting rooms, though she was sure one of them had to be a privy chamber.

"Were are my servants chambers? I require their assistance," Maggie asked her new husband.

"All the servants' chambers are across the hall, but I have given them the night off. I told them that we would not need them. What do you need them for?" he replied.

"This robe was dreadful to put on I thought I would have my bed maids help me out of it, and help me into a gown," Maggie said.

"Let me help you," Aidan said and walked over and shut the door behind her.

Maggie's mother had told her not to argue with her husband, so Maggie gave a nervous nod.

"How do we get this thing off?" Aidan asked with a friendly smile.

"My maids put it on over my head seems how there is no opening in the back, but all this fabric is a lot to handle," she said in a quiet voice.

Aidan bent down and gathered up all the fabric around her feet. Then pulled the fabric put to her waist, "it might work better if you were to put your arms up," he said and Maggie did. Finally after wrestling with the fabric Aidan managed to get the virgin robes over her head.

Maggie stood looking at her husband in nothing but small clothes covering her sex. Her breasts were bare and the cold breeze from the window had given her skin bumps and made her nipples hard. She dropped her arms and went to cover her breast with her hands.

"Don't, you have no reason to hide your beauty from your husband," Aidan said.

So she dropped her hands to her waist and allowed him to stare at her.

"You are beautiful Maggie, you do know that right?"

"I have been told so, but my body is still growing I am sure that I will have better breast soon," she said embarrassed.

"They are perfect as they are now," he said back to her and lifted his eyes from her breast and looked at her face.

Maggie could feel herself blush.

"Now what did you want to change into? I instructed that your clothes be put in the wardrobe over there," Aidan said and pointed to the cabinet in the corner of the left hand side of the room.

Maggie walked over to the wardrobe and pulled out a dark pink gown with red beads sewn into the top and around the bottom of the bell sleeves. In all of Maggie's fourteen years she had never dressed herself, spoils of being a Princess. She was thankful that she had left her hair down today so she would not have to work on that as well. She slipped into the gown easily enough but when it came to lacing it up the back she was lost.

"You don't by chance know how to lace up a gown?" she said almost laughing.

Aidan gave a giggle, "No my lady I do not. I apologize for sending the servants off, I did not realize how much work you women go through to get dressed. Would you like me to go grab one of my sister Ailis's maids?" he replied.

"I would be very grateful if you did so. You wouldn't want your wife looking a fool," she said, and she and Aidan both started laughing.

Once Aidan and his sister's maid arrived Aidan went off to change while the maid helped Maggie look presentable. When Aidan returned he was wearing the crown that his parents had given them as a gift, and he was caring her crown in his hand.

"For the future Queen of the West," he said and placed the crown atop her head.

"My thanks, the Future King of the West," she said back with a smile.

"Shall we head down to the celebration? I am sure all of our guests are ready and waiting."

Maggie gave a nod and took his elbow.

Outside the Great Hall you could hear the room within was full, loud voices carried out into the hall.

"Are you ready to great our guest again?" Aidan asked her with a heart melting smile. Maggie gave a nod and they entered the hall.

"All rise for Prince Aidan McCue and his wife Princess Margery McCue," the herald announced as soon as he spotted them.

The hall grew quiet and everyone rose from the benches at the long tables. Aidan led her to the front of the hall in front of their table, and within seconds a great line of people were there waiting to congratulate them on their marriage.

After Maggie had been hugged and kissed by about four hundred people her legs were sore and aching from standing so long, and she was relieved to finally sit at the table. They had a great ten course feast with every delicacy she could hope for. They had jugglers and fools entertaining the guest during the feast, one fool bumped into a juggler and caught the juggler's sleeve on fire and the whole hall burst out laughing at the scene. Maggie took big gulps of her sweet honey wine, she was very found of the honey wine it was the best wine she had every had. Aidan was enjoying mead and was soon laughing along with the guest and the fool's performance.

The plates from the last course were being cleared away when King Cynon stood and yelled for everyone to shut up, he was obviously drunk. "A toast to my son and his beautiful wife, may you live and rule long!" he said with his horn of ale high above his head.

The hall got loud with cheers and the King sat back down and started laughing with his Queen beside him. The music started playing and it was tradition for the bride and groom to dance the first dance. Aidan stood and took Maggie's hand and led her to the middle of the hall. They were both tipsy from the alcohol and Aidan stumbled once on the last step, but Maggie didn't think anyone noticed. Aidan started spinning her on the floor and Maggie was laughing at the look on his face. She had never been so happy.

After the first dance Aidan and Maggie grabbed their chalices and walked around to every table. The first table they came to was where the Ice Queen and the South's King were seated.

They approached the Queen first, "that was a beautiful wedding," the Queen said to them.

"My thanks, Your Grace. And congratulations on your new son, what have you named the new king?" Aidan replied.

"He is named after my father, King Conell Mathis III. Beg pardons for not bringing him, he is still too young for such a journey," she answered.

"Not to worry I am sure I will meet your king soon enough," Aidan said and the Ice Queen gave a nod.

The King of the South was not as friendly. He was rude and gave smart remarks with everyone of Aidan's questions. Aidan had heard that King Abhay had banished one of the lords from the King's own council, and when asked about it the King got up and walked away without an answer.

"You will have to forgive my husband, we have had traitors every where lately and it has weighed heavy on him," his beautiful copper queen said to Aidan after the King was gone.

"Not to worry, Your Grace. The pressures of ruling a kingdom are great," Aidan replied and they soon moved on to the next table.

By the time they had visited every table the sun had left the sky and the moon had replaced it.

Aidan leaned down and whispered in Maggie's ear, "It's time for us to retire."

Maggie's stomach tightened, the part of the marriage that she had feared was upon her and she was not ready for the task. She gave a nod and tried her best to hide her fear.

"It has been a long and tiring day, me and my wife will now take our leave. I thank you all for coming and wish you all a safe journey home," Aidan said in a loud voice that echoed off the walls.

Maggie glanced at her mother right before they left the hall and she gave Maggie a smile and a nod, Maggie nodded back and left the hall.

On the way back to her and Aidan's chambers they could hear the knights and guards celebrating in the tents outside. There had not been enough room to allow the knights and commons into the castle, so King Cynon had thirty great tents seat up below so everyone would be able to celebrate her and Aidan's marriage. They reached the room and Maggie's legs started shaking, her hands were sweaty and she was breathing quicker.

"It is alright, you will be fine," Aidan said and opened the door to the chamber.

Maggie walked in and Aidan closed the door behind her.

SNOW CAP MOUNTAINS

Wodan, Weland and Etzel sat around the fire in a small cavern. Wodan had been chosen by the dwarfs to be the new Leader of the Dark Dwarfs after Gundahar had been murdered. The day after they burnt Gundahar's body Wodan had the dwarfs gather all their belongings and the gems and silver and they moved to a mountain closer to the White Woods. When they found the cave of their new home they found skeletons of fifty three men. The skeletons were dressed in pricey armor made of the finest silver and most had gems embedded in it. They found very nice weapons too. The men dwarfs stripped the corpses and got ride of the bones before they brought the women and children to the mountain. It was not as cozy as their last home, but at least Ser Fintan did not know where they were.

"Ser Fintan traveled with one hundred knights, I am sure they will travel back to Ice Storm with him. We need to take them by surprise and kill as many as possible before they can get to us. Knights are harder to kill then common men, they are trained well. Ser Fintan will have to pass this way to return to Ice Storm and he will not expect us to attack this far from our old home," Wodan informed his friends.

"How many fighting men do we have?" Etzel asked.

"Fifty men who are seasoned in fighting, ten young men that have never fought in their life, and five boys who are almost men that I would like to keep out of the fighting," Wodan answered.

"So it will be almost two to one and they have the advantage?" Weland asked.

"We have the advantage! I plan for most to be dead before they even see us. We know the mountains, they do not," Wodan said.

"I want boulders placed above the road, so we can crush them and block their path. Also with some luck the snow will cover them, so by the time we reach them most will be dead or dying. We can leave no survivors to go running to the Queen, if she thinks the wolves have gotten her knights she will give us no trouble," Wodan continued with his plans.

"What if they come looking for them?" Etzel asked.

"We will get rid of the bodies, they can look all they want but they will not find them," Wodan replied.

Just then Gundahar's sons Alberic and Ing entered the cavern that the three were in.

"I want to help. I want to avenge my father," Alberic said.

"Me too," said Ing.

"What have you two heard? How long have you been there?" Wodan said surprised by there arrival.

"We heard enough. You three were my father's closes friends, but he was my father it is my right as much as yours to avenge his death," Alberic replied.

"You are just boys who have never fought a man in your life. Your mother could not handle loosing you two after loosing your father, it would destroy her," Wodan said to the boys.

"Our mother would understand," Ing said.

"You think she would? Ok go get her then, bring her here and let's see what she thinks," Wodan replied.

The boys looked at each other with scared looks and Wodan knew that Brunhild would never allow this.

"Go on. If you mother approves than I will not deny you. Go," Wodan said.

The boys walked slowly out of the cavern.

"Brunhild will never allow her sons to fight, not after just loosing Gundahar," Weland said.

"I know and I am counting on that, I want to keep those boys safe. They will be reckless with grief and get themselves killed," Wodan replied.

"You cannot blame them though, what would you do if it were your father? May haps we should let them help, they could be on top of the mountain and release the boulders," Etzel said. "You can not blame them for wanting to kill the man that killed their father."

"We will see what Brunhild says about it. I will not make decision about her sons without her," Wodan replied.

Within the hour the boys returned with their mother, it was obvious they had not told her of their plans.

"What is it Wodan?" Brunhild asked bluntly.

"Brunhild sit," Weland said to her.

She looked at him through squinted eyes, but sat none the less.

"Brunhild your sons have come to us wanting to assist in avenging Gundahar. They want to help us bring down Ser Fintan and the other knights," Wodan informed the widow.

"This is madness! I just lost my husband now you want to take my sons?" Brunhild yelled at Wodan.

"It was your sons who asked this of us. If you approve we can have them help up the mountain, they would not even have to swing an axe," Wodan said.

"Approve! You think I would approve? No! Not a chance, they will stay here with me," she replied.

"Let me go over our plans with you Brunhild, Gundahar was their father you can not blame them for wanting to see his killer die," Wodan said calmly.

"Fine Wodan, tell me your plans but don't think that it will change my mind!" she said loudly, her voice echoed off the walls of the cavern and pebbles rained down upon them.

Wodan explained their plans of blocking the road with boulders and snow. When he was finished Brunhild looked just as mad as she had before.

"Wodan, Weland, Etzel I appreciate that you want to see this man pay for what he did to my husband, I do. But I can not risk loosing my sons as well. I am sorry, but when this battle takes place I want my sons in the mountain with me," she said to the three dwarfs.

All three gave a nod of understanding.

"Mother, you would rather us stay behind with the women and children than to go bring fathers killer to justice?" Alberic asked.

"I would rather my son's live long lives safe from harm. Than let them go off and risk being killed," she answered. "I will hear no more about it. Alberic, you and Ing will stay here and that is the end of it," Brunhild said to her sons and walked out of the cavern.

"I am sorry boys, I understand why you want to do this, but I will not go against your mothers wish," Wodan told the boys.

The look on their faces was heart breaking and Wodan felt bad for not letting them be involved. The boys walked out with their heads down and their feet dragging.

"Ok it's been one week since Gundahar's death, so Fintan will be heading back to Icestorm soon. I want ten men on the mountains as look outs at all time. We also need to get all the men together and start getting the boulders ready to block the road. I will go over our plans tonight and on the morrow we prepare for battle," Wodan said to his friends. Weland and Etzel nodded in agreement.

At first light sixty eight dwarf men left and set out into the mountains. The boulders were easy to find, it was moving them that was difficult. They rested the boulders on logs that had rope tied to them, so when the enemy approached the dwarf would pull the rope and release the boulder. They covered the boulders with snow so if the boulder missed the target the snow would slow them down. The dwarfs did this on all four mountains that were surrounding the road. If his plan worked, Ser Fintan and his men would have no escape, they would be surrounded by boulders and snow on all sides. With luck the boulders would kill most of the men and the dwarfs would not have as many to fight.

By the time the last boulder was ready the sun was setting in the west and the sky was growing dark. The dwarfs went back to their cave in the mountain and sealed the entrance. Wodan would not have watchers in the night, he didn't want to risk losing what men he had to wolfs, plus he didn't think Ser Fintan would be foolish enough to travel at night. All the battle axes they had were placed at the entrance of the cave, along with leather slings they used for throwing stones. Wodan instructed that all men be dressed for battle in the daylight hours.

That night they feasted on salted meat and wine that they had stolen from Ser Fintan's men. When Wodan finally crawled into bed his head was spinning and his stomach was turning.

The next morning Wodan decided he would take the first watch. He left Etzel in charge and him and nine other men set out up the mountains. Each man was armed with an axe, a sling and a horn to sound the alarm. If the horn was sounded then the remaining dwarfs would come out and climb the mountains to assist with the attack.

Wodan chose the mountain closest to North Star and started his climb. When he reached the boulders he was out of breath and his legs were cramping. He sat down in the middle of two boulders and kept his eyes to the north. It was a chilly autumn day, but warmer than usual in the mountains. The sky was clear with not a cloud in sight, the sun was reflecting of the white snow and was almost blinding to look at. Wodan wrapped his cloak tighter around him and looked out into the mountains.

At midday Gunner an older dwarf with a long grey beard came to replace Wodan. Wodan was happy for the break, his ass had gone numb from sitting in the snow for hours and his legs were cramped so bad he almost fell when he stood up. He massaged his thighs, and then set off slowly down the mountain. The way down was steep and the snow and ice posed a threat. Half way down he steeped in a snow drift that brought snow up to his waist, it took him half an hour to climb out. By the time he reached their cave Wodan was so tired he could hardly stand. He decided that he would rest awhile before taking over for Etzel. He laid down in his bed with his axe still in his hand and his snow covered boots still frozen to his feet and fell asleep quickly.

He awoke to his wife Lorelei trying to wrestle his boots off his feet. His wife was very plump with breast as big as his head. He often wondered how she didn't topple over from being top heavy. She had stringy brown hair that went down to the middle of her back that was braided. Her round face was red from trying to pry his boots off.

When she saw he was awake she said, "Why didn't you take these things off? Now you've gotten the bed wet."

"I am sorry dear; I was so tired I didn't want to mess with them. What hour is it?" he replied.

"Late, the entrance has already been sealed. Not to worry the watchers say the road is clear," she replied.

He nodded and helped her get his boots off, then rolled over and went back to sleep.

He was the first one up, long before daybreak. Wodan waited by the entrance until the sun touched the sky, so the boulder could be removed from the entrance. He stepped out in the crisp autumn air. The cold breeze kissed his cheeks and rustled his beard. He crunched through the snow to the closest mountain with the boulders. It was a long climb and when he reached the top he was breathing heavily. He looked to the north, the sun had just started to light the sky, and half the world was still dark. To the east the snow on the top of the mountains sparkled like diamonds from where the sun hit them. He sat down in the cold hard snow and waited, and watched.

Two hours passed; there was still no sign of Ser Fintan and his men. Wodan climbed back down the mountain and let another dwarf take over his watch. Not much was going on inside the mountain where they had made their home. Wodan ordered no digging until Ser Fintan had been taken care of. So the women rushed around trying to make their new home livable and the men paced back and forth like caged dogs. All men who would join in the attack stayed close to the entrance so they could get to their weapons easily and up the mountains in time.

"Any sign," Eztel said as he approached.

"Not as of yet, Ser Fintan will be here soon, he needs to return to his Queen. A couple more days at the most," Wodan replied.

Etzel gave a nod with a crinkled brow and walked away.

Wodan grabbed his battle axe and walked outside. He sat down on a nearby rock and started sharpening the blade with a whetstone. He was still sharpening his axe when he heard the horn, their horns had been fashioned to sound exactly like a wolf howling so as not to give the enemy warning of their attack. Wodan threw the whetstone on the ground and ran as fast as is stunted legs would go towards the cave. The men inside the cave had heard the alarm also. The entrance was crowded with men grabbing their axes and slings and rushing out and up the mountain. Wodan saw that everyone was getting their weapons and he turned and returned back outside.

He climbed quickly up the same mountain he had been atop that morning. Three men were already up there when he reached the boulders. He looked to the north and saw the light blue banners and silver armor glittering in the sun. The knights were at least a league away which gave them enough time for the other dwarfs to get in position. Etzel and Weland would be stationed on the other mountains to make sure everything went as planned. Wodan had ordered that the boulders not be released until they heard the horn the second time, so the knights would not have time to escape. He crouched down by the nearest boulder and wrapped the rope connected to the log around his wrist. The other dwarfs with him did the same with the other boulders. By the time Ser Fintan was close everyone was hidden and ready.

Wodan watched as the knight's new horses brought them closer. They did not seem to suspect anything which was good, it would have been harder if the knights new of the attack. Ser Fintan was in the front of the party, his black cloak flapping in the wind. Closer and closer they came, they were almost in position. Then for no obvious reason the party stopped. Ser Fintan dismounted his stallion and looked up towards Wodan. Wodan ducked deep behind the hidden boulder, he could not help holding his breath. Ser Fintan walked over to the nearest bush and started to take a piss. Wodan released his breath in relief. The other dwarfs were looking to him for the single, and he shook his head for them to wait.

After Ser Fintan had relieved himself he mounted back on his stallion and the party started coming towards them again. They were in position! Wodan gave the nod to sound the horn, and the dwarf next to him lifted his horn to his lips and made a loud howl. Once the horn was lowered the ropes were pulled. Within seconds there was a cascade of rocks and snow falling off the mountains onto the knights. When the boulders hit the ground the snow came up and made a big white cloud blocking all view of the attack. Wodan got to his feet and ran as fast as he could down the mountain and toward the buried knights. He could hear horses and men screaming as he was making his way down.

All the fighting dwarfs he had were surrounding the pile of snow and boulders and waiting for any survivors to emerge from beneath. Wodan had his battle axe securely in his right hand and was gripping it so tight his knuckles were turning white. They waited for what seemed like hours before they saw the snow start to move. He held his left hand out to let the other dwarfs know to wait for the attack. They watched in silence as the snow slowly started to fall away from the first man to emerge.

The man finally got himself free from the snow and stood on top of the pile. He had lost his helmet in the attack and his forehead was bleeding badly. Wodan could see it was not Ser Fintan and a little piece of him was disappointed he wanted to kill Ser Fintan with his own hands. The injured knight started digging with his hands in attempt to find his party. Wodan gave a nod to one of the dwarfs with a sling in his hands. The dwarf loaded a nice size rock in the sling, whipped it around his head and released. The rock hit the injured knight right in the temple and he fell back into the snow.

Before long more knights emerged, this time there were five. Wodan knew he would have to start the fight soon before one of them could run off. Wodan signaled with his left hand to prepare and all the dwarfs crouched down and got ready to climb the pile of rocks and snow and dead knights. Once all five men were out of the snow and on their feet Wodan gave the signal. All dwarfs climbed quickly and quietly up the pile, when they reached the top they gave no cry of warning but went straight for the attack. They caught two knights unarmed and killed them quickly. The remaining three were more difficult, it took three dwarfs each to take them down and kill them. The white snow quickly drank up the blood from the slain knights.

Wodan was standing on the edge waiting for any more survivors when a hand came up from the snow grabbed his ankle and pulled him straight on his ass. Before Wodan hit the snow he swung his axe and cut off the hand with a single swing, blood sprayed from the arm of the unknown man covering Wodan in a spray of red. Wodan climbed back to his feet and watched the bleeding arm grow into an arm and shoulder and then a head emerged from the snow. Before Wodan could even see the man's face he lifted his axe high and berried it in the top of the silver helmet. His axe was stuck and he had to put his foot on the dead head to pry it free.

Then the survivors were emerging two and three at a time. Before long every dwarf was hacking at a stubborn knight that refused to die. The fighting went on and on. Every time they thought they killed the last one, another knight would emerge from beneath the snow. Wodan was on his eighth kill when he spotted the torn and tattered black cloak. He buried his axe in the knight's throat that he was fighting and ran over to the cloak. Silver armor with spots of fresh red blood shown through the snow. Wodan swung his axe and landed it right into the armor, though it was half buried so he didn't know which part of the body he had struck. He pried his axe free and struck again and again and again until the snow had all melted from the fresh blood and Wodan could see a man laying face down in the snow.

Wodan dropped down to his knees and pulled the dented helmet off the body, he had to make sure it was who he thought it was. With all his weight he pushed the body until it flipped over. With a clank of armor and the crunching sound of broken bones the body turned and Ser Fintan's dead eyes were starring up at the pail blue sky.

CRYSTAL KEEP

Two days after they set forth Aldreda and Julian finally emerged from Elf Forest. Aldreda saw the first sign of autumn on the last row of trees, the tops of the maple trees were starting to loose their green color. The nights had been cold and the days were warm. It was midday and the sun was high in the cloudless blue sky. Something off to the east was sparkling like a star in the night.

"What is that?" Aldreda asked and pointed to the east.

"Crystal Keep, the highest tower has a great crystal taller than any man on top of it. You can see it shinning leagues away, we will not reach the city until nightfall. Once we get to the city you will need a last name being human and all, I was thinking Black."

"A bastard name?" she said disappointed. "Why not your name, as your wife?"

"I guess we could use that as well, I was just thinking no one pays any mind to a bastard so it might help," Julian answered.

"I would much rather like Blair," she said to him with a pleading smile.

"Very well, wife," he teased back.

She was happy with that even if it was just a cover. Soon after this business with Lord Mullen was done she would talk her father into performing the ritual to bind them together and she would be like what the humans called a wife.

She kept her eye on the shining crystal as she rode east. The warm breeze kissing her cheek as her horse trotted to keep up with Julian. She was not fond of this saddle, she had never ridden a horse with a saddle and she found it more a nuisance then a help. It was a lot of work to saddle a horse and she would rather hold on with her thighs then have her feet in stirrups. But she was trying to play the human part and not the elf that she was so she tolerated it and kicked her horse to a gallop.

Aldreda looked around, she had never seen this much emptiness. To the east was the Sapphire Sea and to the west were flat grass plains. She had never been out of the forest before. She had always thought the rest of the world was the same as what she was use to. She felt so naked, not being hidden from trees and brush. It was quiet, no animals crying, and no birds singing their songs, just the sound of the wind blowing through the grass. She could faintly hear the waves of the sea and there was a slight smell of salt in the air. She didn't want to seem as nervous as she was, so she forced a smile every time Julian looked her way.

She thought she would try talking to keep her mind off of being out of the forest. "So my love, how long have we been married?"

"We are newlyweds, just last week. I don't know the last time my father got word from Kevin," he answered.

She could see his thoughts were elsewhere, he had been so quiet since they left the Great Willow. "And am I from your village?" she said trying to keep the conversation going.

"I think not, Kevin knows almost everyone from the village. What about the village we passed on the way here."

"Then how did we meet?"

"Hunting," he replied.

"Very well. So I am from the village by the sea, and I was off hunting when we met and instantly fell in love. You courted me and we had a small wedding last week, right?"

"Sounds good," he said with a forced smile.

She could see he was not in the mood to talk, so she did not push the conversation further.

The sun was behind them slowly setting in the sky turning it to purple and a deep blue. The crystal was barley ablaze when they reached the great stone wall of the city. The great iron and oak gates were opened to allow passage beneath the wall, and Aldreda was amazed at the sight of the wall passing above them. She had never seen a structure like that before in her life. Once inside the city her nose filled with the smell of smoke and urine, it was not a pleasant smell, the city reeked. Light and music poured out of the buildings windows and doors. She heard yelling and laughing mixed together as one. She kicked her horse forward and trotted as close to Julian as she could get. He looked over at her and gave her on of his heart melting smiles, and she forgot how scared she was for a moment.

After passing many buildings they came to an inn and Julian pulled his horse to a stop. A young boy about ten years of age came running up to them and Aldreda thought he was going to attack them. She rushed behind Julian and he laughed at her.

"You stayin here tonight?" the boy asked.

"Hoping to," Julian answered.

"I'll put your horses up for a copper," offered the boy.

"Let me make sure they have a room first than I will take you up on that offer," Julian replied and tied the horses up then took Aldreda's hand and led her toward the inn. "You don't have to be so nervous, I will let no harm come to you," he whispered in her ear.

"I have never seen anything like this before, I was expecting something like your village. This is much bigger," she whispered back.

"This is a city, wait until we reach Rosegarden it is twice this size," he answered.

That made her feel worse, she was ready to return to the safety of her forest. They walked hand in hand into the smoky inn. Tables full of men and women filled the hall. There was a big hearth on the north end of the hall that put off more smoke than heat. It was very loud inside and Aldreda squeezed Julian's hand harder. A fat, bald man with a red face, and two chins stood behind the bar in grease stained clothes.

Julian led Aldreda up to the man then said, "We require a room."

"You're in luck got one left on the top floor. Aint that big but it's got a nice size bed big enough for da both o' you," the fat man replied.

"We'll take it."

"One silver will get you da room an food," said the man behind the bar. Aldreda reached in her purse at her hip and handed the man his silver.

The man came out from behind the bar and waddled toward the stairs, the couple followed. Four stories up and one left turn later they stood out side a beat up wooden door.

The man opened the door and said, "dis is it, supper gonna be in ten minutes tops." and walked away back towards the stairs.

The room was quit small, the straw bed in the middle of the room took up most of the space. "It will work for a day or two we won't be in the room much," Julian said to her and gave her a convincing smile, she smiled back at him nervously.

After paying the boy to tend to the horses, Aldreda and Julian grabbed their satchels and headed back into the inn. They took up an empty spot on the bench at the table in the far corner. A woman came along fatter than the man that had showed them the room, and filled their glasses up with ale. The woman was almost to fat to squeeze in between the tables. Aldreda sipped the ale, she had never been found of ale. Julian had her try it once a year ago, she still did not like it. The hall soon filled with the smell of burnt meat. The fat woman and two skinny, younger women came along with skewers of charred meat and carved slices off onto the plates at the table. Then they brought out some hard bread and placed four loafs at each table.

After eating all she dared to eat, Aldreda tried to wash the taste out of her mouth with the ale, but that only made the taste worse. Julian ate all the meat and bread on his plate and the fat woman filled his glass three times with ale. After empting his third glass of ale, Julian stood from the bench and took Aldreda by the hand. It was so loud in the hall with drunken men he did not even try to talk, he just led her up the stairs to their room. Once they reached their room Julian lit a brown wax candle that gave off more smoke than light and Aldreda shut the door behind her.

"Will we seek your brother out tonight?" she asked in a hushed voice.

"No, not tonight. He will be easier to find on the morrow. Plus you don't want to go walking the streets at night after the men have been at their cups," he said to her. Julian sat down on the corner of the bed and started taking off his boots. "We should get some sleep," he looked over and said to her.

She nodded back, she didn't know how much sleep she would get in this strange place but she would try.

He must of seen the worry on her face because he said to her, "Don't worry love, I won't let any harm come to you."

"Do you plan for your brother to come with us to see the King?"

"I do not know if Lord Hearon will allow him to leave, or if he even wants to go himself. We will see on the morrow."

She thought on that awhile and watched Julian strip his clothes off.

"Are you going to bed with me?" he asked her after seeing her still dressed.

"Yes," she said and started removing her own clothes.

She climbed in the cold, lumpy bed, naked and scooted as close as she could to Julian. He wrapped his arm around her as she laid her head on his chest. She could hear his heart beating, and it comforted her a little. She closed her eyes and tried to relax to go to sleep, but this place had strange sounds and smells and sleep was not coming. She lay awake for hours listening to Julian's heart, then finally sleep took her.

The smell of fresh bread baking woke her she opened her eyes and realized that Julian was no longer in bed. She sat up startled and frightened. She threw the quilt off her and quickly got dressed. She pulled the hood of her cloak over her head and made her way down the stairs. She saw Julian when she reached the bottom of the stairs, and her heart was instantly relieved. He was sitting at the table closes to the hearth nibbling on some bread. He didn't look up at her until she reached him.

"Why didn't you wake me?" she asked as she took a set beside him.

"You looked so peaceful I did not want to disturb you," he said back and leaned over and kissed her gently on the lips. She returned the kiss.

After they broke their fast on warm bread and fresh milk they set forth to find Ser Kevin. The streets of the city were crowded and people paid them no mind as they rushed by.

"Don't walk to close to the windows, you might get a chamber pot poured on your head," Julian warned.

Aldreda got as close to the center of the road as she dared. He laughed and followed her. They walked past the market that was already full of customers. Past a brothel where the whores cried down to Julian. Aldreda watched as Julian tried not to notice the whores and laughed at him. They went past another inn and five pubs, and then they finally came upon the gates to Lord Hearon's castle.

The castle was the biggest man made structure Aldreda had ever seen. "Someone lives there? It's huge," she whispered to Julian.

"Just wait until we reach Rosegarden," he whispered back.

The gate protecting the castle was twenty foot tall iron spikes surrounded by a stone wall of the same height. The castle was massive, made of white stone with four large pointed towers reaching towards the sky. The tallest tower had a great crystal on the top of it that reflected rainbows into the sky. Aldreda stepped closer to the gate to try to get a better view of the castle, when a guard yelled down at her from atop the wall.

"What is your business here?" the guard asked.

"We have come to find Ser Kevin Blair. Do you know were we might find him?" Julian yelled back.

"Ser Kevin is in the castle today, who seeks him?"

"His brother Julian with news of his family. Might I speak to him myself?"

"I will go see if he can come out to see you. Stay here," the guard said and then disappeared. Aldreda and Julian waited and watched the lively city.

Finally after what seemed a lifetime, a tall man in steel armor that was polished so well it reflected the sun emerged from the gate. "Julian to what do I owe this unexpected visit?"

He was slightly taller than Julian, but had the same dark hair and hazel eyes. His shoulders where broader and he had a thicker chest than Julian had, but she could tell they were brothers.

Julian embraced the man in a hug and said, "Brother this is my wife Aldreda. Aldreda this is Ser Kevin Blair."

Ser Kevin gave a bow and kissed Aldreda on the right hand and said, "I did not know you got married, father did not mention anything the last time he wrote. Is this why you have come so I can steal your beautiful wife."

Aldreda blushed.

"No I have come to tell you what has become our village. Kevin, Lord Mullen attacked our village, everyone is dead."

His brother looked shocked at the news and it was a while before he replied. "My shift ends at nightfall, are you staying here in the city?"

"Yes at the inn by the wall to the city," Julian replied.

"Good, meet me at the pub called the Sailor's Stop come nightfall we will talk more about it then," Ser Kevin said.

Julian gave a nod and him and Ser Kevin clasped forearms and went their separate ways.

They found the Sailor's Stop before nightfall and grabbed a table in the far corner, so as not to be disturbed. A serving wench came over with a flagon of wine and some glasses. Julian paid her two coppers and told her if she saw a knight named Ser Kevin to direct him in their direction. The wench took the coppers and walked away. They were on their second cup of cheep wine when Ser Kevin finally entered the pub. He spotted them strait away and took a seat across from his brother. The wench brought another cup over and Julian filled it for his brother.

"So Julian what is this news about the village?" Ser Kevin asked after the wench had left.

"Lord Mullen came to the village the day before the attack and was saying that we owed him his due for living on his land. Father tried to talk to him and explain that every other year he got his share of the harvest come Samhain, but Mullen would not hear it. Lord Mullen said we would have his share of the harvest by nightfall the next day or face his wrath. The next day we were in the field gathering the harvest. I met Aldreda at the river to tell her about Lord Mullen, I wasn't gone from the village more than an hour when I saw the smoke. Everything went blank after that. Aldreda says that I slipped on the rocks and cracked my head," Julian answered his brother.

"And after you awoke?"

"I awoke in the woods, Aldreda could not get me back to the village with me knocked out," he lied to cover up that she was an elf. "By the time I got back to the village everything was burnt to ash. Everyone in the village was dead or dying, not one person left uninjured. Our house Kevin, it was burnt to the ground with father and Ludwig still inside. I found their bones. No one survived for long, I am the only one living from our village now."

"Did you see the attackers?"

"No, but who else would it be if not Lord Mullen's men. He threatened us the day before."

"So what is your plan now?"

"Aldreda and I are going to Rosegarden to bring this matter to the King," said Julian.

Aldreda had not said a word the whole time she sat there watching Ser Kevin's reactions. Now Ser Kevin's brow wrinkled and he pursed his lips tight together.

"And what do you expect the King to do? You did not see the attackers! You think the King is going to take the word of a low born villager over a high born lord? Lord Mullen is the one that pays the King taxes, not you. What harm has the King taken with the village gone? None, but if he losses Lord Mullen and his men then the King takes a hit to his purse. Trust me brother I have been around high lords and kings, they care nothing for low born villagers. Lord Mullen will deny the charges and then find you and kill you too," Ser Kevin said loudly to his brother.

"Then what would you have me do, nothing?" Julian asked angry from his brother's response.

"I would have you go back with your wife and forget about Lord Mullen. I grieve for father too, but I would rather still have you then have you killed also. Trust me brother, you can't play the high lords game. Lord Mullen has hundreds of knights and men, plus he will deny everything to the King and the King will believe it. You have no other choice, go back or die trying to get justice," Ser Kevin said softly with emotion in his voice, he could see how much his words were hurting his brother.

Julian's eyes were red and his face was redder. Aldreda could not tell if he was more hurt or angry, she feared what he would do.

"Do nothing? Just forget it? Our father is dead Kevin, and our brother," Julian said in almost a whisper with his voice cracking in the middle of his words.

"And you will be dead if you try to face Lord Mullen or go to the King," was Ser Kevin's response.

"If I don't go to the King there has to be another way. You're a knight you have friends, or we could pay swords," Julian tried.

"Pay swords with what? And you think Lord Mullen won't pay twice as much for those swords to turn on you? If there is an attack on Springs End then the King will respond and not for our side. Julian, I am sorry but there is nothing that we can do."

Julian emptied his cup, filled it then emptied it again and slammed the cup down on the table. "Well brother, my thanks for your help. Now if you would excuse us, I and my wife must return to our room," Julian said and grabbed Aldreda by the arm and yanked her to her feet.

"Julian wait," Ser Kevin called to Julian's back.

Julian ignored the call, and dragged Aldreda faster out of the pub and towards the inn. Aldreda was having a hard time keeping up with Julian's long angry steps, and by the time they were half way to the inn she was almost running. Julian still had a tight grip on her arm and his grip was tightening. By the time they reached their inn she had a red mark in the shape of his hand.

Back in their room Julian slammed the door behind him, "Do nothing, that is his advice, do nothing!"

"What are we going to do now? Are we still going to Rosegarden?"

"You heard Kevin and unfortunately he is probably right! The King will take Lord Mullen's side, and as soon as we leave Rosegarden we will be killed. But there has to be another way!" Julian yelled back at her.

She knew he was not angry with her, but she was still frightened. She had never seen Julian like this before. She decided not to ask any more questions for awhile. So she undressed and slipped into bed.

The next morning Julian woke her gently, "Aldreda, we need to set off."

Aldreda opened her eyes to Julian sitting next to her and looking caringly at her. "What?" she said sleepily.

"We need to set off. We are leaving Crystal Keep," he answered.

She stretched out in the bed, then pulled him close to her and kissed him roughly. They had not made love since his village had been burned, she was yearning for his touch. He kissed her back, but when she tried to pull him on top of her he pulled away.

She looked deep into his eyes, "What is wrong my love?"

"I am just ready to leave," he said looking down at the floor.

She slipped out from under the quilt and found her linen dress and slipped it on. She grabbed her cloak that was hanging on the peg on the wall and tied it around her. She pulled the hood up to cover up her pointed ears.

"I am ready, where are we off to?"

"Rosegarden. I don't care what my brother says we have to try."

FIRE HARBOR

King Abhay's party crept closer to Fire Harbor. They had been off the main road all day which made the wagons slower. The sun was setting on the Bloody Sea and the sky was pink and purple when they finally reached the gates of the city. The big iron gates to the city were still opened and guards cried down from atop the wall. Xolan was on the King's right riding his black stallion. Prince Akash and Prince Akhil rode on the Kings left. The Queen's curtained wagon was right behind them, and around the party were all the guards. The guards in the front of the party rode ahead to clear the road for the King. Xolan kept his eyes open and tried to channel all his powers to see if they faced a threat, the city had an uneasy fill about it. The party went down the main road of the city towards Lord Rajesh's castle. The villagers all looked on with worried eyes. The city had grown quiet with the King's arrival. No cheers and cries of joy, no welcoming celebration, nothing. The only sound Xolan heard was a child crying, that soon grew quiet as the party passed by.

Xolan had been to many cities and had never entered one so quiet it gave him an uneasy feeling as he sat high atop his stallion. The wagon's wheels creaked as the four horses pulled it forward. Xolan looked back at the wagon and saw the Princess looking out the curtain that had been pulled back. It was a gloomy autumn evening with the sky turning darker and the clouds hiding the moon that should have appeared. A drizzle of rain started when the party was half way to the castle, and the Princes' complained about it loudly. Xolan looked around at the villagers peering out their windows with cold eyes. They were not happy to see the King that much was obvious. The King felt their anger also, Xolan could feel him getting tense.

Finally after what seemed like a lifetime the party reached the wall that surrounded the castle of the high lord. The wall was made of yellow sandstone that appeared almost brown at this hour. The gates were made of wood and iron and had five guards standing outside them and at the least ten up top on the wall above.

Xolan yelled, "Open the gates for your King."

And one of the guards on the ground nodded up at the men on the wall. Soon the gate began to creek open with screaming rusty hinges. Inside the castle walls were more guards standing in the courtyard and on the steeps to the castle. They all watched as the King's party came slowly in the gates. As soon as the last horse had entered the gates were closed quickly, and bared with a large log.

Xolan was the first to dismount his horse. He looked around at the worried guards and could sense that something was wrong. He wanted to get the royal family inside fast. He escorted the King quickly inside the castle then came back to retrieve the children and the Queen.

Lord Rajesh quickly met the party at the door, "Your Grace I was not expecting you for another day, my apologies for not having my guards escort your party through the city." Lord Rajesh said breathless from running to meet them.

"I have enough guards to escort me. How is it going? The villagers did not seem happy to see their King."

"There have been riots all over the city, the people want their Lord and Lady back. Most of Fire Harbor's guard left shortly after I arrived. The only guards I have are the ones I brought with me and a couple old men that aren't worth a copper."

The King looked troubled by the news, "Might we get my family to their rooms and then discuss this matter further?"

"Of course, Your Grace, I will have my servants show the Queen and the children to their quarters," Lord Rajesh answered and waved a servant girl over and gave her the instructions.

Once the Queen and children were gone, Lord Rajesh escorted Xolan and the King towards the Great Hall. Lord Hugart's old castle was a quarter of the size as the castle at Dragons End. The halls were bare with nothing showing but the yellow stone that the castle was made of. The floor of the castle was a red marble that swirled down the hall. Once in the Great Hall there were five long tables and two big chairs for the High Lord and Lady. The walls were bare in here also the only thing showing was black smoke and ash marks above the hearth. All the candles in the chandeliers had been lit with made the room seem emptier. Lord Rajesh took them to the nearest table and asked them to have a seat. He and Lord Rajesh waited for the King to take a seat before himself and Lord Rajesh took theirs.

"Tell me of your troubles," the King said to Lord Rajesh.

"Where do I begin? I can barely leave the castle gates with out being attacked. Three buildings by the harbor have been burnt down due to the riots. The boys are depressed, and weep for their mother and father and won't speak to me. My guards are trying to keep the peace, but there are more commons than guards and I have already lost five men to the riots. I do not wish to trouble you, Your Grace, but I don't know how much longer I can hold the city," Lord Rajesh confessed.

The King thought on what Lord Rajesh had said Xolan sat quietly as to not disturb his thoughts. The King did not need any more troubles and Xolan feared for the King.

After a long silence the King finally spoke, "The commons want a Hugart to be Lady I will give them one. Lord Rajesh you are not married and need a wife, you shall marry the oldest Hugart daughter Rashmi."

"Your Grace, she is but a child," was Lord Rajesh's response.

"Her youth is a good thing, men want a young wife that can give them many children. If you do not want to bed her right away you do not have to, I will not order what goes on in the marriage bed, but I am ordering you to wed the girl. The commons will behave with her as their Lady," the King said.

"Yes, Your Grace. What about the boys?" Lord Rajesh responded.

"I will take them back with me and they will learn respect and how to be a ward and squire and be grateful for it," the King said in an angry voice. "I will stay here awhile so my guards can help your guards get everything under control, your dungeons might be full by the time they are finished. Send a falcon instructing my brother to send the oldest Hugart girl here and you will be married to her, and there will be peace before I leave," the King ordered.

"Yes Your Grace, I will have the bird sent right away," Lord Rajesh answered.

"Good, now I am weary from the travel. Might you excuse me so I might get some rest?" the King said.

"Yes, Your Grace. I will show you and Xolan to your rooms personally," and with that Lord Rajesh stood and escorted them out of the hall.

Lord Rajesh Smeltzer led the King and Xolan down the dark hallway to the stairway on the west side of the castle. Every fifth steep a torch was lit to light the way up the narrow yellow stairs.

"Lord Rajesh I have noticed there is nothing on your walls," Xolan said as he followed up the stairs.

"Yes, I have not had time to hang any banners or sigils of the house. The walls were full of the flame of the Hugart house, and I had them removed when I arrived," Lord Rajesh answered.

"I see. You must be glad to be so close to your brother in Bloodstone though?" Xolan said.

"I suppose. I have been living at Dragons End for so long I guess it will just take me awhile to get use to the place," Rajesh answered back, "Ah, here we are," he said and turned to the right on the forth floor. Lord Rajesh showed the King to where the Queen was staying then asked Xolan to follow him.

"I know you like to be close to the King so I have had the servants set up your room on the same floor," Rajesh said to the wizard.

"My thanks for that," he answered.

They passed the stairs again and walked to the far end of the hall. Lord Rajesh stopped at the last door and opened it wide for Xolan. He entered and looked around the room, it was very spacious. A big canopy feathered bed was in the middle of the room, with a nice size table to its right. There was a balcony that looked out onto the bay. Xolan walked out onto the balcony and looked out. The night had turned the water black and the clouds in the sky made it hard to see anything else of the scenery.

"This will do just fine, my thanks again Lord Rajesh," he said.

Lord Rajesh bowed his head and closed the door behind him. Xolan was weary from the trip. Before long he stripped off his robes and climbed into bed.

Xolan woke before dawn and was sitting on the balcony when the servants entered. "Lord Rajesh has a great feast to break your fast, ready in the dinning hall m'lord," the servant girl with dark hair and eyes said to him.

"I will be down shortly," he said back to her looking towards the bay.

"Yes m'lord," she said and rushed out of the room.

It was a nice autumn day with just a hint of coolness in the breeze. The Fire Bay was a sapphire blue with white tipped waves crashing against the shore. The waves were always bigger in the autumn and posed a threat to the ships. Each ship at the harbor swayed with the motion of the waves coming up, and down in time. Xolan got up slowly from the chair he was sitting in and went back into his bedchamber to dress.

When Xolan entered the dinning hall he saw Lord Rajesh sitting at the table with the Hugart boys toward the end. Xolan walked over to great them. The boys looked terrible. Dark purple circles under their eyes, hair and clothes a mess and when he got close enough to them they smelt like a barn animal.

"When was the last time you two bathed?" he asked one of the boys.

The boy looked up at him with empty eyes, but said not a word.

"Good luck getting them to talk to you Xolan, they have only said about half a dozen words to me," Lord Rajesh said.

"At Dragons End they will learn respect that I promise," Xolan said back then gave the boys one last look.

"I trust you slept well and the servants were good to you," Lord Rajesh said to the wizard.

"I slept great. It was nice to sleep in a feathered bed again," Xolan said and clasped Lord Rajesh on the forearm before taking a seat next to him.

Shortly after Xolan had taken his seat the Royal Family entered the hall. Lord Rajesh, Xolan and the boys rose from their seats in respect. The King was the first to enter with the beautiful Queen on his arm, the children followed their parents like little ducklings.

"Good morrow Your Grace, I trust you slept well," Xolan greeted the King.

"I did. It is nice to be in the South again," the King said and helped his wife to her seat, then took his.

After the royals were seated everyone else sat back down and the feast began. The servants had it right, Lord Rajesh had a great feast prepared to break their fast. Eggs fried with fire peppers, bacon, fish, and ham. Fresh bread and butter were placed on the table. Fruits of all kinds with a platter of cheese. And pastries powdered with sugar. By the time they were done Xolan was stuffed full.

"I received a falcon in reply to the one I sent to Dragons End this morning, Your Grace. Your brother the Prince said he would send the Hugart girl at first light," Lord Rajesh informed the King.

"Send her where?" one of the boys said in a whisper.

The King looked over at the boy that had spoken and said, "Your sister Rashmi will be coming here to Fire Harbor to wed Lord Rajesh."

"Wed?" the boy looked confused.

"Yes, wed," Xolan shot back at the boy.

The boy looked down at the table quickly and did not speak again.

"That is good news Rajesh. With luck she will be here by nightfall," the King said.

"May haps, if not then on the morrow, Your Grace," Lord Rajesh replied.

"I am glad you are finally getting married Rajesh. The girl is young and should give you many sons," Queen Kala said to her brother.

Lord Rajesh gave a nod of agreement but no reply. The Hugart boy that had spoke up glared at Lord Rajesh with hatred in his eyes. Lord Rajesh pretended not to notice.

"Xolan once Rashmi arrives I would like you to help Queen Kala prepare her for the wedding," the King said to him.

"That is not a mans job, I can handle getting a bride ready for her wedding," the Queen said back before Xolan could answer.

"I am sure you can I have no doubts in you, but I would still like Xolan to help," the King said back to his wife.

She did not seem pleased, but did not argue the matter further.

The rest of the day Lord Rajesh showed the King and Xolan around the castle and within the walls. They discussed the wedding and the Hugart boys. The King went over what he expected to get out of this marriage. Xolan followed behind quietly and listened, only speaking when spoken to first.

The autumn days were getting shorter, it was an hour past sunset and the King, Lord Rajesh and himself were sitting in the Great Hall enjoying some summer wine. One of the King's guards entered the hall and approached the King, "Your Grace, the girl has arrived," the knight said with a bow.

"Very good, Xolan will you go meet our guest and show her to the room Lord Rajesh has had ready for her?" the King turned to him and asked.

"Yes, Your Grace," Xolan answered and placed the chalice of wine on the table and followed the knight to the courtyard.

The girl was atop a grey filly, with a black woolen cloak that swallowed her up. Her face was hidden by the hood. Xolan walked over to the filly and the figure hidden under the cloak, "Welcome home my lady. I trust your trip went well?" he said when he reached her.

She looked down at him and for the first time he saw her dark brown eyes, "Yes my lord the trip was well, my people were glad to see me enter the city," she said with a forced smile.

Even though she was so young she was very pretty, copper skin that looked darker without the sun. She had an oblong face with high cheek bones and a little round nose. Xolan reached up to her to help her off her horse, she took his shoulders and he lifted her down with ease. Once on the ground she was at the least a foot and a half shorter than he was, he was sure she would grow taller in time.

"My lady, Lord Rajesh has had your old room set up for your arrival. Will you come with me please?" he said to her in a gentle voice.

She had not seemed to loose her manners as her brothers had. "Yes my lord, it would be nice to see my room again," she said and followed him up the stairs into the castle.

She kept close behind him walking fast to keep up, almost like she was afraid to be alone.

"Have they been good to you and your sisters at Dragons End?" he asked her.

"Yes everyone has been very kind. I was sad when they informed me that my sisters could not come back with me. My lord, they did not inform me on why the King has summoned me back here, could you be so kind as to inform me?"

"On the morrow I will answer any questions you have, tonight you need your rest. I am sure your brothers will be happy to see you."

"Yes, I will be happy to see them as well," she said.

Once Xolan was sure the Hugart girl was safe in her room he placed a guard out side her door and retired to his own room.

The next morning he awoke to the castle in a frenzy trying to prepare for the wedding. Xolan found the King quick enough, talking to Lord Rajesh in the Great Hall.

"Ah Xolan I was wondering when you would find me. How was Rashmi when she arrived last night?" The King greeted him.

"The girl was very polite unlike her brothers. She had not been informed of the wedding though," Xolan replied.

"Nor will she be, until it is time for her to be wed," the King said with a smile, "I will not have her doing anything stupid."

Xolan gave a nod, he did not like not letting the girl know what was to become of her, but did not dare argue with the King. With the eggs missing and the wedding and Fire Harbor the King was getting more on edge with each passing day.

"Xolan you will find my wife in the girl's chambers getting her ready, would you be so kind as to assist her and make sure the girl is in this room by midday," the King asked of him.

"Yes, Your Grace," Xolan said with a bow and left the hall and headed toward the room he had left Rashmi in the night before.

When he entered the room was full of servants rushing around to get the Queen anything that she asked for. Rashmi stood in the corner of the room next to the Queen in a beautiful cream silk gown with baby pearls sewn into the bodice. The girls black hair was left down and reached the small of her back in waves. The Queen was talking gently to the girl and every now and then the girl would nod.

"Xolan, my husband sent you I trust?" the Queen asked when she spotted him.

"Yes, Your Grace. How may I help?" he asked, Xolan had no idea how to get a girl ready for her wedding, but he would try to do what ever his Queen asked.

"Oh nothing I still think it is silly that my husband insist on you being here, no offense," the Queen responded.

"None taken I do not know enough of girls and women to be of any help. But if you do require anything I will do my best to oblige," he replied.

The Queen gave a nod then turned back to Rashmi and continued lacing up her gown.

Xolan tried to stay out of the way so he sat in a cushioned chair that was in the corner of the room. The girl still seemed to be unaware of why she was brought here, and for a moment Xolan almost had pity for her.

The sun was almost in the middle of the blue sky above, "Forgive me Your Grace, but it is almost time," Xolan said to the Queen.

She looked at him and said, "So it is, I must go and find my husband. Xolan will you be so kind as to escort Rashmi to the Great Hall?"

"Yes, Your Grace," he said as he bowed his head in respect.

The Queen gathered the bottom of her gown and walked quickly from the room. The girl stood there looking at her reflection in the looking glass without notice of the Queen's departure.

"My lady, we must head to the Great Hall," Xolan said to the girl when it was time to go.

For the first time since he had entered the room Rashmi looked into his eyes. "What is happing in the Great Hall that I must attend my lord?" she asked in a whisper.

"A surprise just for you," he told her.

She gave a slight nod and took his arm and let him escort her out of the room and down the yellow stoned hall. The girl did not make one sound on the way until they reached the door.

"My lord what am I to do?" she asked in the whispered voice.

"Your duty, do not bring more shame to your family. Do whatever is required," Xolan told her.

For the first time since she arrived the girl let her fear show, her brow wrinkled and her eyes starting to tear.

"None of that now, you don't want everyone to see you sad. You must be strong like your mother and keep all emotions hid," he said to her.

She gave a nod and wiped her eyes with the back of her hand, and then the doors opened.

Lord Rajesh stood at the head of the hall with the priest to his left, the King and Queen stood under the dais, and everyone else in the castle including the servants and guards were seated. It hit her, the reason why she was brought back to this castle. She gave his arm a hard squeeze digging her nails into his bare skin, and shot him a pleading look.

"I am sorry my dear, remember your duty," he whispered in her ear and started walking her down toward Lord Rajesh.

Xolan handed the girl over, and took an empty seat in the front row. He glanced around the room and saw the Hugart boys seated on the opposite side of the hall with guards on either side of them, no doubt the King had threatened them to behave. Rashmi did all that was required of her, and hid her emotions until the ceremony was at an end. Even then she cried silently as to not draw attention to her displeasure. When the priest was finished the couple walked down the hall and exited the room with cheers. The servants and guards went back to what ever duties they had and the royal party and the Hugart boys went to the dinning hall for the celebration feast.

Xolan was the last to enter the hall and all had already been seated. He took a seat next to Lord Rajesh and the feast began. The Hugart boys were crying, and would not touch any of the food that was placed in front of them. Before long the King ordered the guards to take the boys back to their room. Rashmi did eat she seemed like a starved child the way she devoured everything that was on her plate. Xolan sat quietly watching her. There were musicians playing harps and flutes with singers standing behind them. The feast ended up being seven courses and after the sweets had been cleared Lord Rajesh stood and asked his new bride to dance. The girl took his hand and let him lead her on the dance floor. She went along with her new husbands lead and matched him step for step. Then the King and Queen joined in and before long, the royal children were dancing as well.

The feast and dancing went on for two hours before the celebration was over. The King instructed Xolan to escort Rashmi back to her room while he and Lord Rajesh discussed other business that needed taken care of. Xolan did as he was asked and waited in the room with the girl until it was time for supper. Rashmi was quiet while they waited. She sat on the bench at her window and stared out with out a word. Xolan thought the girl had been through enough so he did not try to force her into conversation.

Supper was more interesting though.

"Xolan, I would like to inform you that you are no longer a babysitter," the King said to him as the first course arrived.

"That is good to know, Your Grace," he replied, he was relieved the girl was making him depressed. "Your Grace, if I may ask when are we heading back to Dragons End?"

"Soon, I am going to address the commons tomorrow and inform them on the marriage, and then as soon as I am sure they will not rebel we can head home," the King informed him.

Xolan was ready to go back, he had been away to long and wanted to be in familiar surroundings.

The feast went on with the servant girls in their brown linen dresses serving course after course and clearing the empty plates. About the third course, the chandeliers were lowered and lit then raised high to bring a glow upon the hall. The music was playing in the background and the children were laughing. The King and Queen whispered quietly to one another. And Lord Rajesh and his new bride sat awkwardly, and ate whatever was placed in front of them. Overall it was a successful day. Xolan was sure that one of the Hugarts would do something stupid that he would have to stop but they hadn't. He sat eating some peppered cheese and listening to the harp in the background when the guard entered the room and approached the King.

"What!" the King's voice echoed off the stone walls, "How?" he asked the guard even louder than before.

"I don't know, Your Grace," the guard replied, he was wearing the red gold armor of the Kings Guard and had a worried look on his wrinkled face.

"Well why are you standing here? Go find them!" the King yelled at the guard.

The guards eyes grew large and his face turned pail, he turned and ran out of the hall.

"Xolan, Lord Rajesh come with me," was all the King said as he stood and started to walk out of the hall.

Xolan jumped to his feet quickly and left his food half eaten on his plate. Lord Rajesh did the same and both men rushed to follow the King. Xolan was having a more difficult time keeping up. Lord Rajesh and the King were a lot younger than he was and he was almost running and still falling behind. The King was heading to the Hugart boys room Xolan realized about halfway up the stairs. He lost sight of Lord Rajesh and the King before he reached the third floor, so relied on his memory to take him the rest of the way.

When Xolan reached the boys room the King was standing by the bed yelling at one of the guards. Xolan looked around and it did not take him long to realize the boys had escaped. A hemp rope was tied to the wardrobe in the corner of the room, and lead out of the window. The boys must have climbed out. Xolan went over to the rope and touched it and tried to concentrate but the King's yelling was making it difficult.

"Beg pardons, Your Grace but I cannot concentrate with all the yelling," Xolan said.

The King looked at him sharply but quieted down. Xolan touched the rope again and closed his eyes.

He was in the boy's body the older one, tying the rope to the wardrobe and yelling at the younger one to hurry up. Then he was climbing carefully trying to put his toes in the creases of the stone. He had reached the ground he took his brother's hand and ran fast. He stopped in front of the stable, told his brother to stay there and snuck inside as the guard turned his back. He got down on his knees and crawled to the first stall. A brown filly was in it, the boy grabbed the saddle from the wall and secured it on the horse. Then led the horse out of the stable by the reins.

He found his brother were he left him. Told him to take his arm and helped him up so he was sitting behind him. The younger boy wrapped his arms around his waist and the horse was kicked into motion. They went to the back gate, he dismounted, carefully worked the lock and opened the gate with screaming hinges. He got back on the horse and his brother wrapped his arms around him once more. They were free. Out of the castle walls. Ridding down the pebble street, the horse's feet ringing off the pavement. They rode out of the city and turned the horse southeast.

Xolan came back, and opened his eyes. He was lying on the floor, holding the rope for dear life. Xolan was always out of it for awhile after his visions and it took him a minute to realize that he was back in his own skin. He blinked his eyes and saw the King standing over him with a worried look on his face.

"Xolan?" the King said in a hushed voice.

"Yes, the boys are heading for the swamps, southeast. They stole a horse and went out the back gate," he replied.

The King looked at him with that worried look again then turned and said to the guard, "Ride them down, bring them back."

The guard ran out of the room, his boots echoing of the floor and growing fainter with every step.

WEST WATCH

Tansy stood behind her pinning her golden curls from her face. Aidan was taking her to the West Woods today with the pair of hunting falcons they had received as a wedding gift. She had chosen to wear a simple blue wool gown so she would be comfortable on her ride. The gown was warm and would shield her from the cool autumn breeze. Once Tansy was finished, Maggie stood looking at her reflection in the looking glass, marriage seemed to of made her look older. She looked more mature, more womanly and less child.

Aidan slipped in unnoticed and startled her when he wrapped his arms around her waist, "Are you about ready love?"

"Yes, Tansy just finished my hair," she said and then turned around and kissed him.

Marriage wasn't as bad as she had feared, the first night was awkward but each day after she found herself more comfortable with her new husband. The bedding part was not so bad either, it didn't last long, and she was finding it more enjoyable every night. Aidan insisted on being together every night until she was with child, he intended to have a son within the year. So every night Maggie climbed into bed naked and waited on her husband. Aidan was always very gentle with her and kind to her afterwards. And every morning she awoke in his arms, that was her favorite part.

She and Aidan broke their fast, then headed off toward the stables. This was the first time she had left the castle since the wedding and she was looking forward to seeing more of her kingdom.

Aidan walked into the stable, "Wait here I have a present for you," he said to her at the door.

Maggie did as she was told and waited, wondering what present he would bring. She watched as he went to the last stall on the left and closed the door behind him. A few minutes latter he emerged with a tan mare. The mare's body was the color of sand and her mane was a chestnut brown.

"She is yours now," he said to her and handed her the reins.

"She is beautiful Aidan, my thanks," she replied as she took the reins from him.

"A beautiful mare for a beautiful princess," he said and bent down and kissed her gently on the lips.

She returned the kiss and then looked at the mare again.

"What will you name her?"

"Honey," was all that Maggie said.

She and Aidan led their horses out of the stable and mounted.

"Try her out, she is very obedient," Aidan said to her once she was in her saddle.

Maggie gave Honey a gentle kick and the mare went into motion. Aidan was not wrong. With just a gentle pull of the reins the horse obeyed. She turned right and left went into a gallop then slowed into a trot. Maggie found it very easy handling this horse and she was glad.

"She does great," Maggie said laughing as the horse followed every command.

Once she and Aidan were joined by Ser Asher, Rory, and about twenty other knights who Maggie did not know, they set off. Out the north gate they went, they came out on the shores of the sea. The brown sand spraying with the horses steps. Maggie looked out to the sea, the water looked dark grey due to the lack of sun light. Autumn had made the sea wild with waves. As they galloped north, the tide came in and kissed at the horse's hooves as they rode. Maggie hoped for sunlight, it was gloomy and the sun would bring out more colors. The world around her seemed shades of blues and grays.

She caught a glimpse of the forest coming closer to her, and the colors arrived. Shades of orange, red, yellow and brown topped the trees and the ground. They reached the edge of the forest and the woods were so thick she could not see but twenty feet in. Lining the forest were maple and dogwood trees, some still with a touch of green left to the leaves. Aidan was at the head of the party and she stopped her mare to his right. Behind them were Ser Asher and Rory, then the other knights. Aidan waited for everyone to catch up before entering the forest.

Once within the sky above them was hidden by branches and different colored leaves. Squirrels and birds above, and little rodents hidden below. A small path had been trampled flat that was big enough for only one horse so the party formed a long line and rode on. They veered off the road and weaved between trees and bushes alike. Maggie could no longer see the ocean, and the only sign that it was close was the faint sound of the waves clashing upon the shore. Aidan was in front of her now leading the way through the thick woods. They passed ironwood trees and oak, hickory and cedar, all with colorful leaves. Belladonna was patched here and there amongst the tree trunks with deadly bright red berries. They passed other bushes and shrubbery that Maggie had never seen before and did not know the names of.

About thirty minutes into the forest they came across a huge lake. Aidan rode his horse right up to the shore and dismounted, "We should water the horses. There will be no more water until we reach The Fork," he said loudly to the party of knights.

He walked over to Maggie and lifted her off her mare with ease. Ser Asher took Honey and led her and his stallion to the lake, while Aidan took her hand and started walking away from where the knights were.

"What do you think so far? Do you have thick forest like this in the East?" he asked. He was very curious about the East, always asking if it was the same.

"The Lion Woods is small and by the Great Lake, but Elf Forest I am told is massive and very thick. I have never been there though, so could not say from experience. That's where the Elf's live you know. They have been there thousands of years before the Kingdoms were Kingdoms," she replied.

"Yes, I have heard of the Elves. Did you know that the little people live in these woods? They say that they are related to Elves. But they live as we do, they have a village on the main road leading to Forest End. They look like people too, just shorter and with pointed ears, they're almost child like," he said.

"Do the little people have powers like the elves do?" Maggie asked.

"Some have powers but not all, and there not like the elves powers. They can't control nature. If anything, they can see the future and that's about it," Aidan replied.

Maggie was interested, she wanted to meet the little people and see for herself what they were like. "Are they kind towards men?"

"Yes, they are a very peaceful people. They mostly tend to themselves but if a man enters their village they are very hospitable," Aidan replied.

"I would like to see them one day, if that would be alright with you," she said back.

"Sure, I will take you there one day. But not today I have other things to show you," Aidan said.

They walked back to where the rest of the party was by the big lake. "What is the name of this lake?" she asked, wanting to get to know her country as much as possible.

"This is Autumn Lake," Aidan said.

Every one of the four kingdoms had a lake named after a season. The North had the Lake of Winter, the East had the Lake of Spring, the South had Summer Lake and the West had Autumn Lake. Maggie knew that she just didn't know that this lake was the one. The names were based mostly by how the climate was most of the year. Since the North was so far north they could have snow on the ground all year round, so it was more like winter. The East and West being in the middle had mild climates, it was hotter in the summer and they did have snow in the winter but most of the year it was a perfect climate. And the South was always hot, even in the winter months when the rest of the Kingdoms had snow the South would be warm.

It was close to midday so Aidan decided that they should go ahead and eat now while they were stopped. Aidan's squire Rory set down a big quilt for her and Aidan to sit on and brought them their food. Maggie took a seat on the quilt directly across from Aidan. Rory brought them fresh baked bread that had been made that morning before they left, some yellow cheese, salted beef, two apples, and a skin of wine. Aidan picked up the loaf of bread, broke it in half and handed the half to Maggie.

"Thank you," Maggie said to him with a smile.

He smiled back and started eating his half of the bread.

"How long will it take to reach the Fork?"

"It will take longer because we are not on the road and have to weave through the woods, but I am guessing it will be at the least three hours. Then we will follow the Fork to the main rode and make our way back to West Watch so we are back for supper," he informed her.

She sat and nibbled on her half of the bread and wished for some butter and honey to put on it. The Fork was one of the famous rivers of the Kingdoms. It was known for it's strong currents and wild rapids. Many a man had died on the Fork. Word was it was more cruel than the sea. Stories told that it was never still, that the gods put the Fork there to remind men of how cruel life could be. Maggie was both excited and scared to see the Fork.

After everyone ate they mounted up and set forth again. They rode around the Autumn Lake heading east. Maple, hickory and sycamore trees lined the lake. They were full of squirrels playing in the branches and collecting whatever food they could find for winter. With Aidan's black stallion Night Terror in the lead the party slowly rode around the lake and back into the woods. Wet dead leaves stuck to the horse's hooves and the mud beneath made a disgusting squishing sound. Maggie was enjoying the scenery and putting her trust in Honey to lead the way.

It was nice to be out of the castle. Back in the East Maggie had rarely left Rosegarden. The West was more rugged than the East with more woods and wild game. The East was mostly flat grass plains with the exception of the one and only hill, Acorn Hill, and Elf Forest that was in the southern part of the kingdom. It was a nice change to get to see the West Woods and Autumn Lake and the Fork.

It was a quiet ride, even the animals in the woods did not make much noise. Before long Maggie was lost in her thoughts. She was thinking about the prophecy that Lennox had given her and Aidan, as a wedding gift. How the first vision was of her with child and Aidan riding off to war. Aidan wanted a child badly, but Maggie did not want the wizard's vision to come true so soon after her marriage. The sooner she was with child the sooner Aidan would leave. She wished the vision would have revealed whom Aidan would go to war with. That was always the problems with prophecies they left out important information that would be nice to know. Not only that, Maggie was not sure she was ready to be a mother just yet. She had been a woman for only a couple months, then a wife for a fortnight. She wanted to get use to being a wife before she had to try to be a mother.

A cool breeze rustled the multicolored leaves and sent a chill through Maggie that brought her back to the West Woods. The forest was getting darker, what little sunlight that was peaking through the clouds was hidden by the trees. She shivered in her saddle wishing that it was still summer and winter was not coming.

Ser Asher must have seen her shiver because he rode up next to her and said, "Are you cold my princess? You can have my cloak if you wish."

"I would be very grateful for it," she replied and pulled her horse to a stop.

Ser Asher dismounted and unfastened the green cloak with the acorns and placed it around her shoulders. The cloak was already warm from him wearing it and instantly Maggie felt the chill melt away.

"My thanks, Ser."

"It's an honor to help you Princess," he replied and mounted back up on his stallion.

The party reached The Fork about three hours after they left the lake. The river was wild with white rapids swirling around the jagged rocks that stuck out from the water. The current was moving fast and moving leaves that had fallen into it, faster than a horse could run. Aidan walked over to her and easily lifted her from Honey. Ser Asher's cloak was so long on her that it dragged on the ground and swept up the fallen leafs as she walked towards the river.

"The autumn weather has made The Fork wilder than usual," Aidan said to her.

Maggie stood at the edge of the river and looked across. The side they were on was covered thickly with trees, but the other side was clear with tall grass only.

"Eagle Nest is on the other side, about a league from The Fork," Aidan told her.

Maggie could see why it was called The Fork, from where they stood the river forked off and started again across the way.

"Come," Aidan said and took her hand.

The bank of the river was all rock no sand to it at all. Dark grey and white and black rocks, some the size of a wagon, some bigger yet. Maggie looked at the green-blue river with its white currents. There had to be at the least one hundred rocks sticking out from the water. Some stuck out like tiny towers on a castle and some rocks she could only see the tops of.

"The rocks are what make the rapids," Aidan said, he must have seen her staring at all the grey boulders in the river.

Some rocks were worn smooth and some had pointed jagged peaks to them. She had never seen anything like it before in her life, even the sea did not seem as wild as this river. There was not a flat or clam part to the river that she could see. It flowed up then dropped, and twirled, and dropped again. Just looking at it made her stomach flutter. Where the river was most active the waves seemed white, then turned to a green-blue, then white again.

Aidan stopped at a huge rock that was the size of their bed chamber, it started at the bank then reached out into the wild water. The water crashed up against it ferociously spraying water high in the air. Some how the gloomy grey sky made the river seem more intense.

"They call this rock the River Dragon," Aidan told her.

Maggie turned her head and looked at the shape of the rock and tried to ignore the river swirling around it. If she looked really hard she could see how the rock did resemble a dragon. That made it even more frightening she realized.

Maggie looked around her and realized that she and Aidan were alone. The rest of the party must have stayed behind instead of following them. The only other one that had never seen The Fork before was Ser Asher so it was nothing new to the rest of the men.

"We can walk out on the rock and get a better view of the river," Aidan said to her with a smile.

Maggie did not want to walk out on the rock. But she also did not want to disappoint Aidan, so she gave a light nod and Aidan's smile grew bigger as he took her hand.

They walked over to the River Dragon hand in hand, the dark grey rock had slick green moss growing on one side of it. Maggie tried to avoid placing her foot where the moss was. The rock had natural made uneven steps leading up it and Aidan signaled for Maggie to go first. Still holding on tight to Aidan's hand she slowly climbed up the Dragon. Aidan placed his hand on the small of her back to steady her as she climbed. Each step was different, some big enough for both of them to stand on, some were barley big enough for half of her foot. She climbed, the closer she got to the top of the rock the more her stomach knotted up and fluttered.

Once both her and Aidan were atop the Dragon, Aidan took the lead. He walked slowly and carefully out toward the river. Maggie followed cautiously behind, looking down at her steps. She stopped and looked up to see where she was standing. To her left was to safe dark rock shore, but to her right was the green-blue river with all its furry. The waves were white where the water was more active. The base of the rock was surrounded by the white water that looked almost cloud like. The water was uneven, high in some spots and low in others, waves going all directions crashing up against the Dragon.

Maggie was both amazed and frightened by the sight. She found it hard to breathe as she watched the wild water moving violently down stream. Frightened, she looked around to find Aidan for comfort. He was standing toward the edge of the rock, at the least four feet in front of her looking out across the river. He looked back at her and gave her a comforting smile, then waved for her to come over to him. Maggie didn't want to go any farther and she was finding it hard to command her legs to take another step. She edged her way, inch by inch, toward Aidan.

Without warning a huge wave crashed up against the rock. Ice cold water sprayed up into the air and rained on Maggie. The shock from the cold and the water startled her, and she stepped back. Her foot landed right on a patch of wet slimy moss and she slipped. Trying to catch herself she turned and tried to grab the rock. Her hand smashed down on the hard stone and she scratched and clawed to attempt to get hold of anything. Her nails on her right hand bent back and a sudden pain shot through her hand. That did not stop her, she fell.

For half a second she was in the air, enough time to fill her lungs with air. She sucked in a breath quickly and was pulled into the waves. The second she hit the ice cold water it felt like she was being stabbed with a thousand knives, and out of instinct she screamed under the water. Her lungs were empty and she panicked. She kicked and tried to swim up, but she did not know which way was up. The strong water was swirling her around like a doll. It pulled her back and forth with unimaginable strength. It was crushing her, but she would not give up she kept kicking.

Then Ser Asher's cloak that he had lent her wrapped around her like a snake trying to squeeze the life out of its victim. She could not move her arms or legs to try and swim to the surface. Her chest was ablaze from the lack of air, and her head started pounding. The cold water numbing her and she was useless against it. She squirmed, and turned, and tried to fight the water, but she was no match against it. She looked around trying to find any sign of which way the surface was. All she saw was light green water swirling around her.

She didn't want to die like this, not like this, not so young, she had not even lived her life yet. She fought again to get loose from the cloak but it was no use. She was starting to get dazed from the loss of air and her head was pounding loudly while her lungs were burning in her chest. She looked up just in time to see the rock, before she crashed head on into it with unimaginable force.

ICESTORM

Ser Florian Gaddy was glad to be back in the North. He had barley seen the Queen during the wedding, lowborn knights were not permitted in the halls with the royals and lords. So he had to leave his love and Queen in Casmas' care and be in the tents outside the castle. The only time he was permitted in the castle was at night to guard the Queen's chambers. But they didn't risk anything and barley spoke a word to each other. The capitol rejoiced with their return, and was filled with new faces from the villagers that had been brought in to the safety of Icestorm's high walls. The Queen rode the entire way in her wagon that was pulled by six northern unicorns and the five hundred knights rode on horse back. Ser Florian rode next to the wagon the entire time, and every so often the Queen would lift her curtain just enough to give him a wink before closing the curtain again.

They had been back for one week, and he still had not had a chance to be alone with the Queen for long. It was killing him, he yearned to hold her in his arms, and talk to her from his heart instead of pretending he had no feelings for her. But she had been very busy tending to matters that happened in her absence. So Florian waited and knew that soon he would have his Queen in his arms again.

He caught himself starring at her while she sat in her silver throne with their son in her arms. The babe had doubled in size since they had been gone and Ana cried the first time she saw him. The council had met to discuss the villagers again and go over any matters that she had missed. Ser Florian wasn't paying much attention to what was being said, he was to busy day dreaming about having his Queen. Until Lord Cormac spoke up and brought Florian back to reality.

"All council members have returned with the exception of Ser Fintan. He was charged with transporting the villagers to North Star and has not returned. Would you like me to send a bird to Lord Landrum inquiring about Ser Fintan?" Lord Cormac asked the Queen.

"Yes, I think that would be wise. If Ser Fintan had already left North Star he might be in trouble some where and need our assistance," Ana replied. "Were the Lord's accepting of the villagers and understanding?" she asked her council.

The council all gave a nod.

"Lord Cormac have you heard any more problems with the attacks?" she asked her uncle.

"No, Your Grace. Hopefully we will hear no more reports with all the villagers safe behind city walls," Lord Cormac answered.

"And what about the boys from each family? How many have we gained here at Icestorm?"

"We gained seventy five boys between the ages of thirteen and twenty," Ser Brain Mathis informed her.

"Very well, is there any other matters that require my attention today?"

The council looked at each other and shook their heads.

"Well then, if you would excuse me I have other matters to see to," Ana said and with that she stood from her throne and left the hall through the back door with Florian close behind her.

Once they were away from listening ears Ana got closer to Florian and whispered, "I think we might actually be alone tonight. Baby Conell's chambers are finally finished and I have had a bed put in the room for Gloria. I also told Ser Ronan that the baby would be alright with you right next door. He wasn't happy about it but he didn't argue with me."

Gloria was the wet nurse that Ana had chosen for the babe. The trip West had made all of Ana's milk dry up so the baby depended completely on the wet nurse for feedings. The babe's chambers were being set up while they were away and were awaiting Ana's approval. His room was right next door to his and Ana's chambers, until he was older.

Since they had been back, Ser Ronan had insisted on staying in Mario's chambers which was right across the hall from the babe's room. So Florian and Ana would not risk anything with Finn's brother being so close. Florian was grateful to hear that he would finally be alone with Ana. They had not been together since the babe was born.

They climbed the steps of the Queen's tower together heading toward their chambers. When they reached the top of the stairs he was shocked to see Lord Cormac had beaten them there.

"Your Grace, might I have a word?" he said as soon as he caught sight of them.

"Of course uncle let me give Conell to Gloria and I will meet you in my chambers. Ser Florian would you be so kind as to escort my uncle to my room?"

"Yes, Your Grace," Florian replied and opened to door to his chamber for Lord Cormac.

Within moments Ana returned. "Uncle what is it that you need to speak to me about?" she asked.

"Ronan said you told him he was to return to his chambers, do you think that wise? The babe should be guarded," Lord Cormac said.

"This floor is full enough, plus Mario's chambers are small and not appropriate for Ronan. He has a very nice chamber that he doesn't use and Mario needs his chamber back. With Conell's chamber now and Gloria, and my maids there is not room enough. The babe will be fine. We have Ser Florian remember," she said to her uncle with annoyance in her voice.

"But one guard for the both of you?" Lord Cormac protested.

"I have many guards. Two hundred at the wall of the castle, twenty at the front doors, and one hundred more within the castle. Then I have two guards at the bottom of the stairs leading up to my chambers. Trust me uncle, I am well guarded you need not worry. Now if you would excuse me I am very tired. I have been going nonstop since I got back and would very much like to rest," she said and before Lord Cormac could say anything else she led him out the door.

As soon as the door was shut Ana slid the lock in place, turned towards him and rolled her eyes. "I have had about enough of everyone telling me how to raise my son. He thinks there is so much danger within the castle, but you wouldn't let anything happen to us would you?" she smiled at him and looked deep into his eyes.

"No, Your Grace," he said to her and took her in his arms.

He bent down and gently kissed her, she reached up and grabbed his hair on the back of his head and pulled him closer to her. And for the moment they were lost with each other. The castle, the servants, her uncle all the worries disappeared as they kissed.

She started pulling him toward her room, "Wait Ana we can't do this now, not with the castle awake," he whispered in her ear.

"Bugger the castle and everyone else. I am your Queen and I order you to make love to me now," she said back to him and pulled him by the arm into her room.

She closed her door and locked that one as well. Then she reached up and put both of her hands on his chest and pushed him back towards her massive feather bed. He sat down, he could not deny that he wanted her just as much. She bent down and kissed him again more intense this time, twirling her tongue around his as she unlaced the top of his tunic. She stopped kissing him just long enough to pull the tunic over his head.

She ran her fingers through his course brown hair on his chest and circled his nipples with her finger. She ran her hands down his stomach dragging her nails on his skin. Then started unlacing his breeches. She had already excited him and his stiff member was the proof. She gave him a squeeze and he rolled her over so she was on the bed too. Propped up on his muscular arms he looked down at her big blue eyes. She wrapped her arms around his waist and pulled him closer.

He reached down and found the bottom of her velvet gown. Starting at her ankles he ran his hand up her leg, he gave a gentle squeeze when he reached the back of her knee, then pushed the gown up to her hips. To his surprise she was wearing no small clothes which excited him more. He pushed the gown higher. Light purple lines traced down her belly, were the baby had stretched her skin. He ran his hand down her stomach to the soft light brown hair between her legs. She was already moist with excitement and gave a slight sigh as he slipped a finger inside her.

They kissed intensely as she struggled to remove his breeches. Once they were far enough down she pushed his hand away and wrapped her legs around his back. He pushed inside her, it had been so long and he wanted her so bad, he knew he would not last for long.

They lay breathless on the big feathered pillows. Florian's breeches to his knees and Ana's gown gathered on her stomach. She rolled over and laid her head on his chest.

"Your heart is racing, I do believe I will have to take it easy on you next time," she said in a playful tone.

"It has been so long my love, but I can still keep up," he teased back and kissed her forehead.

"We had better dress, it won't be long before I am needed again," she said and got up from the bed and straightened her gown.

Florian laid there a little longer trying to catch his breath. When he sat up Ana was brushing out her honey hair. He pulled his quilted tunic back over his head, and laced his breeches back up. Then left Ana to finish making herself presentable.

The rest of the day drug on endlessly. Once one matter was taken care of someone else would come to Ana wanting something. Ser Florian was tired from their afternoon lovemaking. As the sun crept across the sky he found himself dragging to follow Ana around the castle. She spoke to every council member about their travels home. Her uncle hounded her again about more guards. Cosmas was sure there was a big storm on the way and they needed to prepare. It was none stop. By the time he and Ana did retire to their chambers they were both fighting to keep their eyes open.

"See, it is a good thing we had a second alone this afternoon," she said as they lay in bed.

He smiled and kissed her on the forehead before drifting off quickly to sleep.

Florian awoke hours before sunrise. He rolled out of the Queen's bed and left her to her dreams. Once inside his chambers he dressed in a grey quilted tunic and slipped the heavy chainmail overtop. He attached his breastplate and fastened his cloak to his shoulders. Then made sure *Ice* was secure at his hip and left to walk the hall.

He peaked inside the babe's chamber. Gloria lay on a cot in the corner wrapped in quilts. He quietly walked inside to get a glimpse of his sleeping son. Conell was dreaming in his bassinet swaddled in furs. The fire in the hearth was low, so he added a couple more logs before leaving. He snuck out of the room trying desperately not to make a sound. As he turned after shutting the door, Cosmas stood right in front of him, his face almost touching his own.

"What are you doing?" Florian said in an irritated whisper.

"I might ask you the same thing Ser," Cosmas replied.

"Beg pardons? I am the Queen's personal knight and guard, charged with protecting her and the King," he said louder this time.

"I was mistaken then, I was told Ser Ronan was the King's guard," Cosmas replied casually.

"When I am not around. What do you want, Ana is not awake as of yet," Florian said hoping to end this nonsense.

"No I didn't think she would be, I didn't come to see Ana this time, I will speak to her later. I came to see you Ser," Cosmas said in the same irritating casual voice.

"Me? About what?" Florian was surprised at that.

"I wanted to warn you Ser. What you and her grace did yesterday was foolish and risky, if her uncle would start to suspect anything, I would hate to think of the fate that would fall upon you," the wizard said with and evil smile.

"I don't know what you are talking about old man, may haps your memory is not what it use to be," he said back to the wizard as calmly as he could.

"My memory is fine, after council meeting yesterday you and the Queen came back here. Dropped the babe off with his nurse, then she spoke with her uncle and shut him out quickly. I remember the door locking and awhile later you and her coming back with a certain glow about you. Tell me, do I remember correct?" the wizard asked.

"After speaking with her uncle the Queen was tired and took a nap. I took the opportunity to catch up on some reading was all," he answered.

"Then why was your door locked as well?" Cosmas shot back quickly.

"I don't need to answer your questions Cosmas I serve the Queen not you, who do you serve?" Florian had enough of this conversation.

"I serve house Mathis Ser, all of house Mathis," the wizard replied.

"And what good would it bring to Ana? These accusations of yours. She is of house Mathis also if I do recall," he said back.

"I wish no harm upon Ana, that is why I am warning you to be more careful and not pull any stunts like you did yesterday," Cosmas replied.

"I have had enough of this wizard, and will talk no more on the matter," Florian said and pushed past the wizard back towards his chambers.

"Just remember Ser, it is treason what you are doing with the Queen. Should anyone find out it will be your life. Ana would be forced to marry again. How do you think she would take that?" Cosmas said and Florian reached his door.

Florian was done with this folly. With no reply to the wizard he entered his chamber and shut the door behind him. What nerve that old man had threatening him. Florian was steaming with anger. The wizard was right though, his relationship with Ana would not be accepted and if known would cost him his life, no matter what Ana did to stop it. But Florian was willing to take the risk. The wizard did not understand, Florian loved Ana more than life and would gladly risk it just to be with her.

Florian was calmed down by the time Ana awoke. He thought it best not to tell her of his encounter with the wizard. She had enough worries trying to run a kingdom and he didn't want to add this to the list. But he couldn't help thinking about what Cosmas had said to him. Did Lord Cormac suspect something? If so, would Cosmas tell the lord what he knew? Florian tried not to think of it and force a smile when Ana emerged from her room.

"Good morrow Ser, I trust you slept well," she said and came over towards him to try to give him a kiss.

He grabbed her by the arms, "We can't be doing that during daylight love, it's too risky." She rolled her eyes at him and gave a playful pout. "Life is more exciting with risks," she played back.

"I am serious Ana, no more during the day," he said a little too harshly.

Her eyes filled with anger and pain, "Fine Ser, I will not force you to touch me if that is not what you want."

He pulled her closer he didn't want to hurt her, "You know I want you every minute of every day, I am just protecting you. What if someone finds out?" this time he did kiss her trying to make her fill better.

"Florian I am Queen what can they do," she replied.

"You are Queen, but you can not change the ways of the world. If we were discovered it would never be accepted and you know that," he told her.

She lowered her eyes, "You are right, I will be more careful. Alright?"

"You know I love you Ana, and want nothing more than to be with you. We are keeping it a secret for your kingdoms sake and the sake of our child," he replied, and bent down one last time and kissed her on the forehead.

They played their parts the rest of the day, her the innocent Queen and him her guard. And Florian avoided the wizard at all cost. Until after their evening meal Cosmas cornered him and Ana.

"Your Grace, I received reply from Lord Landrum. He states that Ser Fintan left North Star a fortnight past and should of arrived back at Icestorm by now. He did also state that on his way to North Star, Ser Fintan had problems with the dwarfs and is sure that they are responsible for him not returning to us," the wizard informed.

"The dwarfs keep to themselves why would they bother Ser Fintan?" she asked.

"I know not, Your Grace, only what was said in the message," Cosmas replied.

"Send men out to find Gundahar the leader, and have him brought here. I will have this matter resolved before Lord Landrum decides to take it in his own hands," she gave the order, and the wizard bowed and left.

A week later three dwarfs were brought to Icestorm. Ana instructed them to be brought to the Throne Room and she would speak to them there. They entered through the back door behind the throne. Ser Florian stayed close behind Ana and stood quietly behind the throne as she took her seat. Three dwarf men stood in front of the dais, one no more than three feet tall with a big belly, and two chins that was covered by a peppered beard. The other shorter than the first and skinny with a hair as black as a crow. And the last had a snow white beard that made him look older than the others. All dressed in fur from head to toe.

Ana looked over the dwarfs in front of her then said, "Where is Gundahar your leader? I summoned him."

The chubby dwarf answered, "Murdered, Your Grace. I am Wodan the new leader of the dwarfs of the Caps."

"Murdered, by whom?"

"Ser Fintan, Your Grace, almost a month past now," the dwarf answered with his eyes down at the floor.

Ana was silent for awhile then said, "I want to know what happened to Gundahar and Ser Fintan. You will tell me everything and leave nothing out."

The chubby dwarf told his story, about how there was a storm and Gundahar offered the knights and villagers shelter. He said that the wolves had killed all the horses and Ser Fintan and Gundahar got in an argument about that. He said Ser Fintan killed the leader out of rage. Then he stated that the dwarfs moved from there home in fear of the Landrums.

When he finished Ana said, "And what became of Ser Fintan? Have you seen him since he left towards North Star?"

The three dwarfs looked at each other, but did not answer.

"I asked you a question and demand an answer, have you seen Ser Fintan?" Ana said frustrated.

"Almost a fortnight past I sent hunters out, they came back and informed me that there had been an avalanche and they saw horses and knights buried beneath the fallen snow and rocks. I know not if Ser Fintan was among them," the chubby dwarf answered after awhile of silence.

Ana did not look pleased with the response, she sat silent in her silver throne. After many minutes she said, "I will have to think upon what you have told me. You are to remain here as my guest for your own safety until I have made my decision on what I tend to do about the matter. I will have rooms set up here. You are not to leave the castle without my saying so, do you understand?"

"Yes, Your Grace. But are we being charged with some crime?" the chubby one asked.

"Not as of now, should you be?"

"No, Your Grace. Thank you, Your Grace," the dwarfs bowed in respect.

Ana waved over Ser Fergus Beckman whom was standing guard. "Ser Fergus, would you find our guest some rooms and make sure they are feed?" she said to him."

"Yes, Your Grace."

"Oh and Ser Fergus, you or Ser Abel are to be with our guest at all times to make sure no harm comes to them. Is that understood?"

"Yes, Your Grace," he answered, and took the dwarfs out of the Throne Room.

Cosmas was standing in the corner of the room during the Queen's meeting with the dwarfs. As soon as the dwarfs were away Ana called him over.

"Cosmas, the dwarf's story seems to have some holes in it that do not make since. What did you make of it?" she asked her wizard.

"I agree, Your Grace. I think they know more than what you have been told," Cosmas answered.

"Find Ser Abel and tell him to find me at once, I do not want the dwarfs to leave before this matter has been resolved. And send word to Lord Landrum. Tell him that I require him here at court and to make his way as soon as possible. I want to hear his side of what Ser Fintan said to him," Ana instructed."

"Yes, Your Grace, right away," the wizard bowed in respect then rushed off to complete his tasks.

ROSEGARDEN

The Capitol was massive, twice as big as Crystal Keep if not bigger. Aldreda rode close to Julian as they passed through the giant oak and iron gates. Off to the east she could see the castle with its towers sparkling gold, it looked to be leagues away. The road leading through the capitol was paved with bricks of different colors, stained dark from all the traffic traveling on them. The horses made a "click, clock" sound with every step. The capitol was alive with people crowded everywhere she looked. On both sides of the road apartments stood four and five stories tall with balconies looking out to the street bellow. The apartments were built of a tan colored stone, not as elegant as the castle and the surrounding wall. Women were standing on the balconies hanging clothes to dry and yelling at the children below playing on the street.

Farther into the capitol a market stretched out before them. A man selling apples was yelling out, "Ripe juicy apples, red, yellow and green, the best apples you'll ever taste."

Next to him was a baker, "Hot fresh rolls, white bread, and black bread, loafs and pies."

Each man trying to yell louder than the other. They moved on slowly through the crowded market. Everything that Aldreda could ever imagine was being sold. Different types of food; fruit, vegetables, beef, and pork, poultry and elk, bread and honeys, wine and ale, all in the same area.

Then the market turned into goods, rare silks and lace from the Islands, wool and linen, velvet and cotton. Dresses and cloaks, jerkins, tunics and doublets, leather breeches and boots. A woman sat on a stool embroidering roses on a leather jerkin busy at her work and paying no attention to the people passing by. Aldreda was both amazed and frightened. This place was huge with more people then she had ever seen before, but it was breathtaking to see everything the capitol had to offer.

After the market, the road forked to the left, it looked to be more apartments, a brothel and a couple pubs. To the right of the fork on the corner was a massive inn four times the size of the one at Crystal Keep. The inn was made of tan stone with a slate roof, and six stories tall. It stretched down the road towards the golden castle. Julian went right and Aldreda turned her horse to follow.

He stopped in front of the inn and said, "We will see how much a bed is for the night, then go look around the capitol."

Aldreda gave a nod, dismounted her horse and followed Julian inside the inn.

The common room was almost empty with the exception of the inn keeper and two serving wenches. A short skinny man with no hair atop his head walked over to them as soon as they entered, his boots echoing off the wooden floor.

"Good morrow to you, are you looking for a room? We have great rooms with feathered beds and privy chambers and we have common rooms with straw mattresses, what would you prefer?" the man said to them as soon as he reached them.

"A common room would serve fine, how much?" Julian replied.

"A silver star for room and food, or five coppers for just the room," the man answered happily.

"A silver it is," Julian said and clasped the man by the forearm.

They paid the silver and the skinny bald man showed them to their room. It was on the second floor and the third door on the right.

"This will be it; supper is served at sun down. We'll ring the bell. Make sure you're on time or there won't be much food left. So what brings you to the capitol?"

"We're here to see the King," Julian replied.

"Well that's not going to happen. The King's daughter Princess Margery had an accident in the West shortly after her wedding. She is missing and the King is not seeing anyone," the inn keeper informed Julian.

Julian did not reply he just thanked the man and shut the door to their room.

"What are we to do now?" Aldreda asked him, they had traveled so far to see the King.

"We have to try at least. We will still go to the castle and see if there is anyone else whom we can speak to," Julian answered he would not give up until he tried everything that he could.

They left the inn and mounted back up on their horses and headed toward the sparkling castle. They passed a smith shop on the way with the black smith hammering away to shape a sword. Beyond the smith shop was a pub called the Prickly Thorn, it looked empty from the outside. On they went toward the castle, passing more elegant apartments and shops. Finally they came to the high stone wall surrounding the castle. Ten guards were on the ground before the gate and above there was at the least thirty more atop the wall.

They rode their horses up to one of the guards and Julian said to him, "We wish to see the King."

"You can wish all you want but it's not going to happen. The King isn't seeing anyone," the guard replied.

"It is an urgent matter that must be brought to the King, Ser, we have traveled a long way to see him," Julian pleaded with the guard.

"What urgent matter?"

"My village has been attacked and all the people in it killed, I must see the King."

"You think the King cares about some village? His daughter Princess Margery is missing they can not find her, he does not know if she is alive or dead and you want to bother him about a village. Piss off, go bring this matter to your Lord," the guard replied.

Julian was trying to control his temper, Aldreda could see the veins in his neck and forehead starting to bulge. "My Lord is the problem, that is why I came here," Julian spat back.

"Then you wasted your time. Be gone with you, the King does not need to be bothered by the likes of you," and with that the guard walked away.

Julian turned his horse and galloped off back towards the inn. Aldreda hurried and did the same.

They reached the inn in minutes, Julian jumped down from his horse tied it up quickly and stormed inside. Aldreda hurriedly dismounted and tied her horse up next to Julian's and followed. When she entered the inn Julian was not there, she climbed the steeps to their room. Julian was sitting on the bed starring intensely at the wall.

"My love?"

"No one will help us, not my brother, not the King, no one cares. Hundreds of people were slaughtered like animals and no one cares," he said still staring at the wall.

"I care," she replied, she hated seeing him like this she wanted to help ease his pain.

"I know you do, but what can just you and I do against Lord Mullen? We are but two people against his hundreds, I just don't know what to do any more," he said in a whispered tone.

"Let's go home," she said and sat down next to him on the bed.

He gave a slow nod.

Julian sat in the same spot and stared at the wall for hours. When the supper bell finally rang he didn't even notice.

Aldreda went over to him and placed her hand on his shoulder, "We should go eat love, and you need your strength for the ride back."

Julian took his eyes off the wall and looked at her for the first time since they returned to the inn. His hazel eyes were bloodshot and empty. He rose from the bed and went with Aldreda down to the common room to eat.

Julian only ate a couple bites of the meat, but he drank two flagons of wine by himself. Aldreda helped him back up to their room and once within Julian fell on the bed and passed out. While Julian snored loudly Aldreda removed his boots and covered him up with a quilt. Then she got undressed herself and climbed in beside him. She closed her eyes. She was exhausted from the stress of the day.

They were back in the forest, naked trees surrounded them. Fresh fallen snow covered the ground and ice hung from the limbs of the trees. Her family was there and all the other elves of the forest. They were all armed and atop their horses. She looked around dazed. They were surrounded, knights and soldiers came at them from the north and south. The knights wore different colored cloaks. She saw green and orange cloaks, black and white, and the red and gold cloaks of the King.

Julian was beside her mounted up on the horse they had found after his village was burnt. He was in mismatched armor and had a long sword and shield in hand. She didn't know what was going on she looked around again. She could see herself with bow in hand and an arrow ready to fly. She was atop her chestnut mare. She saw herself look at Julian and tell him that she loved him.

Then the soldiers reached them. The song of metal on metal rang out throughout the forest. She heard screams of pain and saw the snow bellow them turn red and melt. She looked to where Julian had been. He was not there, she looked around desperately to find him. He was fighting one of Mullen's knights. Each blow the knight gave Julian blocked. Finally after many blows, the knight's sword was knocked away. Before he could draw it up again Julian was shoving his sword in the man's neck under his helmet. The knight fell to the ground and Julian moved on to a different knight.

The elves were fighting too, with weapons and powers. The trees would bend down and knock knights right off their horses, then an elf would finish the knight before he could stand up from the ground. Aldreda saw herself loosening arrows as fast as she could, with no pause. Each arrow hitting a knight in the neck or shoulder where their armor did not protect them. She saw her father fighting three knights at once. All were on foot and pounding at each other. Her father had the best of them, until one of the knights hit him behind the left knee. He was falling to the ground . . .

"Aldreda, Aldreda, wake up," someone was shaking her.

She opened her eyes, Julian was sitting up in the bed with his hands on both her shoulders.

"Aldreda?" he said in a worried tone.

She blinked a couple times trying to figure out what was going on. *A dream*, she thought. Then said "what is it love," and smiled up at him.

"You were rolling around and screaming," he told her.

"It was a dream," she said relieved.

Then she remembered the last part, the vision was not finished. Julian woke her she did not know what became of her father. "Julian we must go. We need to return to the forest," she said and got up quickly from the bed and started dressing.

"Now? It's the middle of the night. Can't we wait until the mourning?"

"No, we must leave now," she said and continued gathering her things.

It took them three days to reach the edge of the forest. They left Rosegarden hours before sunrise, and rode fast from sunrise to sunset. Only stopping when the only light in the sky was from the moon and stars. Aldreda led the way riding ahead of Julian desperate to get back home. She and Julian had barley spoken since they left Rosegarden. Aldreda felt bad for that but longed to see her father and tell him of her vision. It was midday when they entered the forest, the sun hidden in the sky by light grey clouds.

The trees of the forest leaves had lost all green and the forest was full of reds, oranges and yellows. Once safely within the forest Aldreda felt at ease for the first time since they had left. It was much darker than it had been outside the forest and she and Julian slowed the horses to a trot. Her backside ached from riding the horse so hard and she was starting to regret not stopping more often.

Julian rode up beside her, "for the first time since we left I can finally keep up with you," he said with a kind smile. He even seemed happier since they arrived at the forest.

"I am just ready to be back home," she said back at him. She had not told him of her dream and wasn't planning on telling him.

"We will have to stop at the village for the night, but we will be back with your family on the morrow," he said to her.

She nodded in agreement and kicked her horse to a faster pace. They reached the village as the forest grew dark and lost all color. It was a small village with about fifty hutches, a black smith, a temple, a single story inn and a tavern. Wood hutches with straw roofs lined the back of the village, with the smith, temple, inn and tavern towards the front. The village was in a clearing in the forest and had trees of all kinds surrounding it. The candles were just being lit and golden light came pouring out of the windows. It was very quiet nothing like Crystal Keep or the capitol. A few voices poured out of the tavern and inn but the back of the village was dead silent.

Aldreda and Julian stayed at this inn on their way to see Julian's brother and Aldreda had liked the inn keeper. The inn keeper was an older woman with brown hair that had grey streaks by her ears.

The woman recognized them when they walked in and greeted them kindly. "Back again? Couldn't get enough o' my cookin'? Well come in come in, just finished up supper better sit," the woman said to them and rushed off towards the kitchen.

The woman returned with two plates and placed them down on the table then returned to the kitchen. They had been served meat burnt almost black, with hard bread and yellow cheese. Aldreda started nibbling her bread and the woman returned with two glasses of tart wine.

Aldreda was starved and ate her food without pause. When she had finished she looked up at Julian. He was staring across the room at three knights sitting in the corner.

"What are you looking at?" Aldreda asked.

He looked at her quickly then turn his head back towards the knights. "You see those knights sitting in the corner over there?"

"Yeah what of them?"

"They have green cloaks with an orange bull."

She wasn't sure what he was getting at so she replied, "So."

"Lord Mullen's sigil is the bull and his colors are green and orange. Those could be the men that killed my family Aldreda," Julian told her in a whisper.

A rush of panic filled her, she did not know what Julian would do. The knights sat in the corner laughing and drinking their ale, while Julian stared. Then one of the knights looked over in their direction and saw Julian starring.

The knight said something to his companions sitting next to him and within seconds the knights and Julian were starring each other down. The knights stood up from their seats and started walking over to her and Julian.

"You got a problem peasant?" the tallest of the three knights asked Julian.

"I was just wondering what Lord Mullen's scum is doing so far away from their master," Julian said back to the knight.

"You got a problem with m'lord do ya?" the knight replied.

"Your lord slaughtered my village," Julian spat back with hatred in his tone.

"Ya hear that boys we got ourselves a survivor," the tall knight said to his companions.

"Now that's a problem, m'lord said there were to be no survivors," the knight to the tall ones right said.

"That he did, what do ya think we should do bout that Jack?" said the knight to the tall ones left. Aldreda figured Jack had to be the middle one because he was the one to reply. "May haps we should take them to da lord and let 'im decide what ta do wit them," said Jack.

"Your welcome to try," Julian said and stood with a dagger in both hands.

The knights drew their swords at their hips. "See this boys, the peasant want to play swords wit us," said Jack.

Aldreda sat there stunned not knowing what she could do. She looked around the room, the woman that kept the inn ran into the kitchen. It was just her, Julian and the knights. The hearth was ablaze with a big fire, licking orange flames up the chimney. That was it, she closed her eyes and tried to control the fire. The hearth cracked and popped in protest. She tried harder trying to clear her mind and forget the danger around her.

Slowly a single flame crept across the wooden floor of the inn. Julian and the knights were to concerned with each other to notice. She opened her eyes and willed the flame to keep going. Slowly it crept and finally met the heal of the knight to Jack's right.

The knight looked down at his foot, "What the hell," and jumped from the flame trying to stamp out his boot.

The other knights looked over to see what was wrong with their companion, that was her chance.

She jumped up from the bench and grabbed Julian's arm, "Run," she said and darted for the door.

Julian kept up with her, running right beside her, the echoes of the knight's footsteps close behind them. As soon as they burst out the door

Aldreda called the wind. A strong blast rose, bringing hundreds of dead leaves twirling around them. Still a hold of Julian she ran towards were the horses had been tied. The horses were frantic, startled by the sudden gust of wind. She let go of Julian's hand and grabbed for the reins of her horse to untie them.

The leaves still swirling around them made her blind she had to rely on her hands to do the job. She was working fast to untie the horse when someone grabbed her from behind. Her hood was knocked down and the man got a handful of her hair and pulled her head back. The cold metal of the blade placed under her left ear. She herd Julian scream and heard fighting. The wind started to die down the leaves gently fell to the ground around them.

With the blade still against her neck she looked down and saw Julian on the ground with two knights atop him.

"That was very stupid," the man whispered in her ear. "What is this," he said, then louder he shouted, "Look boys I caught me self an elf."

EPILOGUE

I am at Xicalli, I just purchased two thousand slaves and two war ships. Get everyone you can to help. Have all your men ready. I will arrive at Gator Swamp in one moon's turn. Be ready. We will avenge my brother and your husband or die trying. Lady Krishna Hugart rolled up the parchment and threw it in the hearth beside her. Raj had come through and before long the King would pay for what he did to her family.

A week past her sons had arrived at her brother's house, tattered and starved. Ratan and Ratnam had informed her that the King had forced her eldest daughter Rashmi to marry the Queen's brother Rajesh. The "new" Lord of Fire Harbor. She had been heart broken at the news of loosing a daughter but then again she was overjoyed to have her sons with her once again.

Even though she had her sons back, the King had all her daughters. The only way she could get Rashmi back was with Lord Rajesh's death. And her other daughters Rati and Ratna were at Dragons End in the castle with the King. It was very risky this plan to avenge her husband, if things went wrong they could cost her daughters their lives.

All of the knights and guards that had served her at Fire Harbor had come to Gator Swamp to serve her. She had her brother Lord Kalidas' guards and knights, and his five war ships. They had The Vipers with Lord Maillett behind them. His wife Lady Rachna was sister to her brother-in-law Lord Filoso. Then, of course, she had been able to talk her sister Lady Kishore Filoso into talking her husband to stand behind them. Lady Sanjana Hamstra of Summer Keep was born a Hugart and convinced her lord husband to join her nephew's rebellion. And Lord Hamstra got his brother-in-law Lord Chittick.

That gave her two thousand men from Raj, one thousand of her own men, two thousand of her brother's men, and at the least two thousand from the other four houses. That was at the least thirteen thousand men to storm Dragons End. If they did a surprise attack the King would not be able to call upon the other remaining houses of the South.

Lady Krishna went to find her brother to tell him of the news and have him get word to the other houses. Her brother's castle was one of the oldest castles in the Kingdoms, made of brown stone with five round towers and three walls surrounding it. Gator Swamp was exactly that, a swamp filled with alligators. There were two walls surrounding the city and another wall surrounding the castle. The outer wall was thirty feet tall and kept the animals away from the city. The inner wall had a mote and drawbridge to keep enemies out if by chance they had defeated the outer wall. And the wall surrounding the castle was the highest of all standing at fifty feet tall with one thousand arrow slits and fifty metal drums filled with oil, to boil and pour on their attackers.

In all its years this castle had never been taken by force. The walls and defenses weren't even the worst part. Any attacker would have to go through the swamps to reach the castle. You could not reach the castle by sea. And the swamps had greater dangers then boiling oil. The swamp people who lived in the swamp lands were savage cannibals who ate the men they killed. A man would have a cleaner death being attacked by an alligator than the swamp people.

Of all the places in the Kingdoms, Lady Krishna felt the safest here. Her sons were now safe here as well and before long her daughters would be with her once again. She was convinced that Raj's plan would work. The King would not expect a rebellion and would not be ready. Lady Krishna walked through the castle seeking her brother with a confidence that she had not felt in years.

She came to the door of her brother's chambers and knocked, hoping to find him here. Lady Kalpana Brunson her brother's wife was the one that answered the door.

"Kalpana, is my brother with you?" Lady Krishna asked.

"Yes he is, come on in," replied Lady Kalpana and she stepped aside to let her enter.

Lord Kalidas Brunson was sitting at his desk looking over different maps of the Kingdoms. "Brother I have received word from Raj, he was able to purchase two thousand fighting slaves and two war ships. He will arrive in one moon's turn. We must get word to the other houses to prepare," she informed her brother.

"This is good news, I will send word. I was thinking with Lord Maillet's permission we should have all the war ships meet at The Vipers. I would have all the ships from Serpent Tongue, The Vipers, Raj's ships and my own there to attack from sea. Then have the men from Summer Keep and Sun's End attack from land," Lord Kalidas replied. "As long as we shoot all birds carrying word from Dragons End the King will not be able to call help. If we attack by surprise I see no way for us not to be victorious," her brother continued still studying the maps.

A knock came at the door and her brother raised his eyes for the first time since she entered the room. "See who that is," he said with a wrinkled brow.

Lady Kalpana stood from the chair she was seated in, and went to the door. A few seconds later Lady Kalpana returned with a servant, a young man with ragged brown hair and a whisper of a beard appearing on his cheeks.

"M'lord there is a visitor, a man dressed in a very nice robe says that he is here to see you and Lady Krishna with word of your niece and nephews," the servant informed her brother.

"Who is this man? Did he give a name?"

"No, m'lord he said he would only speak to you or Lady Krishna," the servant replied.

Her brother looked up at her, "are you expecting anyone?" he asked.

"No," she answered.

Irritated he stood up and said, "Come let us go see who this visitor is and what he wants."

Lady Krishna followed her brother out the door and towards the entrance of the castle.

When they reached the entrance Lady Krishna's stomach turned in knots and her face got hot with anger. A tall man with peppered hair and beard, with a long staff in one hand, wearing a red silk robe, was standing there admiring one of the tapestries. She knew at once who it was the Red Wizard.

"Xolan, what are you doing here?" she said to the wizard.

He turned from the tapestry, "Ah Lady Krishna, I must say I expected a better welcome than that."

"Forgive my sister, she has forgotten her manners. To what do we owe the pleasure of your unexpected visit?" he brother said and nudged her with his elbow.

"The King sent me, might we go somewhere to talk, my lord?" Xolan replied.

"Why of course Xolan right this way," her brother said and lead the group toward the Great Hall.

Lady Krishna walked behind the wizard, she did not trust him to be at her back. If there was anyone in the Kingdoms who could ruin their plan it would be Xolan.

Her brother entered the hall with Xolan right beside him and her behind. Xolan turned to her, "My lady I must say you are looking better than you were the last time we saw each other."

"The last time we saw each other you were taking my children away from me," she spat back.

"I am sorry about that my lady. That is why I have come, because of your children."

"Have you come to give them back to me?"

"Not exactly. You see my lady your sons have run away from Fire Harbor and I was wondering if they had come here to you."

"What madness is this Xolan? First you take my children, and then you loose two of them! I have not seen my sons since you sent me here!" she said loudly hoping that he would believe the lie.

"That is too bad, I saw a vision of your sons escape. They were heading this way, if they did not arrive here then I fear the worst for them," Xolan said to her.

She knew what he was looking for so she gave it to him. Forcing herself to cry she said, "What are you saying Xolan that my sons are dead?" With tears running down her cheeks she could see that the wizard was starting to buy it.

Her brother stood silent and playing the part as well seeming shocked at the news.

"I can't say that your sons are dead my lady. It's just if they are not here, you yourself know how dangerous the lands are around this castle," the wizard said.

She made herself cry harder. Her brother put his arms around her, "Come you should sit down, I'll get you some wine. Xolan would you like some?"

"That would be most welcome my lord," Xolan replied and took a seat next to her.

After her brother left the room to fetch the wine Xolan leaned close to her and said, "that is not the only reason I came my lady, I have also came with news about your daughter Rashmi."

"Did you loose her too Xolan, or just kill her like you did my husband," she said through tiers.

"Not at all my lady, she has been married to Lord Rajesh, she is now the Lady of Fire Harbor," Xolan replied.

Krishna fought back her anger as best she could, she would like nothing more than to kill the wizard right now where he sat.

Lord Kalidas returned with two chalices and handed one to her then to Xolan. "Sweet summer wine Xolan I am sure your travel here was wearing, let me offer you a room for the night. You should not travel through the swamps after dark." Lord Kalidas offered the wizard.

"That would be very kind my lord, I will leave at first light you have my word," Xolan replied.

"Please stay as long as you like," her brother said.

She could not figure out why he was being so kind to the man that helped the King kill her husband, but she knew her brother, and knew there had to be a reason for it.

She sipped at her wine and starred at the wizard through her tears. She had cried so much of late it was nothing to bring them on now, even knowing that her sons were not dead. "So Xolan why has my daughter been married off so soon, when I left Dragons End you told me they would be married when of age. She is still just a child."

"The commons in Fire Harbor wanted Lady Hugart so we gave them a Hugart to be their Lady," he replied and took another big drink of the wine.

So her people wanted her back as well, that could be a good thing when she tried to take back Fire Harbor after dealing with the King.

She was deep in her thought and her brother had started talking to the Red Wizard. The boys were already in bed for the night, but if Xolan stayed the risk of him finding them would be great. She would have to hide them somewhere safe after the wizard retired and keep them there until Xolan was away. She was trying to figure out where to hide her sons when Xolan tried to stand and brought her out of her thoughts.

Xolan put both hands on the arms of the chair and tried to push himself to his feet. Failing he fell back down in the seat with an "oomph." She gave a confused look to her brother, and he smiled in return. Xolan was looking at the two of them with eyes as big as saucers. The pupils of his eyes were huge hiding the dark brown/black of his eyes.

"What . . . have . . . . you . . . done," Xolan said slowly and slurred.

"What are you talking about Xolan, what's wrong with you," she said back with confused look.

Xolan swatted at her, missing her by a foot.

"By the gods Xolan what is wrong with you!" she shouted angry that he would even attempt to strike her.

"It's Night Shade, I put some in his chalice," her brother said to the both of them.

Xolan tried to look in her brother's direction with his head cocked to the side and looking like a fool.

"Oh do not worry Xolan it's not enough to kill you, just enough so we can get that staff away from you and put you some where safe," her brother said with a wicked smile.

This was great! She had not even thought of that herself. If the King did not have his wizard he would be weaker. Xolan tried to stand from the chair again with wobbling legs. He fell and landed on his back starring at the ceiling. Lord Kalidas went over to where Xolan was sitting and picked up the wizard's staff and placed it in the corner of the room. Xolan lay on the floor swatting at the air like he was being attacked by a swarm of bees.

"That was absolutely brilliant! But what do we do with him now?" she said to her brother.

"We'll keep him in the dungeon until we have taken over Dragons End then he will have to decide his fate. He is sworn to serve the King and when there is a new King he can swear his fealty or die," her brother answered.

"Didn't he come with men, I don't see the King sending his wizard with out guards," she asked.

"When I got the wine I ordered that the men that came with him be killed," he replied.

"What about the King? He will start to suspect an attack once Xolan does not return and we cannot wait a moons turn for Raj," she asked.

"No we cannot, we will have to attack before then if we want to surprise the King. But we had no other choice, Krishna, the wizard knew the boys were here even with you acting like they were not. He is a wizard, I am just glad that he was so concentrated on you that he did not notice the Belladonna in his wine. I will send word to everyone and hopefully the gods will give Raj good speed and we will not have to wait a moons turn. We also need to find a way to get word to Kalyan at Dragons End to let him know of the attack so he can get us in the castle. Come, we don't have a lot of time help me get him to the dungeon so we can finish with our preparations," Lord Kalidas said.

She took Xolan's feet and her brother grabbed his hands. The wizard was heavy and it was slow going down to the dungeons. They ended up dragging him most of the way once they reached the stairs. They drug him to the lowest floor of the dungeon and put him in the farthest cell. Xolan was muttering nonsense to entire way. Once they finally got him in his cell they shackled his hands to chains on the wall and propped him up in the corner. By the time they were done she was filthy and exhausted.

CHARACTER OVERVIEW

I.   **Royal Houses**

II.   **High-Born Houses**

III. **Low-Born Houses & Non-Human Beings**

I.

The Queen of the North
Ruler of Icestorm Castle
House Mathis
Sigil: Unicorn
Motto: "Cold as Ice"
Colors: Blue and White

Queen Ana Mathis First of her name. Ruler of Icestorm Castle the Capitol of the North. Queen of the North, of men, giants and dwarfs. And protector of the realm.

King Conell Mathis III thought to be the son of Ana Mathis and Fin Mathis. Actual son to Ser Florian Gaddy. Babe King, whose mother is ruling for him until he is of age.

King Finn Mathis missing during hunting tripe, thought to be dead. Cousin and husband to Queen Ana.

Princess Arian Mathis sister to Queen Ana, second in line for the throne.

Lord Cormac Mathis uncle to Queen Ana, father of King Finn. Husband to **Lady Irnan Mathis**.

Their children:
Ser Brian Mathis Master-of-arms, Captain of the Queen's Guard
Ser Ronan Mathis Personal guard to King Conell

The Queen's Council:
Ser Fintan Landrum of North Star
Ser Ben Goldberg of Giants Keep
Lord Cormac Mathis
Ser Gawain Degoyler of Snowflake Landing
Ser Conair Gribbens of The Horseshoe
Ser Jake Wiker of Rivercross
Ser Bedwyn Schmitt of Thor
Lady Aoifa Perrenot of The Pines
Cosmas The White Wizard of the North
Seer Genevie gifts of prophecy and healing

Queen's Guards
Ser Florian Gaddy personal guard to the Queen, and secret lover
Ser Brian Mathis Captain of Guard, Master-of-Arms
Ser Fergus Beckman
Ser Abel Lynch
Ser Damiano Devitt
Ser Julius Bedel
Ser Lino Acuff

Servants of the Castle
Mario Yoke Squire to Ser Florian
Itala Queen's bed maid
Clara Queen's bed maid
Gloria Wet-nurse for the baby King

King of the East
Ruler of Rosegarden
House Carrender
Sigil: Rose
Motto: "Love and Honor"
Colors: Red and Gold

King Tristan Carrender, first of his name. Ruler of Rosegarden the Capitol of the East. King of the East, of man and elf, and protector of the realm. Husband to **Queen Helen Carrender** of house Hearon.

Their children:
Princess Margery Carrender A.K.A. Maggie. Eldest child, fourteen years of age
Prince Jon Carrender heir to the throne, twelve years of age
Prince Jason Carrender ten years of age
Princess Katlynn Carrender A.K.A. Kate, eight years of age

The King's Brothers:
Prince Alexander Carrender
Prince Teagan Carrender youngest brother to the King. Husband to **Lady Hallie Carrender** of house Hearon, sister to the Queen.

Their children:
-**Hanah Carrender**
-**Harding Carrender**

King's Uncle:

Lord Jared Carrender husband to **Lady Jaquelyn Carrender** of house Turk. Their son:

Ser Jaron Carrender, Commander of the King's Guard. Husband to **Lady Jazmyn Carrender** of house Hearon, sister to the Queen.

Their children:
- **Burton Carrender**
- **Byron Carrender**

King's Council:

Prince Alexander
Prince Teagan
Lord Jared
Calvan Hearon
Seer Pascal Prophecy, healing and wisdom
Gabriel The Great Wizard of the East

King's Guard:

Ser Jaron Carrender Commander
Ser Clifford Turk of Dolphin Keep
Ser Asher Merriman of Acorn Hill
Ser Byron Chitwood of Golden Rock
Ser Burke Stoddart of Lionsgate
Ser Clive Mullen of Springs End

Princess Maggie's maids:
Tansy
Violet

The King of the South
Ruler of Dragons End
House Cvetkovich
Sigil: Dragon
Motto: "Fight Fire with Fire"
Colors: Yellow and Red

King Abhay Cvetkovich first of his name. Ruler of Dragons End the Capitol of the South. King of the South and protector of the realm. Husband to **Queen Kala Cvetkovich** of house Smeltzer.

Their children:
Princess Kaja Cvetkovich
Prince Akash Cvetkovich heir
Princess Kali Cvetkovich
Prince Akhil Cvetkovich

King's Brother:
Prince Amar Cvetkovich husband to **Lady Rachana Cvetkovich** of house Maillett.

Their children:
Abhilasha Cvetkovich
Akanksha Cvetkovich
Amit Cvetkovich
Amrit Cvetkovich

Royal Council:
Prince Amar Cvetkovich King's Hand
Lord Rajender Maillet of The Vipers, Master-of-Arms
Lord Anand Filoso of Serpent Tongue, Commander of the Guard
Lord Kalyan Brunson of Gator Swamp, Commander of Goods
Lord Aravind Hamstra of Summer Keep, Master of Word
Lord Jitinder Chittick of Suns End, Chief Captain
Lord Punit Beckom of Foxrun, King's Justice
Lord Yash Kouns of The Red Islands, King's Justice
Sage Zuri wisdom and healing
Xolan The Red Wizard of the South

King of the West
Ruler of West Watch Castle
House McCue
Sigil: Crown
Motto: "Strong as Steel"
Colors: Blue and Red

King Cynon McCue, first of his name. Ruler of West Watch the Capitol of the West. King of the West and protector of the realm. Husband to **Queen Aileen McCue** of house McNeely.

Their children:
Prince Aidan McCue, heir to the throne. Sixteen years of age.
-Husband to **Princess Margery McCue** of the East.
Prince Ailin McCue
Princess Ailis McCue

King's Brother:
Prince Cadogan McCue husband to **Lady Athne McCue** of house McNeely, sister to the Queen.

Their children:
Barry McCue
Bedelia McCue

King's Council:
Prince Cadogan McCue
Lord Domnail McCue
Lord Donal McCue
Seer Isabel wisdom, healing, prophecy and supernatural powers
Lennox The West Wizard

Royal Guard:
Ser Angus McCue cousin to the King
Ser Aodhan McCue cousin to the King
Ser Alastar McCue cousin to the King
Ser Brady McCue cousin to the King
Ser Braden McCue cousin to the King

Other members of the castle:
Rory McDaniel Prince Aidan's squire
Ser Asher Merriman Princess Margery's guard
Tansy & Violet Princess Margery's bed maids
Dermot McNeely King Cynon's ward
Peter High Priest

II.

Lord of North Star
House Landrum
Sigil: Eight Pointed Star
Motto: "By Skill and Valor"
Colors: Black and Silver

Lord Modred Landrum husband to **Lady Alice Landrum** of house Wiker.

Their children:
Finlan Landrum heir to North Star
Ser Fintan Landrum member of the Queen's Council

Lord Landrum's ward:
Olwen Beckman Cousin of the Queen, Nephew to Lord Landrum

Lord of Lionsgate
House Stoddart
Sigil: Lion
Motto: "Family First"
Colors: Green and Gold

Lord Herman Stoddart husband to **Lady Kacey Stoddart** of house Mullen.

Their children:
Kalie Stoddart
Kara Stoddart
Kayden Stoddart heir to Lionsgate

Lord Stoddart's Brother:
Ser Burke Stoddart of the King's Guard

Lord of Springs End
House Mullen
Sigil: Bull
Motto: "Live and Love"
Colors: Green and Orange

Lord Midir Mullen husband to **Lady Rochelle Mullen** of house Stoddart.

Their children:
Rolland Mullen heir to Springs End
Ser Clive Mullen of the King's Guard

Lord of Gator Swamp
House Brunson
Sigil: Alligator
Motto: "Loyal and Strong"
Colors: Green and Black

Lord Kalidas Brunson husband to **Lady Kalpana Brunson** of house
   Hugart.

Their children:
Lakshoni Brunson
Lalit Brunson
Lalita Brunson
Lochan Brunson
Laxman Brunson

Siblings to Lord Brunson:
Lord Kalyan Brunson of the Royal Council
Lady Krishore Filoso
Lady Krishna Hugart

Lord of Fire Harbor
House Hugart
Sigil: Flame
Motto: "Embrace the Flame"
Colors: Orange and Black

Lord Raghu Hugart convicted of treason and died while questioning. Husband to **Lady Krishna Hugart** of house Brunson, sent to Gator Swamp after husbands death.

Their children:
Rashmi Hugart wife to Lord Rajesh Smeltzer, the brother of the Queen
Ratan Hugart Lord Rajesh's ward
Rati Hugart of the Queen's ladies
Ratna Hugart of the Queen's ladies
Ratnam Hugart Lord Rajesh's squire

Brother of Lord Hugart:
Lord Raj Hugart was of the Royal Council, banished after Lord Hugart's death

Lord of Fire Harbor
House Smeltzer
Sigil: Stingray
Motto: "Blood is thicker than Water"
Colors: Blue and Black

Lord Rajesh Smeltzer Queen's brother, appointed Lord of Fire Harbor
after Lord Hugart's treason. Husband to **Rashmi Smeltzer** of house
Hugart.

Lord Rajesh's ward and squire
Ratan Hugart
Ratnam Hugart

Lord of Autumn Way
House McClure
Sigil: Thunder Bolt
Motto: "Courage is Everything"
Colors: Grey and Yellow

Lord Gwern McClure husband to **Lady Fiona McClure** of house McMahon.

Their children:
Fergal McClure heir to Autumn Way
Fergus McClure
Finley McClure
Finnan McClure

III.

The North
Dark Dwarfs of Snow Cap Mountains

Gundahar leader of the Dark Dwarfs of the Snow Caps. Husband to
   Brunhild, their children:
-Alberic
-Ing

Other Dwarfs:
Wodan friend of Gundahar, husband to **Lorelei**, their children:
-Siegfried
-Sieglinde
Weland friend of Gundahar, husband to **Grimhilt**, their children:
-Gunther
-Wieland
Etzel friend of Gundahar, husband to **Kriemhild**, their children:
-Nerthus

   The Dark Dwarfs are cursed by the gods and men, and condemned to
a life underground. They unearth gems and metals from the mountain for
the Queen.

The East
Elves of Elf Forest

Bronimir Leader of the Elves, husband to **Cateline**, their children:
Elis
Dionisia
Aldreda lover to Julian Blair (a human)
Bronimir's family is blessed with the gift of prophecy along with the other
    powers of the elves. His is the most powerful family.

Other types of elves include:
Oak Elf have the power to influence the forest
Willow Elf have the power of healing
River Elf have the power to influence the rivers and rain
Animal Elf have the power to influence animals
Ocean Elf have the power to influence the ocean and storms
Wind Elf have the power to control wind
Wise Elf the elder elves who have the power to see what will be

    The Elves live in the Great Willow, in the middle of the forest

House Blair
Village in the Southwestern part of Elf Forest

Justin Blair father to:
Ser Kevin Blair knight at Crystal Keep
Julian Blair lover to Aldreda the elf
Ludwig youngest son

Magister of the Island Azec

Magister Kimo Xenos, the Magister, husband to **Kilikina Xenos**, their children:
Kiana Xenos
Konani Xenos
Keoni Xenos
Kekos Xenos

The Magister's servants: (not slaves)
Kaleo Captain of Magister Kimo's ship
Maile
Leilani
Melika
Keanu

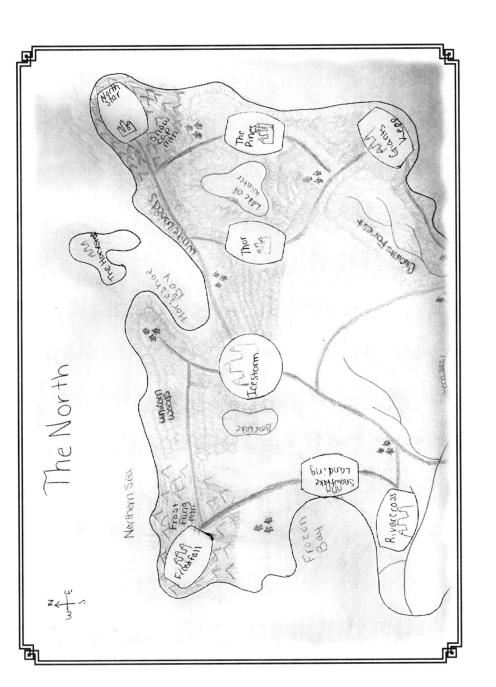

The North

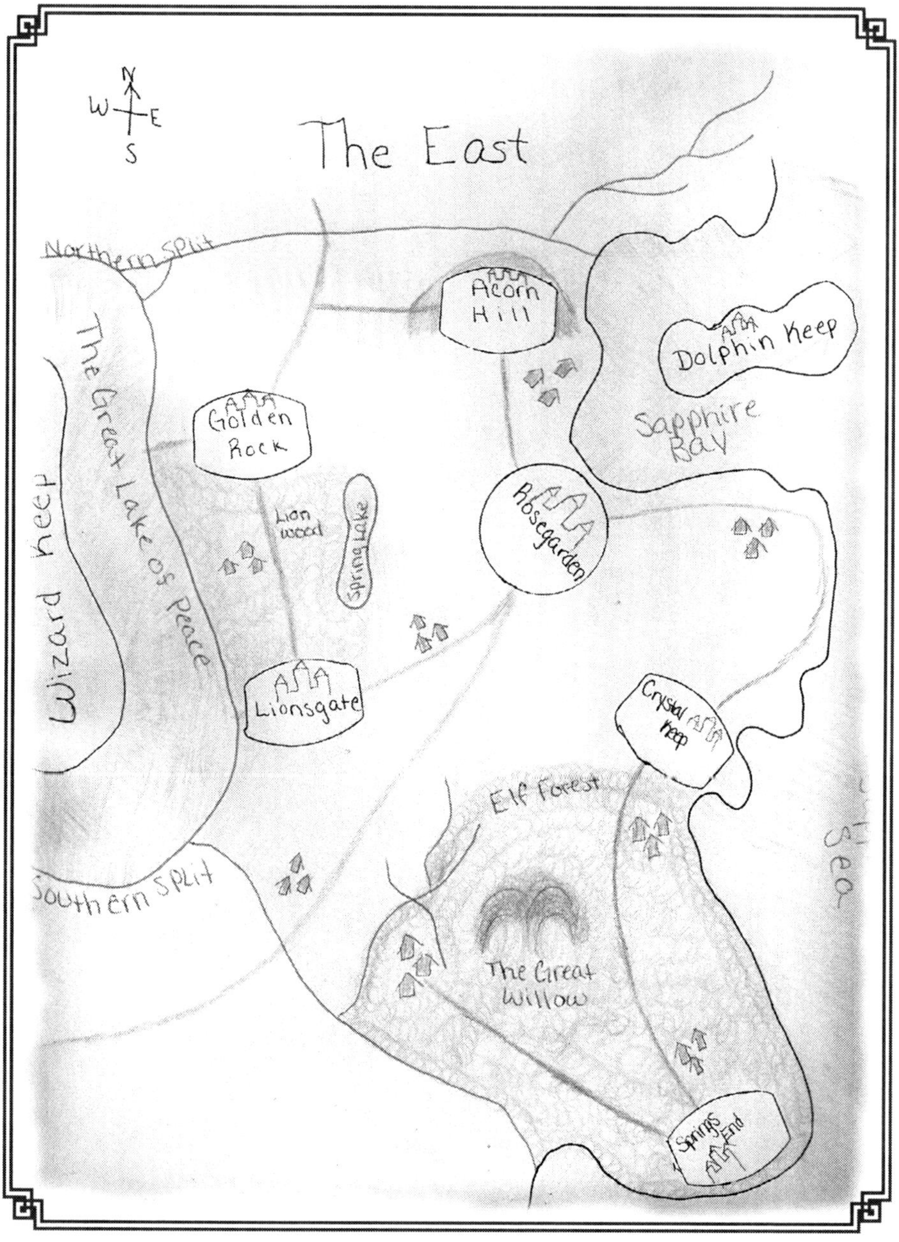

The East

N
W E
S

Northern Split

Acorn Hill

Dolphin Keep

Sapphire Bay

The Great Lake of Peace

Golden Rock

Wizard Keep

Lion wood

Spring Lake

Rosegarden

Crystal Keep

Lionsgate

Elf Forest

sea

Southern Split

The Great Willow

Springs End

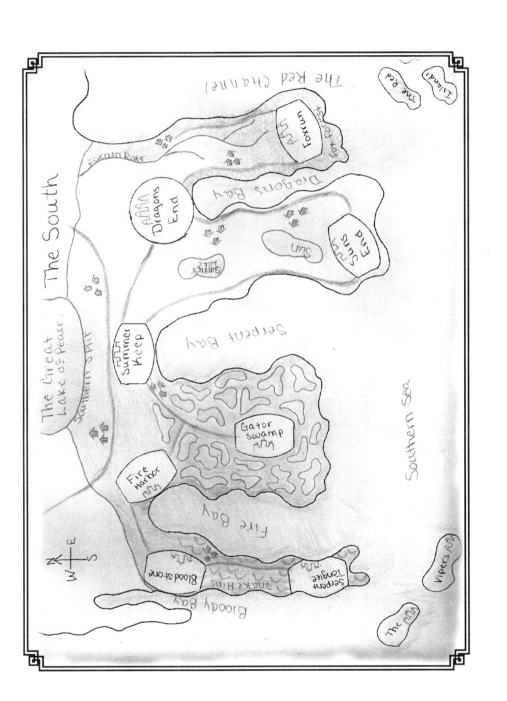

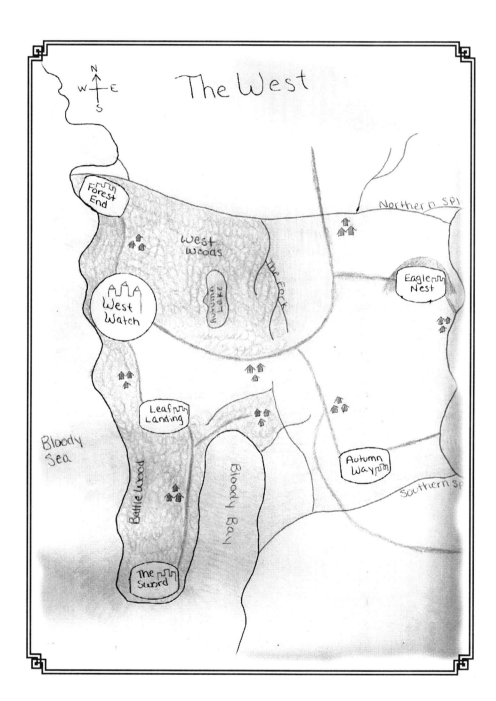

CPSIA information can be obtained at www.ICGtesting.com
Printed in the USA
BVOW031908110412

287461BV00003B/57/P